Trudi Had Not Seemed to Enjoy the Party ...

She had worn a distraught air, her eyes sliding frequently to the front door, the fingers of her restless hands tense. She had sent Solomon upstairs alone ...

He moved toward the bathroom. "Hey!" he called. "You in there?" Someone had left the water tap partly open; a steady drip-drop answered Sorge's call. "Trudi!" he roared. "What the hell are we playing? Hide and seek? Damn it, woman, I'm tired!"

It was only after he had stood, unmoving, for a full five minutes, his words rocking in gentle waves about him, that it came to him that Trudi was not in the house.

THE PAST AND PRESENT OF SOLOMON SORGE "should appeal to all those who haven't yet had enough of Herzog & Co."

—*Library Journal*

Winner of The Award of Excellence of the Friends of American Writers

The Past and Present of Solomon Sorge

Judith Barnard

WASHINGTON SQUARE PRESS
PUBLISHED BY POCKET BOOKS NEW YORK

This book was originally published in 1967 by Houghton Mifflin Company.

A Washington Square Press Publication of
POCKET BOOKS, a division of Simon & Schuster, Inc.
1230 Avenue of the Americas, New York, N.Y. 10020

Published by arrangement with the author
Library of Congress Catalog Card Number: 67-12903

ISBN: 0-671-61832-6

First Washington Square Press printing May, 1986

10 9 8 7 6 5 4 3 2 1

Printed in the U. S. A.

To my parents
Ruth and Harry Barnard

1

SOLOMON ALEXEI SORGE sat in bed, writing, waiting for his wife to join him. *Fifty-six,* he scribbled on the line headed *Age,* thinking that his wife would have to retype the information; he couldn't send in a form filled with his scrawls. *Birthplace: Odessa, Russia. Date of Birth: February 17, 1908.* A hell of a time to be born. Particularly in Russia. Particularly and especially for a Jew in Russia. But when would be a good time for a Jew to be born in Russia? *Father's name: Boris. Mother: Sarah.* Father dead; mother in Israel. *Brothers and sisters: Leon* killed twenty years ago this month in the Normandy landing; *Yetta,* a foolish woman married to a foolish, enormously successful insurance agent; *Daniel,* member of the Irgun, shot by the British while attempting to blow up a hotel in Tel Aviv, 1947—poor mama: one son killed at the side, so to speak, of the British, the other by the British. It was a lesson in power politics but of course one could not expect her to see it that way; two sons in three years . . . not to mention her relatives not requested on the form: three uncles, two sisters and assorted cousins who disappeared into the ovens of Auschwitz, Bergen-Belsen, God knows where; her parents killed by Cossacks in Bialystok; her mother- and father-in-law who died natural deaths in Odessa (how did that happen?); a second cousin experimented upon by Nazi doctors but still half alive and living with mama now in Haifa. Yetta and I, mama and cousin Anna; we survived. A miracle. Or a masterpiece of stage-craft, of cunning. On whose part? Ours or God's?

Sorge looked at his watch. Two o'clock; the moon had moved past his window. What else did they want to know—the editors of this latest status volume, *Notable Men of America*—that he was willing to tell them? *Occupation of father: Rabbi.* A thinker, God help him, caught between Zionism and socialism. A man of contemplation who made the fatal mistake of trying to mediate between revolutionaries and the Lord. A sweet, loving man who wept for his Jews, the persecuted, as well as for the Russians, Poles and Germans and all who were persecutors. He wept when his synagogue was stoned and raided, he wept when there was no matzoh for Passover, he wept for the temptations that would face his children and for his inability to reconcile opposites in his worlds. A good man who wept too much. *Education:* grammar school and high school in Chicago. A bewildered family fleeing to America before Stolypin's necktie could encircle papa's neck. Relatives along the way helped us; all of them dead now. *BA, MA, PhD in Political Science, University of Chicago, 1930, 1931, 1934.* Not the easiest of times to stay alive and in school. But no one wants to hear about the depression now. The new breed has forgotten it. *Married: yes. Wife's maiden name: Trudi Loeffler* born in Teschen, Austria of a luckier (smarter?) family than mine: they all got out in the twenties and made modest fortunes for themselves in the land of opportunity. Where is she, by the way? How long does it take to empty ashtrays and start the dishwasher? *Children: David,* attorney; *Nathan,* MD; *Harriet Sorge Kiernan,* housewife married to an apostate Catholic now a despairing, doctrinaire Unitarian. Trudi had never made a fuss. She was as calm while two sons fulfilled every Jewish mother's dreams for her children as she was when her daughter, not even bothering to argue principles, ignored religion as a factor of any weight in marriage or parental relationships.

Sorge looked at his watch again: 2:30. He had gone to bed at a little before two; Trudi had said she would straighten up from the party and follow him. He considered getting up to find her—she would never hear him call; the house was too big—then settled back; she was a grown woman, capable of coming to bed when she was ready. *Present occupation: professor. Publications: Face to Face Groups in a Metropolitan Sub-Culture* (1939); *Military Attitudes and the Hypodermic Theory of Information* (1942); *Face to Face Groups in a Suburban One-Party Political System* (1946); *Secondary Groups in the Educational Hierarchy of a Parochial School* (1949); *Apperception and Non-Status-Oriented Community Participation* (1955); *Information Flow and Group Mobility* (1959); *Negroes in Suburbia: A Projection of Political Groupings* (1963)—the only book I ever wrote that might be called a best seller—*and articles in the American Journal of Sociology, American Political Science Review, etc.* And a biography of my father, planned and completed in my mind, only a few words on paper; I can't seem to get it right. To do him justice.

Quarter to three. He was tired and becoming impatient with Trudi's vagaries. She belonged in bed, with her husband. "Trudi," he called, his voice muffled by the empty bedrooms around him. Once the rooms had been bright and busy, cluttered with projects, catcalls, the blueprints and fears of growing children: luminous settings for Trudi's sensuous, mystic, mother's smiles and his own exhilarating sense of well-being and accomplishment in spite of the fate of the rest of his family. The rooms had changed with the growing years; Trudi had decorated and redecorated them to match the changing tastes of the children; projects became more complicated, blueprints simpler, fears more abstruse. And habits had changed. As the children stayed up later and later at night, so had he and Trudi; putting off their own climbing upstairs until the three near-adults with whom they shared their home were asleep and unaware of the rhythms of their parents' mattress. Then the children departed, in a rush, and their rooms, unnaturally neat, dusted, ordered, stood silent, arrested in their development, monuments to a past of echoes and shadows that Sorge could barely bring to life. If it were not for the carefully pasted, carefully dated photograph albums in the bookshelves, he would have no certainty of those fleeing years.

His house was still and aging. He was waiting for Trudi. He sighed. After twenty-nine years of marriage, and unchaperoned by offspring, a man should not have to chase his wife to his bed. He threw back the covers, slid his large, white feet into leather slippers, and left the bedroom: a huge man with stooped shoulders, thick black hair, enormous finely shaped hands, the beginnings of a paunch, heavy eyebrows and eyelids flanking a prominent, proud nose. "Trudi!" he called and descended the stairs in blackness.

The dark was littered with smells: stale liquor, crushed cigarettes, ashes of pipe tobacco, the perfume Susan Hazlitt wore as an inner sheath, the incense Barry Rosenthal had burned in his exposition on Byzantine religion, drying leftovers of chicken tetrazzini, olives, pickles, celery, assorted cheeses, nuts, coffee—the blended odors of a crowd and its indulgences that hovered long after the party was over. Sorge switched on a light. The scene sprang from its smells: nothing had been cleared away; it was as if he had just shut the door on the last guest—Frank Spiros, drunk, verbose, inconsolable since his divorce. Trudi had done nothing: not a plate scraped, a glass emptied, an ashtray dumped. She had stood here as he did now, looked at the mess—and had done nothing. What then had she done? Relived the hours? She had not seemed to enjoy the party; she had worn a distraught air that warred with her hostess smile, her eyes sliding frequently to the front door, the fingers of her restless hands tense. He had put it down to fatigue, and something unanalyzable that could wait until morning. She had let him go upstairs alone, had sent him upstairs alone, had stood here in the aftermath of the party—and turned her back upon it.

He moved toward the lighted kitchen, framing one of the jocular-admonitory comments with which he had trained her from the time she was a bride of sixteen and he an assistant professor of twenty-seven. Whatever was bothering her could be disposed of; she had always been amenable to suggestion, to a little soothing care. But the kitchen, tumbled and disorderly, was empty.

The bathroom, then—powder room, Trudi insisted. "Hey!" he called. "You in there?" Someone had shut the door but left the water tap partly open; a steady drip-drop answered Sorge's call; when he turned on the light, his mirrored face met him. His eyes had a startled, sensitive look.

"Trudi!" he roared, standing in the middle of the living room. "What the hell are we playing? Hide and seek? Damn it, woman, I'm tired!"

It was only after he had stood, unmoving, for a full five minutes, his words rocking in gentle waves about him, that it came to him that Trudi was not in the house.

He raced from room to room, short of breath, his wife's name exploding in sharp bursts into corners, closets, window embrasures. He took the stairs three at a time, slippers flapping, fingers blindly reaching for light switches as he looked—he knew he was being ridiculous—under beds, behind couches, in dresser drawers, beneath lamp shades. He leapt up the stairs to the unused third floor, sneezing in the dust, cursing the burned-out bulb, his wife's name a steady, murmured undercurrent on his lips: no longer a demand, but a question.

The basement. She had gone down to get something; she had fallen; she was lying there now, leg broken, or neck, or unconscious, or awake and unable to answer him, afraid, waiting for him to come. He saw her clearly and cried out. So much time wasted upstairs—he should have thought—he should have known . . . "I'm coming, Trudi! Don't move!"

The basement stairs were dark; the basement was dark. His certainty of her death, or near-death, plummeted him down the stairs and through the four damp rooms, as he pulled the strings that dangled from light bulbs; as he whispered her name, then slowly left him; for the first time, he began to be angry. The absurdity of trying to save himself by manufacturing tragedy. Faced with the sordid, he clutched at the dramatic: all the time avoiding the most natural place to look.

He climbed the stairs to the kitchen and paused at the door to the garage. He had used Trudi's car to buy liquor that morning; he had filled the gas tank. He had cashed a check for a hundred dollars at the bank and had given her seventy. But that was hardly important: they had a joint checking account with eight hundred odd dollars and though tomorrow (today) was Sunday she could find places to cash her checks—she was known at every damn discount store between Waukegan and Gary. He had done everything but buy her a ticket to Hawaii. Why Hawaii? "Wouldn't you like to live in Hawaii, Sol? Think of all the ethnic groups you could tear apart and put together in your own image." But that had been mockery; she had often mocked his work.

With a grunt, he yanked open the door. The two cars hulked side by side—mechanical counterparts of their owners snuggling in bed. He pushed a switch and watched the garage door slide up along the ceiling. Warm summer air flowed past the gasoline and carbon monoxide; the locust tree at the curbing bent in the breeze. In the silence, his breathing was heavy. She had not taken the car.

He slouched by the door, facing the cars, the tree, the dim shapes of houses across the street. A good neighborhood, a successful neighborhood. Old, established Evanston, a block from the lake, where money spoke quietly, gently, easily. A proud neighborhood where the painters came every year to refurbish outside and in, where garages held all the latest lawn and garden equipment for the Puerto Rican gardeners who descended in swarms of chattering efficiency from April to October, where elms were sprayed every spring and sidewalks plowed every winter. A neighborhood where all were settled, their children at the best colleges, or married; their grandchildren dressed from Field's or Saks; windows discreetly shuttered twice or three times a year for trips to Jamaica, Europe, occasionally Africa and, when time was short, Mexico or Canada. He and Trudi had been the first Jews on the block; since then two or three had followed, but not an influx; the neighborhood was balanced, carefully friendly, private. He had worked hard, in the early years, to get here and to stay here; to send his children to college; to take his wife on trips around the country, around the world; to feel, more than once, earned fulfillment. Where had she gone? Where that she could find more than she had here? And—he thought of it for the first time—with whom?

The telephone rang. Trudi. She had gone for a walk—hit by a car—had a heart attack—lost her way—a victim of amnesia—he had maligned her. Tragedy again. Damn it, it could be.

But he did not say her name when he answered. "Well?"

"Sol?"

Susan Hazlitt. He neither needed nor wanted her; it was too much effort to shift gears, to make the normally smooth transition from his wife to another woman. Impossible, now, to funnel lust into socially-accepted bon mots. "Susan, my dear, it is past three in the morning—"

"I know, Sol, but your lights are all on, like the White House in a crisis. Is there one?"

"One what?"

"A crisis."

"Oh." Not Susan. Someone would have to know, but not Susan. Not yet. "No."

"Just . . . no?"

"I lost something." Never tell a lie if you can help it, said the rabbi, my father. "I was looking for it."

He got rid of her. Her voice was smooth and heavy, as embracing as her perfume in his living room. Her last words—"If you need any help"—were meant to wrap him like a comforter, but now, at this hour, in his messy kitchen, there was no comfort, for Susan was not Trudi, in no way resembled her, and never had, nor had he sought resemblance, even on those occasions when she had taken Trudi's place in bed beside him.

No comfort, but confirmation. Trudi was gone. Had she been here, bustling about to create order in her home, or lying, stretched taut, beside her husband, Susan Hazlitt would not have telephoned: the windows would have been dark, the house wrapped in the sinless sleep of its neighbors. Had she had been here, anywhere, in any of the rooms, he, Solomon Sorge, would be at ease in his bed, not standing in the middle of the kitchen with a headache and tears of exhaustion in his eyes.

He stood. The smells of the house hung about him, magnified by silence. He had lost all his senses but one: his eyes stared at a patch of floor and saw nothing; his ears were clogged for there was nothing to hear; only his large nose was alive—it twitched like a dog's, recognizing individual odors, trying to find strands of order in chaos. Damn it, at least she could have thrown out the garbage before she left.

2

ALL RIGHT, he had accepted it. Accepted something; the fact that a state of affairs existed. He might even say—the thought rankled when he woke the next day—he had taken the affair too easily, had accepted all too readily, without the requisite pose of bereavement. After that first mad flight through the house, after the self-deception of a Trudi injured or dead, after Susan Hazlitt's too careful offer of help, he had stood alone in the kitchen, recognizing only the offending smell of garbage. Trudi was gone; it was left to him to clean up.

Until almost five in the morning he cleaned up. In a frenzy of thoroughness and efficiency, he stacked glassware and plates, scraped and drained them, loaded them in the dishwasher. He emptied ashtrays and set them to soak. He stuffed garbage down the disposal and, eyes closed, listened happily to the roaring of chewing blades and water flushing pulp down the pipes. He dampened a dust cloth with polish to wipe clean all the living room and dining room furniture; he vacuumed the rugs, wood floors, and tile in the kitchen. He scrubbed the toilet and washbowl in the powder room. Finally, with something called "Jubilee" saturating a damp sponge, he polished all the kitchen appliances and cherry wood cabinets, the brass lamp hanging over the round wooden table, the chairs encircling the table, the varnished window sills and white porcelain drawer pulls. Finished, he looked upon gleaming surfaces, clean stretches of uncluttered countertops, neat, symmetrically-placed furniture with every pillow fluffed to its intended contour. Was this how a woman felt after housecleaning, this accomplishment and pride in order, this possessiveness? Sorge began to understand Trudi's fury when he walked in on cleaning day and laid his behind on a chair, his feet on a hassock, his cigar in an ashtray. He simply did not fit in that clean room; something Trudi had been unable to explain to him over his stormy protests. Now he understood because now, this dark morning, no one fit in the still order he had created.

He went upstairs, then, after cleaning his house as if for a bride, and rather desultorily went through Trudi's dresser drawers and closet. He knew he should have done it earlier; but, even now, it did not seem important. Unless he found all her summer clothes gone and could deduce from that that she had, indeed, gone to Hawaii. But none of her clothes seemed to be gone. Blouses, sweaters, underthings neatly stacked, skirts and dresses hung on padded hangers, shoes lined in sentinel rows beneath, woolens and winter coats in garment bags with tiny moth cakes hanging among them. Hats (she hated hats but needed them for Temple on the high holidays) were boxed, pushed back on the closet shelf. Purses stood side by side on the same shelf: blacks, browns, blues, greens grouped together. She never wore any other color; he wondered why.

Then, without making the effort to picture Trudi somewhere, anywhere, alone or with someone, without a suitcase, wearing the black linen she had put on for the party, he went to bed. It never occurred to him that he would not sleep: those accustomed to trouble, to disaster, learned how to sleep when they had to; they needed their strength. And he slept, until Sunday noon.

Perhaps, like his grandfather and father in the days of the pogroms, he slept with a fairy tale: it can't happen here, but even if it can, it will be over in the morning. He awoke and reached out his hand for Trudi. Who was not there. Who, if he thought of it rationally (for, after all, one could not compare this disaster with that of the pogroms), could not be there (for such petty prayers were not likely to be answered). Sorge's own disaster—the sudden, complete, unexpected, uncalled-for erasure of his wife—was only a tragedy insofar as it disturbed the even tenor of his life, as it disrupted his steady climb to success and security in the teeth of a fate that had devoured most of his forebears and family. For, after all, was Trudi as significant as untold thousands in pogroms, as millions in ghettos and concentration camps? It had been said that one could not weep for millions; one could only weep for the single. But, with the memory of millions, could one wail with sincerity for that single? Solomon Alexei Sorge, in bed of a Sunday morning, wondered what had become of his wife and why he could not weep or fear or, at the very least, mourn.

"Because you're in shock," said Yetta. "It's terrible, terrible. A Jewish wife doesn't leave her husband. It's a nightmare. You're numb with tragedy. I always knew you were more sensitive than you liked to pretend."

Sorge balanced on the hind legs of a kitchen chair, drinking coffee, black, boiling, and wondered, as untold times before, why he chose his sister as confidante. She was a tragic Pippa—who but Yetta could have achieved that?—preaching the doctrine of God's presence in his heaven and the rightness of the world contingent on certain alterations in the Jewish scheme of things. Simultaneously—and Sorge admired this: it was either art or artlessness—she worshipped the glory of God and His cruelty to Jews, the wonders of the earth and its harshness to Jews, the brotherhood of man and men's brutality to Jews. Leaping over the crags of philosophical thought that made suffering and joy inextricable, she deified both, understanding neither. In common with most preachers, or disciples, of their own truths, she had a simplistic mythology awesome in its purity; her answers were almost always wrong.

She dyed her hair black or red or blond with the waxing and waning of the moon; her nails were painted by a manicurist who thought birth control a sin and tried to convert Yetta with each vehement stroke of the emery board; she wore bright, well-made clothes, bowled on Wednesdays, played mahjong on Thursdays, worked in the Michael Reese Hospital Resale Shop on Fridays. Her cleaning woman was named Quelardeen; she came from Georgia and groaned each time she knelt to wash the floor, so that Yetta had to leave the room, unable to bear her own guilt. She thought housework a form of slavery that deserved the highest pay, but did not raise Quelardeen's daily ten dollars for fear her friends would blame her for destroying the delicate balance of the market. She shopped frequently and read novels. She claimed to have a perfect marriage. "You're a sensitive, soft-hearted man, and you've had a terrible blow."

Sorge recaptured, momentarily, the panic of his early morning housecleaning, the cessation of thought, the refusal to concede his aloneness. There had been a kind of grandeur in such massive reactions; surely he deserved better than soft-hearted or even—though it was perhaps closer to the truth—sensitive.

"You always try to hide yourself," said Yetta. "To be unfeeling. Cold and distant. But you couldn't fool me. Yetta, I said to myself, he's suffering. He's not so far from us."

Above, perhaps, thought Sorge. My father thought otherwise but somehow conveyed that to me. One must be above to survive. The farther above, the easier (more impressive?) the survival.

"What's a family for," asked Yetta, "if not to weep with?"

There were too many tears in my youth, thought Sorge; tears and joyful despair. Yetta has fulfilled our heritage for us both; I decided long ago to abandon it. But he knew he was lying and he disliked lying to himself: would I prefer being a bastard, or, like Sartre who appreciated it, orphaned at a tender age?

". . . intuitively that something was wrong," said Yetta. "I told Doris Raschman at Sisterhood the other day: something is wrong, I said. Something isn't right."

Something is always wrong in Yetta's world; how, otherwise, could she exist? She has solved my dilemma by weeping for each of the millions who have been killed and if the tears begin to dry after the four hundred thousandth or so, her voice still retains its quivering indignation and multiplied sorrows. What, then, has she left for her family, for me? Stupid question; she has for me precisely what she has for the unknown, with the added fillip of being able to offer a shoulder to demonstrate, personally, close at hand, in the reality she has misused, her empathy and the extra reservoir of tears she maintains for precisely such occasions. And the recipient, exhausted by the whole procedure, must admire, if nothing else, her energy. Or would she call it love?

". . . could almost have predicted Trudi would leave you."

Sorge looked up. "What?"

"Well, have I finally got the great man's attention? The mighty intellectual is willing to listen—"

"What did you say?"

"You don't have to raise your voice, Solomon. I know you don't like my sarcasm."

He stood over her. "What did you say about Trudi?" he roared. He knew his bulk intimidated her, and his voice; he used them consciously, calibrating decibels when he no longer could tolerate her coy knitting of troubles.

She drew a martyred breath. "If you'd been listening to me, I was talking about being a sister. The importance of being a family. Being needed. Loved. Having someone to turn to. I was telling Doris Raschman about it the other day—poor thing, she really knows what trouble is, her son—"

Sorge clenched his fists.

"So you don't care about Doris Raschman. Or her son. You don't care enough about other people, Solomon. You're cold. You have to change that, you have to learn to love. That's just what I was telling Doris. I met her at Field's, we just ran into each other, and she said should we have some coffee and I looked at my watch—I don't like to drink too much coffee, you know, it's a stimulant, after all, and it makes me run to the washroom all day—anyway, I looked at my watch and said it's almost time for lunch, let's eat together and she said fine. She should go on a diet but God knows with her troubles she's got to eat. A human being can only worry about so many things at once. So we ate in the Walnut Room, and Doris started telling me about her son and I said we all have troubles, take my brother who's going to have trouble with his wife, it's been coming for years. Doris, I said, Trudi isn't happy. Something's wrong, I said. And Doris, with all her *tsuros,* was very interested, she met Trudi at Sisterhood a few times and she liked her—everyone seemed to like Trudi, didn't they? That's a knack I never had; I'm a woman of strong opinions and I'm not afraid to say them out loud—to people's faces if necessary. But thank God I have friends, two or three good friends; it's a miracle to have that many the way people misuse friendship these days. I don't think Trudi had so many friends either, but everyone seemed to like her, women as well as men. She didn't seem to let anyone get too close to her, if you know what I mean. Friends have to be close to each other, but people did like her. Not that that made her happy. It takes more than being liked to be happy. So I told Doris I was worried about you, and about Trudi. Of course I never mentioned the fact that Trudi was having an affair—''

Sorge stamped one huge foot and shook the house. ''Stop this!'' he bellowed, the depths of his anger as frustrated and helpless, as childlike as the stamping of his foot. ''Talk coherently or get out of here and leave me alone!''

''Don't scream at me!'' screamed Yetta. ''I'm not deaf and I'm not one of your children. I try to talk to you, I try to help, I try to understand and what do I get? Thanks? Gratitude? Even a little love? What I get is screaming.'' She waited while two tears formed and began their slow descent down her powdered cheeks. ''I don't understand you, Solomon,'' she went on more quietly, settling back comfortably in her chair. ''This is a terrible day. You called me; I came. I came to help. And what do I find? Nothing. You don't cry, you don't talk, you don't telephone to find Trudi, you don't call the police—all you do is yell at your sister. This is what I rushed over here for? I left my Sammy alone with his lunch for this? Don't make faces at me; sit down, I'm talking to you. It's like I told Doris; he doesn't care about anybody, I told her. No wonder Trudi's upset. I saw her once, her eyes were red from crying. That sweet little thing, so tiny, I always wondered how you two—well, that's none of my business, but a sister, a loving sister, wonders about these things. It's part of her job. My job. When papa died I said to mama, 'We're the women of the house, we have to take care of the boys.' Can you imagine? I was only seven but I recognized my responsibilities—shared with mama, of course. But mama was in a bad way, crying all day, worrying about living in a strange country—

it was still strange to her—without papa, not speaking the language—well, she spoke a little, but . . . not having any money, and she leaned on me. Only seven and she leaned on me. Of course I spoke English and she treated me like another woman. I never had a childhood. Not that I'm complaining; I didn't want to be a child; I wanted to take care of you and Leon and Daniel, *oleve sholom.* And then when mama married Max of course it was all my job to see that you were all right. Mama had a new life to make. And I didn't mind, I wanted to do it, I wanted to take care of you. A Jewish family is strong because it holds together. And I did hold us together, didn't I, Solomon? I did give you a good life? I talked to you about school and you told me about the girls you knew; even when you went to college you were living with us and you confided in me. And that was right; mama couldn't understand these things. And when you married Trudi I thought, she's a nice girl but not smart enough for Solomon. And not big enough. That did occur to me, Solomon. She was too tiny. You would always worry about hurting her. I don't agree with mama that we should ignore the sexual act—it's part of our lives. If it's handled with delicacy. I told mama that. She cried. She would have slapped my face but I was already too big. Do you know when I was marrying my Sammy and I told her I wanted a—well, you know what I wanted, Sammy and I didn't want children right away, after all we were still young—I told mama and she almost fainted? I had to go to the doctor myself. So I didn't talk to her about my fears for you and Trudi but I worried. I never minded worrying about you. I always wanted only the best for you, for all of us. The best, the easiest. And I tried, I did what I could to help. But I've tried to know my place, too, and if I didn't you've told me often enough. What I put up with from you! Just because I told mama I'd keep an eye on you. I did tell her that, you know. She saw that I cared about you, that I wanted to help you, and she was marrying Max and I think she didn't quite know what to do with you, anyway. So I told her I would, I promised her I would. And when I married my Sammy—I wasn't going to get married, I was going to devote myself to you but Sammy wasn't a danger, a threat—do you know what I mean? There wasn't so much . . . so much passion that I would forget my family. My Sammy's a good man; you know that, Solomon. Of course he doesn't talk much but he's a good man and a good provider. And a good father. So I could watch over both of you. But it hasn't been easy, let me tell you, watching you grow up, with all your success and people reading your books and students looking at you like you were God or something, and then to see you marry a sweet simple girl who loved you and make her unhappy, let her have an affair she probably didn't even enjoy, though that wouldn't be any of my business either. . . ."

"Enough." He was terribly tired; his bones ached, his neck was stiff, his stomach empty, shrunken. Perhaps he called Yetta here because her wrong answers made his own correct, reinforced his private visions, made reality of his myths, but none of that seemed important when he faced her. He should have kept the hours private, to examine his reactions, to examine himself. "Go home, Yetta."

"I can't go home, Solomon. You need me."

"Go home. All I need is to be alone."

"Solomon, *talk* to me. How can I help you if you don't talk? Did you quarrel last night, you and Trudi? Did you, do you ever hit her? Or, oh, Solomon, you couldn't—you didn't—force yourself on her?"

"Dear God," muttered Sorge and burst out laughing at the wild improbabilities of his morning.

"Hysteria," said Yetta firmly. "Good. I'm glad to see it.

You must *feel,* Solomon; then I can help you. But don't swear at me."

Sorge sat down. "I was not swearing, my dear Yetta. I was calling on God to send a gust of wind through my kitchen and carry you away to points unknown. Go home, Yetta. Go home to your Sammy and his lunch."

Two more tears appeared. "You don't want me?"

"I'd rather be alone. Think things out."

"What things?"

"Among others, the fact that my wife has disappeared."

"Of course she has; what have I been saying? You haven't acted like anything happened at all and I've been trying to make you feel something. It's terrible, terrible. You have to suffer. I want to help."

"By informing me of a mythical affair."

"You don't believe me."

"Not one damned word."

"I asked you not to swear at me. If you would let me finish . . ."

"Yetta." He stood again and moved to the back door. "Trudi was incapable of intrigue, she was inexperienced and innocent. She had a good, full life and she knew it. If she were here, she would be disgusted with you. As I am. Now will you go home?"

"So now I'm a liar."

"I'm not Doris Raschman, my dear. I don't take kindly to leaps of the imagination. No, not a liar. A colorist. You know," he added, the desire to talk coming upon him so suddenly he had no time to remind himself that it was Yetta to whom he was talking, "on Sunday mornings we'd sleep late and eat a quiet breakfast and laugh at the idiocies of the *Tribune* and then go out to buy the Sunday *Times.* Sundays were always slow days; we stretched them out. Trudi once called Sunday a story by Scheherezade."

''Oh, Solomon,'' Yetta was weeping now; the reservoir had at last been tapped. ''You do care about her, I'm so sorry, you never talk very much and Trudi *was* crying once. And it seemed to me you ignored her, no, not ignored so much as walked around her and sometimes you'd say excuse me and sometimes you wouldn't. You didn't take her into consideration the way my Sammy does with me; Sammy and I share decisions, we share our thoughts. Of course Sammy doesn't have as many thoughts as I have but he's a good man, a good provider and we *live* together. I don't know about you and Trudi. Did you live together, Solomon? It's hard to know about other people. Every time I decide somebody has a good marriage they get a divorce. I'm not always a hundred per cent right in my judgments. I admit that. And I'm not really sure that Trudi had an affair, I just think so; I never dared ask her. Once I met her on the near north side and her face was shining; she was coming out of one of those rebuilt coach houses. Solomon, what can I do to help? We've got to stand together in this; it's terrible, terrible. Maybe I should call Sammy and ask him to come over?''

''I think not,'' muttered Sorge, demonstrating a capacity for self-control new to him. ''Sammy likes to rest on Sundays. Somehow I'll manage alone. Maybe I'll take a nap.''

''Oh, you poor thing,'' cried Yetta. ''You're exhausted. You probably didn't close your eyes last night. That I can understand. I should have known. You go upstairs and lie down and I'll start your dinner.''

Sorge's control began to slip. ''Yetta ,'' he groaned, opening the door. ''Go home this minute and I shall forgive all your excesses and sins for all time.''

Deliberately, Yetta took a sip of cold coffee. ''You'll forgive me?'' she asked calmly. ''For sending me away?'' She looked up, her face suddenly contorted. ''Why are you trying to get rid of me? So you can have one of your women over for company? Maybe you got rid of Trudi so the field would be clear! Look at your face! I'm right, aren't I? The nail on the head. Little Yetta isn't so stupid, is she? Not as stupid as poor Trudi!"

Sorge moved to the table, stuffed Yetta's cigarettes and lighter into her purse, picked up her coat and walked back to the door. "I am about to throw some of your worldly possessions into the back yard. I intend to follow by throwing you into the back yard. If you come back, either alone or with your inflated insurance salesman, I shall spy on you from the upstairs window and keep my doors locked. You are a stupid woman and you force me to act like a child. I cannot tolerate stupidity, nor the dislike I feel for myself at the moment. Do I make myself clear?"

"Something's going to happen," said Yetta. "And you don't want me here."

"Yetta . . ."

"Anyway, you're just upset. I can always tell because you start talking like Nero Wolfe."

Sorge's laughter burst from him; my God, no wonder I always call her; is anyone so comforting? He tossed her purse and coat onto the back lawn and moved to take her in his arms, lift her off the chair and kiss her warmly on her forehead. "I love you, Yetta. You are everything a man dreams of. Now go home; I'll call you tomorrow."

"And today?"

"Today I will clean the rest of the house. Alone."

"And tonight?"

"I shall sleep alone. Unless, of course, Trudi walks in from her vacation in Hawaii."

"From what?"

"Didn't I tell you? Trudi is vacationing. I don't know when she'll be back; I told her not to hurry."

Yetta wiggled out of his arms. "Solomon, no one will believe that."

"My dear," he said pleasantly, "I don't give a tinker's damn what anyone believes. Trudi has gone to Hawaii. If anyone asks you, that is precisely what you will answer."

"But it's a lie."

"It may be. I haven't even decided how often to use it yet. But if I do, and until you hear otherwise from me, it is my story and you will honor it. Whose problem is this?"

"Ours, Solomon. Nothing is stronger than the family. We suffer together."

He kissed her again and edged her through the door. "I accept your share in the problem if you accept my lead. If you'll leave me alone when I tell you to. Is that clear?"

"Solomon, don't send me away. Please, I beg of you, don't send me away. All my life I've waited for something like this, for a time when you would really need me, when the family would depend on me. I used to dream about accidents, illnesses, tragedies that I could prevent or repair. All my life I've looked for a day like today. Let me stay, Solomon; let me stay and help. I'll cook for you and we'll talk like you and papa used to talk, we'll decide what to do, we'll work together to find a solution, a way out. Maybe you want me to get in my car and look for Trudi? I'll do whatever you say, whatever you want. But let me share this terrible time with you, let me make it *our* worry. I've always wanted to be necessary to you; this is the time. I'll talk or I'll be quiet, I'll cook and clean—a man shouldn't have to clean house; I'd never let Sammy so much as wash a dish or dust a chair—I'll do just what you want. But don't make me leave. Please don't make me leave."

His back ached and he felt hungry without the desire for any specific food. He longed for a bed, for the dim, silent coolness of his room. Mostly for silence. But Yetta was watching him, pleading. "Make a list," he said. "Go home and make a list of all the places she might have gone. Call me tonight and read it to me."

"You really want me to leave?"

"Make a list."

"I could do it here."

"At home. With your husband. For me."

"I have to leave?"

"I am asking you to."

"You'd be home if I called?"

"I'll be home, waiting."

"You really want me to go and leave you alone? In this big house?"

"I really want you to go. Please, dear Yetta. For me."

She stood, uncertain. "The police should be called."

"When and if I decide."

"Maybe a detective . . ."

"When and if I decide."

"What are you waiting for, Solomon?"

He looked at her. "I don't know," he said. "Now go home."

3

SUNDAY NIGHT. In the cold months they would eat dinner at a small table before the living room fireplace, warmed by the curling flames of a birch fire, the rest of the house shadowed and still. In the summer they would carry trays to the patio and sit beneath the huge pin oak that had once supported rope swings and a tree house. There was always music—Bach, Vivaldi, quartets of Mozart, Beethoven, Shubert—Sorge's favorites. When they talked, their voices were low, savoring the silence, the dusky, fragrant air. They were comfortable. I *know* we were comfortable. There was no tension; we were at ease with each other. When the telephone rang it would be one of the children, to talk for awhile, to share events, to let the grandchildren say goodnight. Their calls would remind us that the silence of the house was newborn, that only recently we were a part of growing up, of noise and argument and giggles and adolescent despair; that, even in our new silence, we were not really alone, and thank God for that. We were happy.

Sunday night. Trudi's Scheherazade Sunday. Sorge sat alone on the patio, staring at Trudi's rose bed, a bottle of bourbon in one hand, notes for his Monday morning class in the other. The silence was appalling.

"Korean spice bush," he muttered, identifying a shrub

next to the patio. His voice scattered the silence. "Three Persian lilacs. One hawthorn. Two burning bush, two Rose of Sharon, two—what the hell are those?" Trudi was the gardener; not he. "Austrian pines in the south corner; Scotch pines in the north. Red Dogwood across the back lot line; perennials in front of them: peonies, hibiscus, funkia, phlox, day lilies, chrysanthemums, and the annuals that Trudi laughs about because they come back each year whether she wants them to or not; marigolds, snapdragons, moss roses. How could she leave her garden?" He was dismayed to hear himself sniffle. He drank from the bottle and brooded at the garden. They had planted everything together: Sorge digging the holes, Trudi holding the bushes and trees straight while he shoveled in peat moss and clayey soil and finally the fresh black dirt they bought by the yard. Together they knelt in the moist earth to hammer in stakes for tomato plants, together they stretched a wire fence to contain proliferating raspberry canes, together they went out before dinner to cut mint for their iced tea. Where Trudi wanted a new garden he dug out sod, turning over the soil, standing to rest on his shovel while she transferred seedlings from flats to neat rows, labeled, fertilized, watered. They pruned bushes and trees together, one standing back to judge the final shape while the other snipped a twig, a branch, a leaf growing from the trunk. When he did the heavy work she would bring out cold drinks and they would sit together, hands stained, bodies sore, foreheads filmed with perspiration, the sunlight making them dizzy, somnolent, a little reckless. Once, on a morning when the children were at Sunday school and the roaring of electric lawnmowers on either side wrapped them in a private world, he reached out to cup her breast and they both rose, swaying a little in the sun, to walk together into the shaded house and upstairs to their room. She had smelled of earth and leaves;

he had lain upon her and closed his eyes, outside again, elemental, immensely strong and pure.

And in the evenings, showered, freshly dressed, they would sit on the patio, screened from neighbors by greenery and color and fragrance, eating and drinking in a shrunken, personal, handmade world. Our world; our yard; our labor. The children played here; once there was a swing set and sand box where the Scotch pines now stand; once there were bare spots in the grass from croquet and baseball; time after time there were scattered paper plates and cups and hats after a birthday party. How could she leave it?

His shoulders were convulsed; he was crying. His insouciance with Yetta had not been entirely feigned; he had been searching for something—as Yetta put it—to feel, something minor, Yetta's comedy, to settle his reactions as a tablet might settle a stomach. Now, alone on his patio, *their* patio, his voice naming bushes to keep the silence at bay, drinking, as he never did, from a bottle, he wept. How could she leave it? Not alone the bushes, not the gardens, not the yard or the house, but the memories inherent in all of them; the *life* of them, her life in them. How could she rip herself from herself knowing, as she must, that anything she did from now on would be a repetition of something she had already done with him?

But some still sober honesty forced him to admit he was not weeping only from unhappiness or self-pity; he was furious, frustrated as when he stamped his foot at Yetta: *he did not know what had happened.* Where had she gone, this woman he had married, in the middle of the night, without extra clothing, without her car—and why? What had gone through her mind in the three or four minutes before she stepped out the door? For that matter—and this came much harder—what had gone through her mind in the three or four months (years?) before the night she walked out? He did not know; he did not have the faintest idea. And the tears now trickling away were more than a little from anger at his ignorance. That was what Yetta had been unable to understand: a man cannot quickly grasp, much less admit or act from, his own ignorance.

He drained the bottle and stood up. In the clear air, a car door slammed, a dog barked, wind rustled the leaves of the oak above him. The silence was so complete he could hear the steady, gentle rustling of the lake a block away. I'll walk. Give her a chance to come back. And explain. But as he turned from the patio the telephone rang.

The telephone had always annoyed him: he liked to gauge instant reactions to his words in facial expressions, not wait to puzzle over the intonations of a magnified voice. He had never understood Trudi's frantic efforts to climb from a bathtub or run inside from her garden to grasp the receiver before the ringing ceased. If she was too late, she became fearful and began ticking off the names of those who might have called for her help: first, the children; then a list of close friends who must have needed her; then mere acquaintances who might have discovered she was the only one to provide something they lacked. In these cases, she always phoned the children. "Did you call me? What's the matter?"

Sorge remembered innumerable times when Trudi had dashed in from somewhere to grab the receiver and shout a triumphant greeting, only to be asked to subscribe to the *Tribune* for three months, or to buy something from the Blind Workers, or did she want the Tiny Tot Photography Studio to photograph her babies in these precious years before they grew up? Then her face grew desolate, lonely; the triumph in her voice replaced by helplessness. "No . . . no . . . no . . ." until Sorge grabbed the telephone and shouted some non sequitur about the Daily Worker, or Burpee Seeds, or passport photographers. It never failed to give him satisfaction, then, to try to picture the face he could not see.

But now, suddenly, there was no other link with Trudi, with the possibility of Trudi. Let your fingers do the walking. Would Trudi walk to him on her fingers? Or fingers and then knees, begging forgiveness for a momentary aberration, a reversion to childish impulses? I have to answer it. And talk. And wait.

"Yes," he said into the blind receiver, hating his disadvantage.

"Dad," said his son Nathan. "Aunt Yetta just called. What's going on over there?"

"God damn your Aunt Yetta," growled Sorge. "It should have come from me."

"What should have come?" asked Nathan. "What's wrong?"

"Yetta didn't tell you?" Unbelievable.

"She hinted. You know how she is. 'Terrible things, Nathan. Your father needs you. You should call him.' Coy. Is it mother? Is she sick?"

Not so unbelievable after all. Yetta would never be the bearer of terrible news whole and entire. She would only suggest tragedy and set events moving. And what could he tell his son? That he had let his wife slip through his fingers? That this was a case for Nero Wolfe or Lord Peter Wimsey? That he was ignorant? "She isn't here," he mumbled.

"Well, where is she?" demanded Nathan.

"Gone!" roared Sorge. "Walked out. Disappeared. I don't know where the hell she is and your aunt should keep her mouth shut."

There was a long silence. Sorge clutched the receiver, seeing Nathan frown, rub his forehead, tap his foot in the little dance that always meant he didn't know what to do next.

But he did know; he was first a doctor. "Do you need a sedative?"

Sorge shook his head.

"Dad?"

"No. I just want to think. I want to walk."

"How long has she been gone?"

"Since last night. This morning. About two o'clock this morning. I've been cleaning house."

"I'll be right over."

"No. I'm going for a walk."

"You think she'll just come home if you're gone?"

Children should not be allowed to see into their parents' minds; some realm should remain private. "I don't think anything; I just want to walk."

"Why don't you come over here?"

"Because I don't want to talk."

"We might be able to figure something out . . ."

"I don't want to talk. I want to think."

"About what to do?"

"About Trudi."

"Oh." Could a son understand that? It was a mother, not a wife, he was worrying about. Or was it? "Kay?" called Nathan away from the telephone. "Where are you?" Sorge heard her voice distantly. "Nothing," said Nathan. "I just didn't know where you were." As if he had visions, or remembered Wylie's book, that all women, everywhere, had disappeared. "No, I didn't think you were in China," he said. "I just wanted to know where you were. Dad?"

"Yes."

"Are you sure you don't want me—us—to come over?"

"Not tonight. Come tomorrow."

"Aren't you teaching tomorrow?"

"Tomorrow." Monday; a ten o'clock class. "Come in the afternoon. I'll teach."

"Maybe you should call and tell them . . ."

"I'll teach. Come in the afternoon."

"If you need a prescription . . . or something to make you sleep."

"Nothing. Goodnight, Nathan." He hesitated. "And don't worry."

"Oh, for God's sake. Dad, call me if she . . ."

"I will. Of course I will. Goodnight."

"Dad?"

"What?"

"Did you quarrel?"

"No."

"But why did she leave?"

"She did not inform me. Goodnight, Nathan." He hung up quickly and backed away from the telephone. Why did she leave? Because, obviously, she wanted to.

He walked from his home in Evanston to downtown Chicago. He was momentarily diverted, and amused, as he strode down Sheridan Road, to recall the importunate peace marchers who had urged Trudi and him to join them on this walk the previous year. He had said then, believing it, that such walks did no good. Well, perhaps he had been wrong. As a step toward peace and harmony they were probably valueless, but as therapy for the marchers, what could be better than a brisk eleven mile walk for a good cause?

And what was Solomon Alexei Sorge's good cause as his enormous frame moved purposefully southward, Lake Michigan to his left, the shops and apartments and sudden proliferation, after dry Evanston, of Chicago taverns on his right? He was thinking of his father. "We never walked when I was growing up. We went to Cheder or home; to a friend's house or a shop; there was little desire to walk for the sake of walking. There was almost no sense of nature as something to be enjoyed.'' So Sorge became a walker, defiantly naming the trees and flowers and kinds of moving water for which there were no words in Yiddish. His father had described the Jews of the Pale as nonwalkers; Sorge walked.

He and Trudi walked. From the campus on the eastern edge of Evanston their strolls took them to Wilmette on the north, Chicago on the south, Skokie on the west. They walked to movies, to concerts and plays on the campus, to visit friends. They walked down the quiet streets of Evanston, past old three-story and new bi-level houses, past elaborate churches and temples of sundry architecture; through the neat, retiring Negro section; along the railroad tracks on Green Bay Road; and always back to the lake: stretches of clean, well-swept sand and gnarled trees swaying in the metronome of rising and falling waves. A good town: a little stuffy, more than a little snobbish, but Chicago seemed far away and perhaps that was reason enough to be snobbish.

But he was in Chicago now. Striding past Loyola University and Chicago had once been a dream. ''It will be different in America,'' said papa.

''Different, maybe,'' said mama. ''But not better.''

''Yes, better,'' countered papa; it was by now a familiar litany. ''Better. There are no pogroms in America.''

Mama shrugged. ''You've been there?''

''And no Stolypin,'' said papa. Stolypin had been assassinated two years before, but no matter. Every anti-semitic prime minister of Russia—and what tsarist prime minister was not anti-semitic?—was Stolypin to the Jews.

''So,'' said mama, ''in America he'll have a different name.''

''Even if that were true,'' said papa, ''there is no tsar to stand behind him in America.''

''Since when has that mattered?''

''The peasants weren't bad. . . .''

''They just hated Jews.''

''They couldn't help themselves.''

''To keep from killing Jews?''

''It was the tsar who forced them.''

''So now someone can force a man to kill another?''

''The tsar campaigned against us.''

''And Ivan was happy to oblige.''

''They thought they were protecting themselves.''

Mama made a face. ''Cutthroat Jewish competition.''

''They were sincere,'' said papa.

''So sincere they drove us out.''

''But in America—''

''In America it will be the same. Just the same.''

''There people are free.''

''Free to close doors on us. Everyone is free *kronye zhydov.''*

''Except the Jews,'' chanted five-year-old Solomon.

''Even the little one knows,'' said mama. ''Such wisdom to have pounded into him at that age.''

''No more,'' said papa. ''Not in America.''

Solomon tugged at his father's hand. ''No more neckties, papa?''

''No more neckties,'' said papa. ''In America they do not hang revolutionaries.''

''You were not a revolutionary,'' said mama sharply, looking over her shoulder at the sleeping ship. ''Don't talk that way.''

''In the Cossacks' eyes I was a revolutionary,'' said papa.

''In Americans' eyes, too, if you talk that way.''

''No, mama. Because I did nothing wrong.''

''You let the Bund hold meetings in the synagogue!''

''The Bund was right in some ways.''

''Everyone is right in some ways to you! You never make up your mind!''

"Hush, mama. It is difficult for me. . . ."

Mama's hand made an angry gesture. "So we stay in *galut*. We couldn't go to Palestine. Home."

"I didn't know," said papa.

"What didn't you know?" asked Solomon.

"Whether I should be a Zionist," said papa.

"Zionist!" spat mama. "You don't need a label to go where you belong. You'll see; it will be just as bad in America. They'll call you a socialist."

"They will be wrong," said papa. "I was not a socialist any more than I was a Zionist."

"You were nothing," cried mama. "So you will be nothing. Everywhere you will be nothing because you will not go home."

And then Solomon, exhausted by the familiar, chanting argument, lurching with the ship, stuffed with the everlasting macaroni fed the passengers, began to vomit and mama gave a triumphant cry. "You see! Even the journey goes badly!"

My only memory of the trip to America, thought Sorge, looking up at lighted windows of apartments that floated past him as he walked. Did I have some intimation that papa's heart would never be the same, that fleeing Russia and arguing with mama, together with his own racking doubts, was too much for him, that he would die in Chicago still doubting, still fearing the wrongness of his decision because America had been far from all he had hoped and argued for? If so, I do not remember it. I was looking forward to being an American.

Papa died and twenty-eight years later mama got her wish: she moved to Palestine. She lived in Haifa, wrote letters to her children urging them to come join a *kibbutz,* survived a war that saw the birth of Israel, and was content. She had bequeathed her children sharp tongues and sharper eyes, an assuredness of the ills of the world, and a guilty doubt of their father's wisdom that equaled that good man's own doubts concerning himself. Fortunate mama, thought Sorge. She will never know what she left us. Two of us are dead; Yetta does not understand; and I would never tell her.

But someday I will write my father's biography. And make all clear.

4

AT WELLS STREET, he turned southwest to Old Town. A Polish professor visiting Sorge's University had decried Chicagoans for calling this area old—who knew better than the Poles what was really old, what deserved the name? But Sorge understood, as the professor had not (coming from a country then celebrating its thousandth year as a state) the need of America to create things old, the perpetual harping on the value of tradition as a symbol for stability and virtue while having no reverence at all for that which was really old. It was a case of national ambivalence: tear down the old but revere tradition; that is, as long as the two are not confused, thus interfering with progress in this land of progress. It is easier, therefore, to create an area such as Old Town, self-consciously coy, mimicking the façade of the past, as suspect as an underaged cut of meat, than to retain monuments to a sometimes remarkable age that, in the mid-twentieth century, have the misfortune to be in the way of a parking lot or a new office building or university campus.

Sorge could sympathize. How could a nation value the few genuine artifacts it had (the most genuine being the Indians) when it did not yet know what it was or where it wished to go? Never did birth pangs last so long or cause so much bedside concern. America was like the young wife who, worried about the permanency of her marriage, changes the furniture arrangement each week to maintain the illusion of freshness, of change synonymous with growth, with excitement. As a student of American institutions, he could understand, but he did not like Old Town: it was a pitiful reaching out for the ghost of a murdered parent.

Still, thinking of his father, and, now, of Trudi, he walked Wells Street. Trudi liked Old Town. She liked to browse through The Emporium and The Town Shop, Valucha's and Frank Ryan, Walls of Art and The Crate and Barrel. She brought home candy sticks, teak trays, faked antique paintings, Brazilian blouses, Danish coffee mugs, Japanese saki sets. "I know I'm indiscriminate," she would say to Sorge's raised eyebrows. "But I love the shops." "You can get most of these things at Field's," Sorge pointed out. "It's not the same," she said. "Field's isn't interesting. Or fun."

Sorge had long since given up arguing Trudi's concept of fun. Years ago, shortly after their marriage, he had thought she was emphasizing, in quarrels, the difference in their ages. "Not important," she said when he first circled the idea of marriage and debated the eleven years that lay between them. "You're mature enough to adjust to a child bride." He smiled; Trudi at sixteen was a mature woman. But later: "It's fun," about her bicycling through the park when the breakfast dishes were undone; "it's fun," as four-year-old David had said after cutting off half his hair with the kitchen scissors. "I don't need another child," Sorge shouted. "There are adult pleasures; fun is for children." She had never acknowledged his arguments; finally, it was her sheer incomprehension that defeated him. "I could probably understand you," she said. "But instinct tells me I shouldn't try." The same quiet, wry humor that once attracted him (her vision of the world always seemed a bit askew) played havoc with his sense of order and progression once they were married.

"You don't like Old Town because it isn't really old," said Trudi. "I love it because it pretends. Like Yetta dying her hair, only in reverse." "Immaturity," growled Sorge. "Man's response to reality," said Trudi and kissed him. "I love you, Sol."

Someone jostled his elbow, reminding him he was not alone. Or that he was. Wells Street was quieter on Sunday night than on Saturday when one was carried along by the crowds, but still there were people: couples. Everyone, it seemed, had a partner: prostitutes walked in pairs, like nuns; lesbians and homosexuals flaunted their mates; college kids were in threes and fours; commuters down for a last fling before the new week were in couples in large, mink-clad groups. For the first time since his marriage, Sorge saw himself outside the pairing-off of society. Amid the bright lights and curio-stuffed windows, the chattering, laughing customers of Old Town blended into a charming advertisement, with Sorge the observer, silent watcher, looking down from his great height, a foreigner appraising the natives. And wasn't he a foreigner? His wife had left him, disappeared; how many of those around him could claim that distinction?

He was at home only because he was in the city, where he belonged. Evanston, though hardly country, often was uncomfortable; Sorge felt torn from the vitality of Chicago. Here, in the city, he walked through hundreds of other lives; every window, every door, every rooftop protected a unique set of circumstances (and if they were not always unique, part of the wonder lay also in their similarities). Nowhere else could he begin to comprehend the hugeness, the fantastic multiplicity of society. He walked through the world he professed to study—the behavior of individuals in the political system—and quietly laughed at himself for his presumption. He walked; the sidewalk returned the pressure of his feet;

hundreds of hostile faces passed his own; the cherished, and necessary, secrecy of the city challenged him, the alien, to try his hand at opening doors. He had set himself up as an expert, he even taught others from his expertise, but the city mocked him as he traveled its streets: he was urban of urban stock, he was learned, he was sophisticated, but by setting himself up as interpreter he had partially removed himself from the center of activity. "If I am not for myself," Hillel said, "who will be for me?" But he added, "If I am not for others, who am I?" Sorge extended it: "If I cannot be of others, what am I?" At which point he usually fled back to Evanston and suggested to Trudi that they attend a Friday night service at the Temple. "We're going to the Hazlitts' for dinner," she said. "Shall I call them? I can say you've heard your voices again." "Never mind. We'll go another night." "To the Hazlitts'?" "To Temple." He never knew whether to be angry with her for wilfully misunderstanding, or grateful for her limning his sudden urges as a child's demand for the uncomplicated. "What is a Jew, papa?" In three easy sentences.

•

He descended a few steps to open the door of the Bratskellar. He was not sure whether he had had dinner that night, but he was hungry. The restaurant, as always, was underilluminated and overcrowded, but the heavy Austro-German decor was sufficiently authentic to be pleasant and the bratwurst and beer superb. Sorge settled at a table in the corner, gave his order, and fell into the kind of stupor he usually experienced when eating alone.

He enjoyed eating; he did not enjoy solitary chewing. He preferred the illusion that jaws are for verbalizing as well as for mastication; thus was man carried one more step forward from his animal forebears. "Chewing isn't romantic," said Trudi. "You'd like your food to slide down whole." They were at Maison Lafite and Sorge was happy, eating Grenadine de boeuf and wild rice, drinking a Rosé de Lascombe, relaxed beside a roaring fire. When he ignored her, Trudi went on thoughtfully. ''Not only romance. Dignity. You'd like to achieve a dignified romanticism. Or do I mean romantic dignity? Like the man who keeps his hat on to hide his bald spot while he makes love to Cleopatra.'' ''Leaves.'' ''What?'' ''Caesar wore a crown of leaves. And I have no bald spot.'' ''No, but you try not to swallow when we make love.''

He put down his fork. Malicious woman! She saved her little insights to stab him when he was least prepared. And yet she amused him more often than she annoyed or angered him. ''You're dissatisfied with the way I make love?'' ''No,'' she said with a kind of fierce coolness. ''No, you're quite good.'' Sorge picked up his fork and began to chew his meat. ''More wine?'' ''Now I've pleased you,'' she said. He filled her glass. ''You've allowed me to preen myself.''

But why the mask of coolness? Sorge ate his bratwurst and tried to recapture that evening, years ago, when she had placated him with sexual loyalty. It was not in Trudi's nature to placate; he recalled his inordinate gratitude on the isolated occasions when she verbally petted him or doled out praise. Yet he knew she had been proud of him: his lectures, his books, his popularity on campus, his generally easy way with their friends. If she had been unable to express pride, he would have understood. But there was something else: ''You force me to it,'' she said when they left the restaurant. ''To what?'' ''To make you angry.'' ''I'm not angry. Do you remember where I parked the car?'' ''On Dearborn. But you were angry.'' ''I'm never angry with you. Watch the curb.'' ''What if I had said I was dissatisfied?'' ''Then I couldn't have preened. But you would hardly have robbed me of my manhood." "No, I could never do that, could I? Your cup—if that's the right word—runneth over."

Crude, he thought, from a woman who is seldom crude. But he said nothing, for he was uncomfortable, faced with possible interpretations of her crudity: either her coolness sprang from overprotesting her own satisfaction to hide the lack of it (in which case he must consider himself something of a failure), or she had found out about—who was it in those days? the wife of an Evanston lawyer—what's her name (in which case, too, he was a failure).

There had been comparatively few women in Sorge's life, most of them after his marriage. He could chart his behavior from the lowest point: the intense, weary college days when he was searching for a girl worthy of his father's son; to the curve's peak: appraising every woman as potential temporary mate; to the plateau of the last few years devoted exclusively to Trudi until Susan Hazlitt appeared, proving he had not yet achieved, or sunk to, the monogamy of his father. At different times his women had called him brutal, demanding, gentle, patient, cruel, selfish, generous, even, once, briefly, sweet. To all of them he had shrugged his massive shoulders, putting his hand over their mouths, or, if it was early in the game, their breasts. He cared neither for categories in this instance, nor feminine analyses; post mortems bored him; it was as if the women, observant even in their passion, had acted the scientist, taking notes for the sexual edification of those to come, or, perhaps, the younger generation.

Trudi, with the exception of that one declaration, had never analyzed, never—though through the years he might have welcomed it—commented. She often played the aggressor, but it was only play; with a grace he admired she left no doubt that their roles were firmly established: he was to fill the vessel; it could hardly fill itself. Remarkable woman, he thought, finishing his beer; she did it without diminishing herself.

Unless the finale of that long-ago evening had tarnished the image without either of them admitting it, then or later; in fact, they had never mentioned it again. When they reached the car she was silent; once she said quietly, "I'm sorry," but he made no answer, not sure how pleased he should be. They drove in silence, their eyes held firmly to the Lake Shore Drive traffic and the exit signs they knew by heart. "Your mother will be asleep," said Trudi as they turned into the driveway. "Probably," agreed Sorge. Ever since she had moved in with them, his mother had pointedly not been a burden. "And the children, too," said Trudi. "I should hope so," said Sorge. "The house is dark," said Trudi. "Mother left a light in the dining room," said Sorge.

So it was in the dimly lit dining room that she pulled him down to the carpet, angrily fighting with her girdle as if he might escape before she was ready. She tugged at the zipper on his pants with one hand, guiding his hand with her other, all the time whispering desperately, "I'm sorry, I am sorry, please, Sol, I'm sorry," until, elaborately, convulsively, she jerked forward and finally sighed too deeply so that, for the first time, he doubted her and himself.

Two o'clock in the morning. Only twenty-four hours since he sat in bed filling out a form cataloguing his achievements. He would have to rewrite the information. *Date: 1 A.E.* After Evanescence. *Item:* The wife of the noted professor has disappeared. He is, therefore, in a special category, an elite—surely a very small one. Fame, in mysterious ways, also comes to him who stands and waits.

He could not go home. He stood outside, solitary on the nearly-deserted street, debating the miles between Old Town and Evanston, the probability of Trudi's waiting for him (.5 if one believed in miracles), the demands of his body: he had eaten; now he was tired.

He began to walk toward the Loop, counting his strides. If I were not so tall I could not cover so much territory; just before he died my father had to look up to me. He reveled in the strength of his legs; power gave him great pleasure. By the time he reached a hotel his fatigue was part of that power, as strong as his will to continue until he reached whatever goal he set himself.

"A single. Just for tonight," he said to the desk clerk.

"Sign here." The clerk was a boy with hair growing raggedly from a widow's peak, a red pimple at the side of his nose; he was bored, sleepy, and had spread his reading material—a piece of newsstand pornography, a James Bond mystery, and a shiny new paperback of *Catch 22*—on the counter in front of him. He looked up from his boredom. "Where's your bags?"

"I have none," said Sorge, writing.

Boredom disappeared. The boy snatched the register from Sorge. "Pay in advance."

"What?" asked Sorge. His fatigue was spreading from his legs; he could not stand up much longer.

"No bags; pay in advance."

Perhaps it was a new rule. Or an old one. When had he ever done this before? He fumbled in his pocket and counted out three dollars and seventy-two cents. He looked at the boy.

"That'll get you the closet. Five-fifty for the room."

"I don't have that much on me. If you have a blank check . . ."

"Now look." The boy glanced at the register. "Sol-o-mon what's the middle name? It looks Russian."

"Alexei. It is."

"You Russian?"

"Me Russian. A blank check . . ."

"You trying to be funny? Pull something?"

His skull was tight, the skin pulling on his cheekbones and eyeballs; his legs trembled. "I'm trying to overthrow the government of the United States. Now if you'll give me a blank check. . . ."

"If you were you wouldn't talk about it."

He sighed. If this boy had for some unexplainable reason gone to college he might have been in my class; for small favors are we thankful. "I have identification."

"They always do," said the boy.

Sorge pulled out his driver's license. "A check, please?"

"You could have stolen that. We're told about people like you. No bags and all."

"And all what?"

The boy waved his hand. "We gotta be careful. Five-fifty, pay in advance, I give you a room. Otherwise, out. We got rules."

"Now look," he said to the boy reasonably. "I'm exhausted. I walked here from Evanston. . . ."

"Jesus H. Christ," said the boy, fascinated. "You got more stories than my old man. Okay, I walked here from Detroit. Five-fifty, you get a room."

"I don't have five-fifty!" shouted Sorge.

"Don't yell at me, Sol-o-mon. This is a respectable hotel. You got any more stories? Where's your girl? Waiting outside?"

He could walk to another hotel. But he was walked out. He could take a cab home. But he didn't want to go home. "I'm willing to write you a check. I have no girl." I have no wife. "I want to sleep. Tomorrow I teach a class—"

"You're a teacher? I thought they kicked all the commies out."

"A few of us sneaked back in. All right. You can call my son. He can describe me, then you'll know I didn't steal the driver's license. Will that do?"

''You know, I kinda like you, Sol-o-mon. I don't really think you're a commie. You're too dumb. Who's your son? The president of Standard Oil?''

''A doctor.'' No, not Nathan. He doesn't need me on top of the hypochondriacs who wake him up each night. ''My other son is a lawyer. Here's his number.''

''You really got two sons, Sol-o-mon?''

''God damn it, will you call my son so I can get some sleep?''

''I never did nothing like this before. Okay, I'll do it. Like I said, I like you. What's his name?''

''The same as mine. Sorge.''

The boy dialed, watching Sorge, daring him to turn and run. Sorge stared back. How can I dislike him? He is a stupid child, trying to liven up a dull evening. But, my God, I am so tired. And what am I doing here, anyway?

''Your name Sorge?'' the boy said into the telephone. ''Yeh, I know it's almost three in the A.M. but there's an old guy here who says he's your father—''

''Where?'' Sorge could hear the voice roar—an echo of his own—through the receiver. ''Where is he? We've been frantic . . .''

The boy rubbed his ear and Sorge grabbed the receiver.

''David, I'm at a hotel. All I want is a room.''

''Where's mother?''

The boy reached toward Sorge. ''Look, Sol-o-mon, *I* do the talking. No cahoots between you.''

''Talk to this numbskull,'' said Sorge into the telephone. ''You and I can talk later.''

''But mother—''

''Just talk to him, David, please. I can explain later.'' Explain what? My sons have been in conference while I ate bratwurst and hiked the streets of Chicago. What shall I explain?

"Your name Sorge?" asked the boy. "Okay, okay, no more yelling. Just describe your old man." He looked at Sorge and his grin slowly broadened. "Okay, Sol-o-mon, I guess you're okay. He wants to talk to you. I'll get a blank check."

"David," said Sorge. "I cannot talk tonight. You've talked to Nathan. . . ."

"Of course I have. He called me. Look, dad, things like this just don't happen. I've been to your house. . . ."

"Is she there?"

"No, dad, she's not there. Look, if you could just give us a reason . . ."

"I have no reason. David, can I go to sleep?"

"Why don't you go home?"

"Because I'm here. Because I'm tired."

"Then come here. We've got the spare room."

"David, I have finally managed to get a room in this wretched hotel—"

"Wretched?" asked the boy.

"—and I intend to sleep here. David, I don't know what has happened. I know you're concerned. . . ."

"Concerned! For Christ's sake, of course I'm . . . Look, did she ever mention a divorce?"

"No. I'll talk to you tomorrow."

"But you haven't told me what hotel. . . ."

"It doesn't matter. I'll call you tomorrow. Go to sleep. And let me go to sleep." He hung up very gently and reached for the blank check. "Five-fifty and I get a room," he said to the boy. "Now give me a key."

"Whaddya teach?" asked the boy.

"The responsibility of citizens to take part in the political process," said Sorge, tiredly hugging his irony to himself. "Citizens like yourself. My key, please?"

"Room 308," said the boy. "You mean voting?"

"Perhaps running for office," said Sorge, retreating. "Wouldn't you like to be governor of Illinois?"

"Me?" said the boy. "Christ, you got more crazy ideas . . ." but Sorge was in the elevator and the boy, with a shrug, returned to the quiet of his magazine nudes in the empty early-morning lobby.

5

"EACH GENERATION," quoted Sorge to his morning seminar, "criticizes the unconscious assumptions made by its parents." He tipped back his chair and looked at the circle of twelve faces bent over hands busily copying his words. What would they say if I told them they're inscribing Whitehead rather than a trusted political scientist, that I've temporarily hauled them out of the constricted world we make for ourselves in defense of a science we can't define? They should know anyway; a political scientist would never make a statement like that. He briefly considered a lecture on what he was coming to call the bastard known as political science; but these twelve faces about him would shortly face their own classes and it was too late for him now to suggest they reevaluate themselves and their work of recent years to include Whitehead's premise. He was only beginning to do so himself.

Quite suddenly, euphoria swept him, as it had, momentarily on his walk last night: a sense of power. He was free to move, to change, to choose any path. The responsibility was to himself. If I am not for myself, who will be for me? Admittedly it was only a start, but had he ever really started? Even as he spoke to his students about Whitehead, about other names, honorable in political and social science—Aristotle,

Pareto, Burke, Weber—he was soaring away, above the seminar room; he was free to change.

He had not been home since the previous night. His sleep in the shabby hotel room had been sound, though he dreamt of Trudi and woke with a taste of his earlier fury at being a non-participant. With some trepidation he called the desk in the lobby, found a day clerk on duty, and requested coffee and shaving supplies from the drugstore on the corner. The clerk brought them himself.

"We're shorthanded," he said, his gray eyes roaming the room curiously. "You paid already?"

"No luggage," said Sorge, opening the tube of lather. "Pay in advance."

"He give you trouble?" asked the clerk. His fingers were curled as if to pounce.

"Why?" asked Sorge with caution.

"There's been reports. Sir. We don't want no trouble. He give you any?"

There is a hierarchy here and my friend of last night is at the lowest point, easily shoved off. They're looking for reasons to shove. For some reason—and the reason is almost never important—they don't like him, don't want him around. So kick him out. And where would he go, carrying his pornography and his mysteries and the occasional *Catch 22* that he probably heard from someone carries cachet and so should be displayed if not read? He could become a statistic: the unemployed for the month of June. He could enter trade school, but why hasn't he done that already? His goal could be to spend his life hectoring customers in an edge-of-town hotel. Someday he'll want to marry, or be forced to. My God, perhaps he is already. But they don't like him here. Or there's a relative waiting for the job. And why the hell should I care? I couldn't even cope with him. "No," he said, lathering his beard. "He was very helpful. Rules of the house and so on."

"What rules?"

"Pay in advance. No girls in the rooms."

"He said that?"

Sorge turned innocent eyes to the clerk. "Shouldn't he have?"

"Yeh, but . . . Well. Sir. We heard he was—you know, setting things up."

A pimp. Extraordinary devotion to the potentialities of one's job. And your uncle or brother or friend of the streets would do the same if he had the job. Anything to brighten the long night and bring in a few paying customers. "He set nothing up with me."

"Didn't even try, huh?"

Sorge cut himself. Why couldn't these people leave him alone? "Didn't even try."

"Oh. You want me to pour your coffee?"

"I'm shaving."

"Well. You got everything you need? Any complaints, you tell me. We take care of our people."

"I'm sure you do. I'll be leaving in half an hour."

He took the elevated to the campus and remained alone in his office until ten o'clock when his class met. As befitted one of the university's star performers, he had two offices, one in the basement of a building of classrooms, the other in a former private residence purchased by the university for use by political science professors and graduate students. The residence acted as a private club: kitchen, library, small offices cozily furnished, reception hall where one of four secretaries planted throughout the house politely turned away non-members, individual keys for the privileged. And it was distinctly a privilege to be part of one of the wealthiest departments on campus: an aura of importance surrounded the members, pervaded and justified their private jargon. The United States Navy granted money for research as did, later, the Army and Air Force; private foundations poured funds into studies of game theory, simulation, information flow, reduction, factor analysis. An intense feeling of excitement lent the house a perpetual air of Christmas: money came in, money went out, the university pointed with pride.

Sorge enjoyed it all—he admired wealth as he admired power—though he also cultivated the pose of amused, wondering observer, particularly when he described to visitors his fellow scientists' borrowing from economics, psychology, sociology, even physics, to develop theories, or, on a less ambitious scale, a few provocative hypotheses. According to those fellow scientists—the ones who garnered research grants in contrast to Sorge whose fame rested on books written and lectures delivered—he had never taken his work seriously enough. Translation: he had never taken the department seriously enough.

"Life is serious business," said Sorge's grandfather to his father and his father to him. Which proposition, for the Jews of the Pale, was as self-evident as the relationship of breathing to living. In the last year of his life, Boris Sorge enlarged on this theme on quiet Saturday afternoons with his son, feeling the Sabbath as well served by reminiscence as by prayer and study. "In the village, before we moved to Odessa, we magnified the seriousness of the petty to avoid being overcome by the real tragedies. We had our humor, which I do not underestimate. And we had our little quarrels and feuds and disappointments, which no one must underestimate for, like the humor, they were our sustenance. Can you understand that?"

"Yes, papa."

"No, you cannot. You never lived in a shtetl. There were times when we did not know if we were alive; each new law made us a little less human, a little more an object. Do you know what they said about us? One third will die, a third will leave, a third we can handle. So, in the face of that, we quarreled, to convince ourselves we were alive. We magnified anything that illuminated normal life: growing children, food, money, animals, household possessions, even our holidays. I remember my mother, your grandmother whom you never knew, going almost daily to the cemetery to wail her problems on the grave of her mother. 'Mama!' she would cry. 'It is I, Rifka, your pearl, who calls you, who needs your wisdom! My Emmy, my ungrateful wretch of a daughter, talked back to me, *me* her mother! To me she talked as if I was Schmuel the beggar, me her mother! She has no respect, the young ones have no respect, times are changing, mama, thank God you're not here to see!' I do not remember what Emmy did; none of us could ever remember what sent mama to her mother's grave."

Solomon, nine years old, big for his age, and silent, listened with reservations. People didn't talk to the dead; if they did there was something wrong with them. Anyway, Jews were supposed to be smart.

"And how she could curse! It is an art that is dying. The old women were masters at it, and your grandmother the finest of all. For insults or infractions or any dispute, she had the proper curse: she would stand in the doorway of our house, staring after the offender, and then her voice would ring through the village, *'Yimach shemoy!'* May your name be wiped out! The most powerful curse of all, for it implied not only that one should be dead, but that his name should disappear forever. Ah, she gave it such feeling, such indignation. She was widely admired."

"Papa?"

"Yes, Solomon."

"You told me swearing was the sign of an uneducated person."

There was a brief silence. "Solomon," said the rabbi with

a smile, "you must understand the difference between swearing and issuing a curse. Swearing is passivity caused by and causing frustration. A curse is active participation in the fate of another; it is an imaginative consignment to torment that involves him who curses: he becomes part of the process, a fellow of the cursed. When you and your friends at school tell someone to go to hell, you are asking him to commit the act; your part is perfunctory and since it is passive, not significant. But *yimach shemoy*—ah, that is a partnership; God and your grandmother are to make sure a name disappears from the Book of Life; your grandmother, with God's will, enters the life of the cursed and changes it. In her fiery indignation and imagination she is the catalyst. Of course, and entirely by the way, your grandmother *was* uneducated."

Solomon smiled, as was expected. He liked to think he, more than the others, understood his father. His brothers and Yetta were younger, mama was always quarreling; only he was a companion for a dying rabbi.

Everyone knew he was dying; Boris himself spoke of it frequently. He had had two heart attacks since arriving in Chicago; he suffered over the insularity of his west side synagogue and wore himself out trying to make his people understand what was happening to Jews in the rest of the world. In fluent Russian, Hebrew, Yiddish, German, Polish, in halting English, he pleaded and cajoled and thundered. "You are all part of Israel! You must understand what is happening, share in it, work for Israel. Perhaps the answer is Palestine, perhaps there are other answers. . . ."

"Rabbi," said Max Rosenthal, who was a grocer. "Rabbi, my son says work for America. Here we are men. My son says forget the past where we were animals and be Americans."

"Were the Jews animals, papa?" asked Solomon.

"Objects," said the rabbi. "Never animals."

"And now," scorned Solomon's mother. "Now you will teach them. In Russia you could not make up your mind what you were, but here in America you will teach others. Have your dreams come true, then, so you can pass them on to others?"

Mama still wanted to go to Palestine. She was sure she could handle the Turks.

"My dreams have not come true, *mein kind,*" said papa, and fell silent, ignoring even Solomon, who scowled at his mother and then picked up a book, to read and share the silence with the rabbi.

The quarrels raged until he died. And not only with mama. There were visitors: rabbis from other shuls in Chicago; newcomers from Russia and Poland; neighbors who shared Boris' uncertainty and came to convince or be convinced. Each had his own definition of responsibility and a share in all Israel. Each used the past to create his own vision of a future. Socialists, Communists, Zionists, assimilationists: they came to Boris Sorge and his silent eldest son to argue, to debate, to shout each other down in passionate affirmation of their own doubts.

"We have the most powerful tools of all," Boris despaired. "Our traditions. And we do not know how to use them."

And not knowing, thought Sorge in his silent office, they could not help their children. Who fled into their own myths called, among other things, political science. If traditions were tools, I would look for others that might have served my father better.

He walked by the lake after the seminar. There were so many things he had to do: call David, call Nathan, get out of these clothes he'd worn since yesterday morning, proofread the dittos of next week's final examinations, check the summer schedule to find out when his class would meet, and go home.

He had to go home. The euphoria of a few moments ago, the insubstantial sense of freedom, had dissolved in bright sunlight and in the vastness of a lake Trudi once called a private pond for the privileged. He could not remember the source of the vision, nor recapture its certainty; standing on the beach where he and Trudi swam every summer, he lost much of his anger in the sure knowledge of betrayal. She might be at home, waiting for him as she did every Monday after his class, to feed him and listen to his rephrasing of the morning's discussion, to help him find weaknesses in argument or presentation for correction before the group met again. It was barely possible that a nightmare on Sunday did not preclude normality on Monday.

So he had to go home. For even if the nightmare were reality, and his wanderings of last night the first step of a journey rather than a temporary mis-direction, home was his starting point and point of return: he and Trudi had invested it with mysticism—security, permanence, concrete extension of what each dreamt the other would become. Their home performed exactly the same functions as the three children, but, unlike the children, stood fast and kept its counsel. They never considered selling in favor of a smaller place: more than anything else, the house stood as a monument, heir to their time spent in repairs, their energy in maintenance, their imagination in decorating. They were always conscious of its solidity, increasing with age, and the tough, tight face it presented to strangers. And when they lay in bed, beneath their murmurs was the creaking of the house, the slight shifting of enclosing, protecting walls.

He stopped on the beach and turned to retrace his steps toward home. For all that they seldom spoke of it, he knew

Trudi shared his feelings about the house, that they had created their mythology together from the moment they first walked in the door to the tune of a realtor's prattling to sell them what they already wanted. Trudi had been pregnant then, with David, their first child; Sorge had just come from New Jersey to take a new position; they had little money but absolute certainty that once they created a home all else—the depression, the newness of Sorge's position, his mother's predictions of tragedy, Trudi's stormy pregnancy—would fade to nothing or, at the least, to manageable proportions.

The house dictated its own use. While the realtor chanted of building materials, lot size, heating costs, taxes, nearby schools and shopping, Trudi and Sorge adopted the rooms. "Your study, Sol." "My mother's room—we can cut a door through to the bath." "The baby's room." "Our bedroom. You could put your sewing machine in that corner." "What would we do with the third floor?" "Someday we'll be able to afford a maid."

The rooms were large, with high ceilings. Sorge, at last in a setting proportionate to his own size, delightedly paced off the square feet, spread his arms in an attempt to span the living room fireplace, measured with his eye space in the kitchen for stove, refrigerator, table, chairs. He ran upstairs, then down, pounding the walls, rocking his feet on the floors, opening and closing windows. "Good for a thousand years," he said and sat down on the stairs to write a check.

"I'm not sure I want it," said Trudi.

Sorge, his pen suspended, and the realtor, halfway through a smug smile, stared at her. She stood in the center of the bare living room, small, fragile in spite of her swollen belly, her childish face promising a mature beauty, and refused to look at them. "The plaster is cracking all over the house, the kitchen would have to be redone, the floors haven't been varnished in God knows how long—they're all worn down. It would cost a fortune to make this place liveable and we don't have a fortune. I think we should look somewhere else."

"A minute ago—" began Sorge.

"It's too expensive," cried Trudi.

"Ah," said the realtor and grimaced. "I do have some, shall we say, flexibility . . . The owner has given me permission to suggest perhaps . . ." and he named another figure.

Sorge watched, fascinated, as his wife dealt with the realtor. Her full lower lip in a pout, her eyes downcast like an unhappy victim of a matchmaker, she managed to look fourteen years old while sounding like an experienced fifty.

"Painting alone . . ." she said; and "Taxes . . ." and "Probably a new furnace before long . . ." and "Did you see the grass? It would have to be torn out and replaced . . ." and "Electric wiring . . ." and on and on until Sorge, convinced they would never have the house, put down his pen and thought of the quarrel they would have when the realtor left. His little Trudi. His wife with her sicknesses and vomiting and pain when the baby kicked her. She had been a virgin when she first came to him; since that night he had enfolded her, guarded her, adored her. They had seldom quarreled. He was twenty-nine years old; for two years he had put his bulk between his child bride and the rest of the world only to come to this moment; to sit silently by while an eighteen-year-old girl, tiny, doll-like, pregnant, fenced with another man over his, Sorge's, house. He had seldom raised his voice to her: now he waited only for the moment when the realtor would leave.

But when he did leave it was with a check, written by Sorge, as earnest money for a house to be purchased for four thousand dollars less than originally asked. "My God," groaned Sorge. "Did you plan that?"

"No," she said. "But you were too eager." She went into

the kitchen and ran a loving hand over the counter. "Won't it be fun to eat in here?"

"You know what he'll say?" asked Sorge. "That we Jewed him down."

Trudi looked at him. "Will he?"

"Of course he will. We did, didn't we?"

"We bargained with him, Sol. Doesn't everyone?"

"How do I know? I've never bought a house before. But to take the chance that we might lose this one, when we both wanted it so much. . . ."

"I knew we wouldn't lose it, Sol. I knew when to quit."

"Where did you learn how to do that?"

"I don't know. I just talked to him."

"That isn't what he'll call it."

"Do you care what he calls it?"

"Yes!" he shouted. "You're damn right I care. I want this house so I can stay in one place, not be forced by hostility to leave it, not be forced to move around, always looking for a place where I'll be welcome. I don't want to live among enemies."

"You're talking like a child."

"I! I'm simply being a realist."

"All right, Sol. As a realist, were you a Jew or a Gentile when you sat down to write that check the first time?"

It was the first time Trudi attacked me, outflanked me; it was the first time I used battle terms to describe our marriage. She stepped out of her assigned role and neither of us cared much for our versions of each other in the aftermath. It was a bad day for me, for both of us; we were careful with each other for over a month, until David was born and we forgot everything else. But we had the house.

6

HE APPROACHED the closed, secretive face of his house as if returning from a journey. He hardly recognized it. None of the warmth and vitality he remembered, associated with it, was reflected on its surface or shone from its windows; it was an anonymous dwelling place among hundreds he had passed in his wanderings, symbol of the mysterious circularity of society he ordinarily admired and translated into writings, but now rather dehumanizing. Unless one postulated the alternative of his grandfather's and father's shtetl. And that, too, was insupportable.

He stood outside the high privet that surrounded the front yard, willing a personality in black shutters stark against gray frame. Trudi had not returned. If she had, if she were now inside preparing his lunch or cleaning or sewing or tucked into a chair in his study reading whatever was her latest enthusiasm, something about the house would reflect her presence. He thought. He could not be sure. For years he had barely looked at the outside of the house, ever since he decided he was too old, or well off, to do the painting himself; he envisioned himself each evening scurrying in, locking the door behind him, and only then opening his eyes, seeing only the womb-like creation of the inner house. He was a little like the fictional ashcan dwellers whose world had narrowed to a thin slice of the present. Which, if true, left the present in doubt now that a major piece of it had disappeared.

"Dad?" David stood in the doorway. "She's not here."

Sorge walked up the front walk and past his son into the house. "I was going to call you."

"You already called me." David followed him into the living room. "Last night. Or this morning. That was a hell of a stunt."

Sorge nodded. "I should have walked home."

"Walked! You never heard of cabs?"

"I was tired. I just wanted a bed."

"Did you sleep?"

"Some."

"Nathan's coming. He'll give you a sedative."

"Why is Nathan coming?"

"Because our mother has disappeared."

And my wife, thought Sorge. But I am not responding satisfactorily. What should I be doing? Tearing my hair, perhaps. Or weeping. At the very least, pacing the floor. Or calling all her friends. Or putting an ad in the personals column of the paper. Trudi. Come home. All is forgiven. No, there is nothing to forgive. All is forgotten. God forbid, she could not want that.

He was ill at ease. A man did not discuss his wife with his sons; in fact, a wise man spent his married years preventing situations in which his sons could intrude as commentators. I have not been wise in my wife's disappearance. But it would do no good for him to plead innocent victim: no matter what he said, his sons, with wives present and accounted for, had been given, as it were, carte blanche to discuss *his* wife, *his* marriage. It was of supreme indifference to all of them that they called her mother while Sorge called her wife: already David's eyes were shining with anticipation of the excursion into the impermissible: discussion of this woman, Trudi Loeffler Sorge.

In any event, in any crisis, Sorge would have been ill at ease. He was not comfortable with his sons. The easiest, most obvious reason would have been to claim they were Bazarovs who had taken their own, mistaken, turning. But he was denied that simplicity; he was not sure what paths his sons now trod. At one time he had presented alternatives, filling the gaps left by secular and religious institutions, but judiciously, cautiously, so that finally there seemed little difference between Trudi's retelling of Grimm's fairy tales and Sorge's chalk talks on atheism, agnosticism, Christianity, Marxism, capitalism, finely shaded and dissected. And in the end we grew apart, rather bored with each other, so that I never asked them which they chose. Not only boredom: at first I was afraid to dictate their answer by the form of my question. Some obvious phases I could follow: Marxist in their adolescence; semi-Titoist in their early college years; abandonment and careful rediscovery of Judaism: they both married Jewish girls and send their children to Hebrew school.

He had wanted to mold and feared to mold, held back not so much by morality as by awareness that he might shape badly. There was, in his sons, promise that he saw and declared his duty to nurture. And when he overcame his reluctance to become a teacher in his home as well as his classroom, he did so by convincing himself that the promise was already there; with his chalk talks he was only opening doors. Those were the few moments of closeness, of good humor that echoed in later years when his sons suddenly treated him as an equal. But that, he supposed, was success: I achieved the socialization of my sons.

Trudi swung between obstructivism and encouragement. When the children were infants she was wildly possessive, keeping Sorge, his mother, their slowly growing circle of friends all at bay. Sorge, after one look at her face as she nursed David, never argued: the babies were no more his when attached to Trudi's breast than they had been when inside her belly.

By the time Nathan, and then Harriet, were born, the possessiveness was less evident, smoothed and perfected into an efficiency so awesome intrusion was unthinkable. Sorge, overwhelmed by the potentials of parenthood, could do little more than admire from a distance Trudi's sureness. Her movements showed no doubt, no hesitation; she changed, fed, bathed her children with confident authority; she knew why they cried and for how long they should be left alone; knew when to sing to them, when to laugh, when to work in silence; in short, knew them as individuals while Sorge was still struggling with them as concepts, and his own role now that he had dared to create them.

He never lost the sense of wonder at his offspring, nor his ironic awareness of disparity between a creator who wondered at his ability to mold and a disciplinarian who roared displeasure at a puddle of airplane glue on the living room rug. But there was so much to be done, both petty and profound. Life is a serious business, his ancestors had said; Sorge was constantly burdened by the knowledge of what he had neglected to do the day before. And Trudi vacillated.

After the perfect sureness and unholy efficiency of her beginnings as a mother, she rediscovered the joys of slovenliness and a measure of humor. Still, Sorge found her erratic and struggled to time or predict her moods. He was still years away from acceptance of, a certain pleasure in, the unpredictability of people; then, in his thirties, he was caught up by the beauties of his chosen field: the promise of statistics, the evolving refinements in questionnaires, surveys, bloc analysis—what he and his colleagues were calling the methodological briefcase of the political scientist who, using his tools with skill and affection, could analyze human behavior much as a chemist analyzed the contents of a test tube, could predict human behavior almost in the same way. Laswell had opened new vistas with his insistence on psychology as a valid tool of political scientists; the idea of a behavioral approach that would lend itself to analysis and prediction was gathering momentum across the country. It was a heady time for scientists, even for those who were forced to spend much of their valuable time defending their work *as* science. But for them, too, there was more than one ray of light: some professors, notably in philosophy, were beginning to talk of the reduction of all behavioral theories to the fixed physical laws of the universe.

Sorge turned his back on his reservations—legacy of his father the rabbi who created his own hell by a refusal to choose the future—and avidly embraced his new world.

But not at home. None of his new tools were effective with Trudi: he could neither predict nor plan her actions, nor anticipate what the next day would bring. And they argued.

"H.G. Wells sprang from ignorant parents," she said after Sorge's chalk talk on Litvinov's role in Soviet diplomacy. She had waited until the children—seven, eight and nine that year—were in their rooms.

"Poor fellow," said Sorge.

"He wasn't stunted," said Trudi.

"No," he agreed. "Though it is always difficult to analyze the unwritten."

"Brilliant parents have been known to give birth to murderers."

"True. Are you outlining my next study?"

"I'm talking about your children."

"In the genre of H.G. Wells or as murderers?" he asked.

"As sacrificial victims of your ego," she said quietly.

The day before, they had gone on a picnic and Trudi, in a quiet moment when the children were off collecting leaves, had told him explicitly how happy she was. Not content: she never went so far. But happy; and Sorge had learned to trust her vocabulary as perfectly expressive: when committed, she matched and strung words in a necklace of definitive description. When uncommitted, she spoke more rapidly, her words vague, generalized, a jumble of carelessness. But she was seldom uncommitted. When she told Sorge of her happiness, her mouth was precise; she referred steadily to that time and that day, leaving no doubt that tomorrow or the next day the sun might not be so warm, the forest preserve so cool and lush, the children so harmonious, delightful to each other and their parents.

Perhaps it was self-fulfilling prophecy. Standing in his living room, facing one son, waiting for another to appear, braced for a full probe into his absent wife, Sorge thought there must have been a pattern in all those years, all those occasions when Trudi described happiness only to recant the next day with criticism, disappointment, anger. I must have seen it long ago, without naming it, for how else could I have treated her half-cocked theories on parents and children and H.G. Wells with humor? It was like conversing with a mental patient: one made allowances for the distorted pattern, treading carefully, always with open affection.

"Would you care to define sacrifice?" he asked.

"Don't talk like a political scientist, Sol," she said. "In this house I choose the terminology."

"That would please you?"

"No jargon and no timid theories to prove the obvious. I'm not talking—"

"Timid—?"

"—about voting habits; I'm talking about three unstatistical children."

"And about yourself."

"No. That would please you, but no. I'm talking about you and the children. Leave them alone, Sol."

"Nonsense. And you know it."

"I warn you, I'm on their side. I intend to give them normalcy."

"If you're not careful, my dear, you'll turn into a middle-aged Natasha."

"As stuffy and nagging as that? If you were her author you never would have done that to her, would you?"

"I would have kept her charm."

"Then let me keep mine. And let the children keep theirs. You're writing us as if we were a textbook. I'm asking you to leave us alone."

"Not in your context. They would be misfits. I intend to give them more than your unsubtle normalcy and you'll help me do it. You might even learn something."

"Litvinov's sex life? Is that how you'll attract my attention?"

"A sadly low estimate of yourself."

"But my own. I won't join you in your trenches, Sol. For God's sake, come out and join the civilians, soldier, the war is over."

Bitch. As allied in medieval times with Witch. She understood him, watched and judged him, and traveled her own path, divergent from his, when he might have come to her for comfort. It was true: the war had undone him. His precarious perch on science as the future had begun to crumble in Hitler's ovens and gas showers. The years following his father's death were bridged: once again he heard the arguments rage and saw the future of the Jews as a project for which there were no adequate tools.

Sorge's mother read the newspapers with a perverse satisfaction that infuriated him. "Your father was wrong, as usual. We all should have gone to Palestine." Trudi, weeping for the massacred, quarreled with her; the house was a melange of shouted accusations. Sorge wandered through the shouting, putting in an inflammatory word now and then when he felt the fire was dying down; he was pleased by the illusion of activity the two women provided with so much energy. Their quarrels reflected the larger debate throughout the country between those Jews who were pressuring Roosevelt and Churchill to do something for the European Jews and those who refused to do anything, fearing a rise in anti-semitism if the war against Hitler became known as a Jewish war. He joined none of the groups that sprang up to advocate measures ranging from trading tractors for Jews to sending paratroopers into the concentration camps. Trudi became active; between bouts with his mother she wrote letters, sent telegrams, passed out petitions. Sorge envied her assurance; finally he signed papers to bring two families from Germany and guide them so they would not become public wards. Beyond that, he did nothing; he was paralyzed.

"Daddy," asked his son David. "What were you in the war?"

A hater. I hated the Germans.

He translated all the fury his father should have felt for the Russians in their pogroms into his own time and space and expended it on the Germans. They were the enemy; the war in Asia barely existed. But they were the enemy not only of the Jews but of his own freedom of action as well. His paralysis was rooted in disbelief, the same refusal to comprehend as that which kept millions of Jews from fleeing while there was still time. Nothing in his researches had prepared him for so vast, so efficient a plot; none of his poses of amused disinterest at man's foibles even approached a protection for the tribal loyalty and disgust with all silent Gentiles—his friends and neighbors—he now felt. He was, suddenly, naked and unarmed. And ashamed of himself.

And so he retreated.

I tried to bring order out of chaos.

In his office he kept maps of Europe and files on generals, political leaders, casualties. He promoted himself to commander-in-chief and planned battles, working them out to the smallest detail on scraps of paper that lay in ragged piles on his desk. He muttered imprecations as he wiped out a battalion, took a hill, liberated a town, landed on a beach. He liked the French "boche" and used it frequently, exploding it in contemptuous bursts of air that riffled the papers on which he fought the war. Occasionally, as in the Sicily landings, his plans were fulfilled by flesh and blood creatures acting out his fantasies; then his outrage at insanity diminished in the unholy joy of a general whose puppets jerk according to plan, even to their own destruction.

When, at Normandy, his brother Leon became one of the puppets, his satisfaction was shaken but not destroyed. The Jews died for the Jews and all humanity. If tribal loyalty was totally unscientific, a military blueprint for saving humanity was not; the war was far more than a Jewish war. Everyone had failed—the bombs had outrun the brains. It was time for a new beginning, a new faith, a modern religion. And so he came full circle: if once he had wavered in his certainty of science, his brother's death and the end of the war reinforced all his earlier beliefs in the absolute necessity of blueprints, planned progression. When Hitler began his march, Sorge the scientist became parochial, testy with his students. When the war ended, science—with Sorge and his colleagues its handmaidens—took over. We were the chosen people, called to fill the gap between physical and social sciences. Or did we choose ourselves and foist ourselves upon an unsuspecting public? Two comparatively primitive bombs were dropped on Japan and we found ourselves the new prophets. Rejoice ye would-be scientists of marginal disciplines; the world is yours. So, like infants, we poked into corners, and there was no one to tell us to stop, because very swiftly we had created our own language and who would dare thwart us if we could not be understood? It was always possible—we preached this—that we were doing something valuable. We knew—our personified science knew—that chaos had not ended with the finale to the war; only that it had begun a new phase.

How, then, could we come out of our trenches?

"Papa," asked nine-year-old Solomon, "will we go back to Russia now that the tsar is gone?"

"Never," snapped mama.

"But they've arrested the tsar," said Solomon, still to the rabbi.

"It is not clear yet," said Boris Sorge. "If the Bolsheviks gain control . . ."

"Bolsheviks!" cried mama. "Bolsheviks or Kerensky—what difference? None of them will welcome us. Ah, I'm so tired of talk! That's what killed Herzl."

"Papa . . ." said Solomon.

"I don't know," said the rabbi. "Your mama may be right. We may never belong in Russia again."

"When did we belong in Russia?" asked mama angrily.

"Under Alexander II," said Solomon, his father's student.

"Always they have an answer," said mama to an unseen audience on the ceiling. "So? For awhile they let us stand up, walk around. They played with us. And then they kicked us. You want to go back to that? We're through in Russia. Finished. I stay here."

"But," said Solomon, "you said we don't belong in America, either."

"We don't," said mama.

"Then where do we belong?" asked Solomon.

"Home," said mama. "Herzl knew." The apotheosis of Herzl gave mama and her cohorts on Chicago's west side great satisfaction, balancing the scales in otherwise intensely practical women who believed in cutting their losses. Papa, who knew more about Herzl, was the challenger.

"Herzl would have sent us to Africa," he said.

"No," said mama firmly. "That was only talk."

The rabbi smiled and exchanged a glance with his son, who suddenly felt like weeping, for he had been guilty of a moment's wish that his father were more like his mother: firm, certain, poised for action. Even if wrong.

If they felt any such qualms, the old men of papa's shul did not show it. They changed little from year to year, shifting their arguments slightly to fit events beyond Chicago, but treading familiar paths lined with a priori guideposts and milestones reaching back to Russia. They sat in a circle, scalding glasses of tea held in tempered fingers, recalling the past, analyzing the present. The rabbi was indistinguishable in the circle; they came to him not so much for leadership as for reassurance that order prevailed; the synagogue was the center of life and the rabbi moved among its mysteries with authority. But Solomon, who sat at his father's feet, longing for an ordinary cup of tea with a handle he could grasp, recognized the difference between the mystical authority of one allowed to touch the sacred, and the authority of leadership—power—in everyday life. His father may have been able to quote passages, pages of the Talmud, but the men who gathered around him—concerned, among other matters, with how to communicate with their sons, searching for a common language—were beginning to doubt the Talmud's applicability to everyday American life. "They make me an anachronism," said the rabbi to Solomon. "And then they come to me for answers. No," he added thoughtfully. "For support where the beams are weakest. And I don't know what to tell them. Their children grow up, the world changes, they want only a part of what I have to give them." "Which part, papa?" "How do I know? Whichever part suits their new life that particular day. How can I do that? Why should I have to?" Because thought Sorge, sitting in his living room opposite his fidgeting son David, because there was a solid rock of belief they never thought to challenge and as long as the rabbi symbolized that rock he would be used by others in their fumbling attempts to cope with a world beyond their understanding.

Always the debates went on, fed partly by English and Hebrew and Yiddish newspapers, but mostly by memories that, like a collective unconscious, spread to encompass all of them, their ancestors, progenitors, and generations to come. We—they—accepted continuity; it was hardly discussed. That it might perhaps be a miracle in light of the conditions we had fled never occurred to them, any more than they questioned the rituals of their faith. Even the assimilationists who came to shout, to argue, to rediscover their own reasoning, never assumed great numbers would follow them; they wanted the core to remain firm, for its existence made their own rebellion meaningful. Their proselytizing was always casual, an afterthought; they did not want to convince too many besides themselves. It was left to us, Americans by virtue of our parents' naturalization, peripheral in that collective unconscious, to question the unquestionable. Or to ignore the questions, the guideposts, the milestones, unaware that it would be next to impossible to find our way back. If we wanted to.

"You misunderstand," he said to Trudi. "But it doesn't matter. I will bring up the children as I see fit."

"I'm sick and tired of your self-pity!" she cried. "All I

ask is simplicity—for myself and for them. *Our* children, Sol."

He shrugged. "A child's prayer. I've gone beyond that."

"To corruption. Let them make their own discoveries; let me make mine. You can argue with yourself in private."

"There isn't time. Can't you see how much I have to do before I die?"

"Tomorrow? The next day?"

"How do I know? I can't leave them without some foundation."

"You poor fool," she said wearily. "You aren't half the man your father was."

When committed, she was precise in her attacks. Sorge constructed hypotheses on the probability of women diluting commitment to their husbands as soon as children were born. Given youth and immaturity, they would probably tend to do so. (Timid theories to prove the obvious, Trudi had said.) But, where once he had talked to her of his youth, his parents, the shouted arguments in his father's study, now, seeing her attempt analysis on the basis of distortion and imperfect knowledge, he shut the door on the past and never spoke of it to her again. If he was to be solitary in his understanding of the complexities facing their children, he would accept it, as he had accepted the confusion willed him by his father: burdens he could carry alone, for he had loved the pathetic rabbi and he loved his immature wife.

Nathan arrived as David's wife was announcing coffee and sandwiches.

"Kay here?" asked David.

"She's coming," said Nathan. "She brought a casserole."

Sorge found the two women—Kay, wife of Nathan, and Helen, wife of David—depressingly alike. They wore stretch pants, were efficient in their housework, and were familiar with current trends in art, literature and music. They received the fringe benefits of mass culture: they could link Marx and Hegel without having read either, they recognized Warhol and Lichtenstein from their pictures in magazines. They moved in groups of equally well-to-do knowledgeable couples who could distinguish a chateau from a state wine and used California brands only for cooking. They cherished firm opinions, preferred foreign films to American ones, saw computer technology as the hope of mankind, and bought important books to rest carelessly on their coffee tables. They read mysteries in secret.

But who am I, thought Sorge, watching Kay approach the house, casserole in hand, to complain if they bore me? My tall, good looking sons seem satisfied—well fed and no doubt well bedded by their tall good looking wives. Kay has learned never to prescribe so much as an aspirin for patients who call the house; Helen has learned enough law to listen to her husband and enough discretion to keep his cases to herself. They are fit companions for my sons—who also bore me.

"Hello, dear," murmured Helen to Kay. "The casserole can be for dinner. I've made sandwiches."

"Good for you," said Kay. "Dad holding up all right?"

"He's remarkable."

"Hungry," growled Sorge, a patient discussed by solicitous relatives.

"Oh, you poor man!" cried Helen. "Let's eat now. We can talk later."

"Shouldn't we wait for Harriet?" asked David.

"Good Lord," said Kay. "Why do I always forget Harriet?"

"Because you don't like her," said David. "Wonderfully selective memory."

"Who called her?" demanded Sorge.

"I did," said David. "She belongs here."

It would be the first time all of them would be together without Trudi. And no one in mourning. A feeling of unreality wrapped them, the difficulty of sustaining any emotion save bewilderment and an oddly objective curiosity. No one—except Sorge, who had sat in the back yard naming her bushes—really missed her: they were too busy with the puzzle she had left them, and calculating just how much time had to be devoted to it before they could return to normal life. With or without Trudi. "After all," came Helen's voice from the dining room where she and Kay were setting places, "the papers are full of disappearances. Do you ever read the personals column? As a sociological phenomenon, of course."

"Of course," said Kay.

Of course, thought Sorge, but David's voice, hastily raised, covered the women's voices. "She'll be here any minute. It's preferable that any decisions be made by the whole family."

"Decisions?" asked Sorge.

"Family decisions," said David, firmly. "We're all involved; we're all in danger of chaos. We may be upset—we *are* upset—but there are problems here that have to be solved, that can't wait too long. You must see that," he added, his glance resting only momentarily on Sorge, then moving on to take in the rest of them, to meet the approving nods of Kay and Helen and Nathan.

"Decisions?" repeated Sorge.

David became thoughtful. "Your will, for one. That should be changed. We'll have to decide about the title to this house, and your car. Dozens of little details."

"My God," breathed Sorge. "This is only Monday."

"Contingencies, Dad. No one likes them but they're necessary. We won't do anything immediately, of course, but we want to be prepared."

"Like the Boy Scouts. Or is it the Marines?"

David shrugged. "We might decide on a time limit."

Sorge had never struck his children. So he did not recognize immediately the itching in his clenched hand. But there it was: he wanted to smash in the calm face before him, the careful mouth that so easily dismissed and buried Trudi beneath "contingencies." His present is his life hereafter; his loved ones—assuming he feels love in addition to professional interest—are actors in a well-rehearsed drama, alphabetized in leather-bound tomes, immortal by virtue of the Law which serves their incarnations.

Trudi had once described David, after a dinner celebrating his first victory before the Illinois Supreme Court: "A hunchback who uses his disability to take advantage of us."

Sorge had been angry. Now he thought Trudi had been rather perceptive. But that was another pain: that she had known all these years of David's inability to feel, of his use of the law to organize the core of his life and to arouse, if not love, at least admiration and sympathy, even, perhaps, dependence through fear—that she saw all this and bore it alone, keeping it from me. I would have listened. At least she might have given me a chance to listen.

He did not strike his son. He brooded in his chair until he heard the front door open and knew that Harriet had arrived. She was dressed in black.

Helen looked at Kay. "Should we have—?"

"No," said Kay fiercely. "Damned exhibitionist."

Nathan, until now silent in his corner, glanced up, his mouth framing and rejecting greetings until, finally, he succumbed to the gathering darkness of the atmosphere. "Wishful thinking, Harriet?"

Sorge, torn between gratitude and the exasperation of fear, rose and took his daughter's hand. "Leave her alone," he said, facing the room. Harriet and I against the world of law and medicine; bless her for her mourning, but it was a foolish thing to do.

Harriet, ignoring Nathan, kissed Sorge. "You should have called me."

"I know." He had called only Yetta; always, it seemed, he called Yetta.

"Didn't she even leave a note?"

"No."

"Nothing at all?"

"Nothing."

Helen called gaily, "Shall we eat first?"

"First?" asked Harriet of Sorge.

"David has a speech," he said dryly. "You'd better fortify yourself."

"It is impossible that anyone could eat at a time like this."

"For God's sake," said David. "Shut up and eat."

Sorge looked at them as they sat around the table. My family. Handsome, well-dressed, content. Except for Harriet, who is never content, but who has achieved the same trappings of success as her brothers and therefore can concentrate on non-material concerns in sufficient degree to compensate for her brothers' stuffiness. The men masticate, Harriet nibbles intensely, and none of them looks at me. While I eat my sandwiches and try to remember how we all looked last Christmas, around this table, with Trudi presiding, and Nathan in charge of the turkey making his traditional, tired crack about the propriety of a doctor carving the bird, and Kay and Helen trying to convince me to read Father Chardin—probably so I could explain to them what he was saying without their having to read him themselves; and David describing—in pompous *A*'s, *B*'s, and *C*'s—his latest case; and Yetta and Sammy scuttling back and forth to see that the children in the living room had not eaten each other in place of the turkey; and Harriet and her husband Michael a little withdrawn, just on the verge of contempt. But always the focus, the center, was Trudi, at the head of the table, quiet, listening, a beautiful woman whose face betrayed none of her feelings. I am no longer certain she liked any of us.

"Well," said David. "Are we ready? The girls can clear while we talk. Leave the coffee pot, Helen. We'll be as informal as possible. All we're doing today is preparing for contingencies, analyzing the situation as it appears at the moment and as it may affect the future. Are we agreed?"

There was a moment's silence. Nathan said, "I'd like to ask some questions."

Mister chairman, added Sorge silently. He should have raised his hand: our leader is annoyed.

"Are they relevant?" asked David.

"I would hardly ask them if they weren't."

"And it can't wait until I've finished?"

"I may have to leave early."

"You'll stay. You're involved in what I have to say."

"I also have office hours at 2:30." He turned to Sorge. "Had she seen a doctor recently?"

"Her regular check-up."

"Nothing else?"

"Not to my knowledge."

"She wasn't ill?"

"No."

"Not to your knowledge. Was she in analysis?"

"No."

"You're sure?"

"Yes."

"Absolutely sure?"

Sorge hesitated. "No. I didn't track her activities."

"Bills?"

"None from a psychiatrist."

"But she could have paid cash."

"I suppose so."

"Now, think carefully. Have there been any symptoms, anything at all, that indicated she was upset, concerned, preoccupied, or otherwise withdrawn from normal activities due to some unspecified cause or fear?"

"Say it in Latin," suggested Harriet. "It's even more impressive that way."

Nathan turned his back to her. "Well?" he asked Sorge.

"No," said Sorge helplessly.

"Normal in every respect?"

"She was just—herself."

"Obviously she wasn't. Any bleeding between periods?"

Sorge's hands clenched. "Not that I know of."

"Regular elimination?"

"She didn't inform me." Nathan once did. When he was a child he would lead us to the bathroom and point triumphantly to the full toilet. But I can't tell him that now. I haven't the courage. Or, even, the desire.

"Intercourse?"

"What?"

"Have you been having intercourse regularly?"

Harriet stood up. "That's none of your God damn business!"

Nathan swiveled in his chair, sighed, and looked at her for several seconds. "Have *you* ever considered analysis, Harriet?"

"Why?" she asked warily.

"With a doctor in the family, you could all do me the courtesy of taking advantage of medical science. If you're frigid, do something about it."

"If I'm—"

"Don't act the wide-eyed innocent with me, Harriet. As a doctor I know too much. My God, you're a brittle bitch. You could be broken in half like a dried stick. You're underweight and tense, you're filled with hostilities that use up all your energy. And you're frigid. I know the signs. You can't go on this way. You're intelligent enough to overcome your repressions. I can recommend an excellent—''

Harriet began to laugh. Sorge, hearing the note of hysteria, stood and put his arm around her shoulders. Kay was murmuring to Helen, ''We've discussed it thoroughly. Nate is quite concerned about her, has been for years.''

Harriet's laughter rose. ''Dr. Hasanpfeffer,'' she gasped. ''And his loyal helpmate, of course. How can I best serve your voyeurism? By repairing to the living room and putting my head in your lap to combine your inanities with the dark tales of my past?''

''You're a sick girl,'' said Nathan. He thought a moment, then said, ''What tales?''

''Enough,'' Sorge put in wearily. ''This is a farce. God, I'm so tired.''

Nathan switched smoothly from sister to father. ''You haven't been sleeping. I brought some sedatives.''

''I have been sleeping,'' said Sorge. ''Let's get this over with.''

''Maybe I should go to bed with Nate,'' said Harriet. ''So he can time my orgasms like birth pains. And I could tell him my sexual history between humps.''

''God damn it!'' shouted Sorge. ''You will not demean yourself in front of me. I will not have it. Now be quiet.''

She shook her head wonderingly. ''I've insulted you?''

''Leave it alone,'' he said. ''It's done.'' He turned to Nathan. ''Are you finished?''

''I don't know,'' said Nathan doubtfully. ''You haven't been very helpful.''

''Because he hasn't offered to let you examine his bedsheets?'' Harriet cried.

''You're upset,'' said Nathan. ''As, of course, we all are.

Obviously something organic was wrong, or some mental disturbance so powerful as to cause her to walk away from all she knew, rejecting at one stroke that which made her ill and the peripheral objects and people which could not help but remind her of her illness. We all flee in one way or another, most commonly in harmless fantasies. But it is amazing how seldom the running away takes the actual form of physical departure. I'll have to check my library—"

"You do that," said David impatiently. "Dad, Harriet, sit down. We haven't begun to discuss the real problems."

Sorge twisted his head against the pressure at the base of his skull. His body ached with fatigue. "Sit down, Harriet. We have to hear him out."

"Why?" she demanded.

"Because he is Trudi's son." How strange. I am the first to use her name. We could have been talking about anyone. She and her. Never Trudi. Never mother. "Trudi's son," he repeated. "And mine. And your brother. Go ahead, David."

Sorge's use of her name had resurrected Trudi from Nathan's terseness. David fidgeted, then said hurriedly, "I won't take long, none of this binds any of us in any way, but we should know where we stand. First, you know—or do you—that in Illinois it takes seven years to establish death."

He paused, but only to marshall his thoughts, not from any inner turmoil. He's lost Trudi again, thought Sorge—he wraps himself in the law and his mother becomes an *X* or *Y* or *Z* in another case. "There is also, in Illinois, what is known as the Family Expense Statute, stating that the husband is liable for any debts incurred by his wife. Do you know of any?"

"Debts?" said Sorge. "No."

"Charge accounts?"

"Of course. I didn't think you meant—"

"That's part of it. I suggest you call any stores where you

have accounts and specify that the charges are to be used by you only. Otherwise you could find yourself with a bill for several thousand dollars if she went on a spree. You'd be stuck with it.''

''You bastard,'' whispered Harriet.

''If Trudi needs to buy something,'' Sorge said, ''she can buy it. I won't stop her. She was always—she's quite economical.''

David shrugged. ''It's up to you. Now, as to property. Did she have her own bank account?''

''No.''

''Good. You couldn't touch it if she did. Everything joint between you?''

''Everything.''

''We'll start with the bank account. I suggest you withdraw everything and put it in an account in your name alone. Have you called the bank this morning?''

''No.''

''Then you don't know what she's withdrawn. Call them as soon as we leave. If anything is left, withdraw it.''

''Bastard,'' said Harriet.

''Now, stocks and bonds. There's no way you can give good title to them unless you post a bond indemnifying the transferor and the brokerage house from a claim by the joint owner or the joint owner's estate. Is that clear?''

''I have no wish to sell any stocks or bonds.''

''You might in the next seven years. Just keep that in mind; I'll be around to help you when you need it. Now, the house. You can't sell the whole interest in it, but you can transfer your interest to a straw buyer who deeds it back to you. That turns the joint tenancy into a tenancy in common; you can then will, sell, or give good title to that half. Clear so far?''

Sorge nodded. He felt Harriet's hand in his.

''The buyer can institute partition proceedings. That is,

he's the owner of half of any property that is partitionable. Obviously, you can't cut a house in half; in the case of the nonpartitionable property, the court can order it sold and half of the proceeds paid to the new owner. The other half is held in escrow for the missing joint owner or her heirs after seven years. With me so far?''

''Bastard,'' said Harriet.

''Now, after seven years, you'll sign affidavits that you've had no word from her, no knowledge of where she is, no sign of any kind that you are aware of her presence or activities. Under the laws of intestacy, the husband gets one-third of the estate, the remaining two-thirds to be divided among the children. The insurance companies will also have forms to be filled out, but even then there may have to be a lawsuit; it's hard as hell to pry the money out in cases of missing persons. However, there's plenty of time to talk about that. The major, immediate problem, as I see it, is your will, and then the house.''

''I'm not selling the house,'' Sorge murmured.

''Not today, of course. But it's too big for you alone and when the issue comes up—''

''I'm not selling the house.''

''Well, we can discuss it another—''

''The major, immediate problem!'' screamed Harriet in delayed, painful mimicry. Her nails were cutting into Sorge's hand; he treasured the pain. ''The major immediate problem, you bastard, is to find mother.''

''I think *you* need a sedative,'' said Nathan beginning to rummage in his pockets.

''Oh, shut up, shut up, shut up,'' sobbed Harriet. ''Don't you see what you're doing? You're murdering her.''

''Take this,'' said Nathan, holding out a small box.

Harriet struck it from his hand. ''Murderers!'' she cried.

Kay and Helen stood up. ''Come and lie down, Harriet,''

said one of them. "We'll take you upstairs," said the other. "This is so hard on you." "A rest will do you good."

Sorge was fascinated by the fact that he could no longer tell them apart. He was delighted. For years, he had thought of them as indistinguishable, but always, through some alchemy, had been able to come up with the correct name when addressing one or the other. Now, with a sharp recurrence of the amorphous sense of freedom he had felt in the classroom that morning, he was able to formulate the thought and, testing it, see that it was so. For a moment he saw them all with the clarity of an expelled partisan. But, no matter what he had toyed with before, he was not yet ready for complete disillusionment—not until he had adjusted to Trudi's absence, to the unknown cause of Trudi's absence—and so he turned away and struggled to acknowledge once again that this was his family, his creation, and still, somehow, his responsibility.

He wanted to tell them that: that he cared about them if not, particularly, for them; that he knew enough to know he should desire family closeness and continuity; that, therefore, he was willing to lie, to attempt a smile at David's brutal dissertation and Nathan's white-coat-and-disinterest interrogation. But he could not be sure of any of it. With Trudi's disappearance, some essential connection had gone and he could feel nothing but faint curiosity for these jabbering, gesticulating men and women who claimed kinship and a stake in his future.

There they stood, grouped around Harriet, trying to move her upstairs and into a penitential bed that would do duty for all of them, trying to assert themselves master of this or any situation. They rely on principles I taught them: objectivity, order, an instinctive mistrust of the normative. They rely on something known vaguely as the scientific method in an age that encourages them as I once did. And the irony lies in my own diminishing sureness as my creatures march forth under my banner, trampling me.

The doorbell rang, the door opened, and Yetta stood in the foyer. She carried a covered casserole in one hand, a Chale from the bakery in the other; behind her, Sammy held a pot of steaming chicken soup. "The least you could have done was call us," said Yetta tearfully, grasping the scene before her. "A family conference and you didn't invite us. And all the time I was cooking for you. Worrying about you. Your own sister."

Sorge's fatigue was like drunkenness: he had lost control of his limbs, his tongue, his diaphragm. Lacking strength to articulate, his voice wandered through speech in a mumbling stream of earnestness which his mind followed or anticipated with hilarity. He had become a clown.

"Never mind," said Yetta, buoyed up by martyrdom. With a deprecatory hand she waved aside Sorge's apologies, explanations, self-criticism and scattered blame of the children. "Never mind me. At a time like this, I'm just something that's around, to be used when you need me." She handed the casserole and bread to Helen, transferred the pot of soup from Sammy's hands to Kay's, leaned beside Harriet to kiss her cheek—"Have you been crying? Of course, you poor dear"—and settled herself on the couch, to look mistily at Nathan and David and shape her mouth into pity and wise understanding. "Sammy and I have talked over the whole situation. It simply cannot go on. I can just imagine all of you, sitting here weeping together, trying to bear up and get through each terrible day, trying to understand this tragedy . . ."

Sorge peered at her; the tears were streaming down her cheeks. She dabbed at them and hunched her shoulders. "I don't understand it myself. Jewish women don't leave their husbands, they make good wives and the best mothers and they keep their troubles to themselves. Or maybe talk to the rabbi. But he's a cold man, our rabbi. Smart and educated, but cold. Not the kind someone would cry to. But she could have come to me! Why didn't she come to me? If she had troubles, I would have helped, I was always ready to help, I even hinted a few times, but she ignored me. She could be cold sometimes, too, Trudi could, though I don't mean to speak ill of her. . . ."

"Nil nisi," muttered Kay to Helen. Helen shrugged.

Nathan stood up. "I have office hours, Aunt Yetta."

"Not yet, Nathan," said Yetta urgently. "Not yet. You'll listen to me. I admire you for trying to go on as if nothing has happened, but I can see your grief and I understand. So Sammy and I decided there was only one thing to do. Didn't we, Sammy?"

Sammy looked up from the *Daily News* and nodded.

Yetta swept the family with a look at once triumphant and compassionate. "We called the police," she said.

7

From the time she was a child, Harriet had all of Trudi's beauty and none of her humor. At birth she had been welcomed with rejoicing, for Trudi wanted no more children but would have persisted in pregnancies until she had a daughter. Now, the family pleased her and for a time she was content. Until she became acquainted with her daughter. "She'll die an untimely death; Atlas without muscles." It wasn't, as she insisted regularly to Sorge, that she feared a creature as unrelentingly intense as Harriet, but that she feared for her in a world and an era—it was 1945 and Harriet was seven—when a modicum of levity was required for equilibrium and sanity. It wasn't, she further insisted, that Harriet frustrated and infuriated her with solemn consideration of puns, stories and the written word; it was concern for her daughter's ability to make friends, eventually to go out with boys, and to tell the difference between lighthearted companionship and intimacy. "Everyone will be Constant to her de Staël; I couldn't bear that."

Sorge was reluctant to agree, even to discuss. He could see, as well as Trudi, that his chalk talks, offered only as foundations for objective understanding of the present, were being stored by his daughter as a farmer, on a sunny day, stores grain against tomorrow's drought or tornado, knowing that, if he was wrong about tomorrow or the next day, the holocaust, when it did come, would be all the worse for having been preceded by an extended period of peace. He could see, as well as Trudi, that Harriet's gloomy dungeons were filled with the grain of his lectures, and each added sheaf only reinforced her conviction of the essential tragedy of humanity and the world. Or, at the very least, the inappropriateness of humor, the inability to be humorous when so much was at stake, with implications so profound.

But, generally, Sorge found her intensity charming. The solemn gaze, the tensed muscles gave dimension to his lectures and homilies and he found himself turning more and more often from his squirming sons to his ardent daughter, directing his speech and gestures to her, controlling his vocabulary with careful definitions and examples, patient with her questions and showing, after a time, by a weary lifting of his eyebrows in his sons' direction, that he expected few intelligent queries from that quarter.

Trudi, after her one outburst, was silent. Occasionally her lips moved as if she were saying a rosary; indeed, Sorge, glancing at her while he lectured, chalk in hand, was often reminded of a nun: her dark, smooth hair, waved forward over her ears and part of her cheeks, was a neat, conservative wimple, her restless hands and moving lips could have been counting beads, her pose had the stillness of absolute serenity—or iron self control.

But there was more to the anomaly than this: there was her abnegation and his own wanderings from her bed. As for the first, Trudi was pulling back, by degrees, from her early religiosity of wifehood and motherhood, building herself to her own plans drawn and stored away since she was sixteen years old, and married. For the second, Sorge was never sure of cause and effect in his early wanderings: whether Trudi's withdrawal preceded or followed them. As is most often the case, and a happy excuse, in infidelities, nothing was planned or predicted: the fruit was offered, accepted, and found tasty. Not that he tasted overmuch, nor—to be truthful—was he petitioned overoften, but a catalogue, drawn graphically, would have shown a pronounced deviation from fidelity. And so the image of Trudi as nun: building a world of her own and, frequently, sleeping in solitary stillness, the blanket smoothly mounded when he came in late to undress, for the second time, in near darkness.

The children were his sounding board in a way that neither Trudi nor his students could be: their youth made his own beliefs more believable, his methods more methodical. What he wanted was to organize time; what better way than to begin with the very young? Twenty years later he would realize he had taught his sons better than he knew; they may have wriggled and muttered and pouted but they heard. He had vowed, with an arrogant naiveté, that he would not mold them, but his insistence on objectivity, his implied definition of facts as unorganized solutions, led them to his own fount of science and away from the personal history and influence of generations past. Harriet, as a child and a young woman, confused her parents with her intensity; too much feeling, diffused, effectively screened what she really felt. At one time Sorge thought he, and he alone, understood her. Within the family the two of them were duo performers who, while recognizing their accompanists, turned to each other for cues and timing. Sorge saw, because it was convenient and pleased him, that Harriet's unrelenting solemnity could be assuaged by precisely that which he himself sought: order, predictability, a sense of discovered place and time. The fact that, over the years, their sessions—private as opposed to the family chalk talks—had no appreciable effect on her seriousness or single-mindedness was irrelevant; he recognized the particular joy she took in sharing with him the potential of their beliefs: find the pieces and the puzzle could be assembled: Shangri-La was around the corner, the grass would be as green on this side of the fence, atoms would split cleanly to dig canals instead of graves, space would be conquered in amity, ocean water desalted, cancer eliminated, supersonic jets made silent, the common cold, cavities, sinusitis, heart attacks all things of the past—and, finally, man's nature itself altered so that brotherhood, equality, freedom, peace would reign and Science, on its own seventh day, could rest and survey its wonders.

It was, of course, as Sorge frequently reminded himself, a game. But not entirely. For Harriet it was gospel, and her faith, joined with the beauty of theory and hypothesis, could draw him into the fantasy—all the more, as he discovered years later when working through his first shocks of disillusion, as that fantasy often edged insidiously into reality. He was appalled, in those later years, when his academic position was secure and he could afford, if only tentatively, to indulge the possibility of his being a traitor, to discover that the game he and Harriet once played was increasingly, solemnly pontificated in professional books and articles and convention papers. When he learned that some renowned men in his field were measuring happiness in units called Euphorias, he did not know whether to laugh or weep.

But by then it was too late to share his laughter, or his tears, with Trudi. If it was desirable—and he was still not sure it was—for a man and wife to share the husband's work, the time for Trudi to do so, or for him to welcome her as a compatriot of sorts, had passed when he chose Harriet instead. There was no mystery about it: he had known that Harriet would immerse herself wholeheartedly while Trudi would have mocked, debated, challenged—would have kept it a game. And in those days, notwithstanding his occasional attempts to convince himself otherwise, Sorge did not want to play games; he wanted desperately to believe in what he preached.

But if he was trying to deny Trudi by framing her into a convent—for whatever reason: to make more palatable his experiments elsewhere, or to eliminate her as a contender for his fantasies—Trudi was not altogether willing to be framed. She never repeated her attempt to change him, but she made of herself—and slightly overdid it—mother and father to the boys: she played catch with them, pitched to their batting, became a den mother when they joined the Cub Scouts, arranged the dinner hour so she could watch their hockey and Little League games, and countered Sorge's enforced intellectualism by memorizing the batting averages of major league ball players and discussing football in companionable argot. And she intruded rather often on Sorge's private sessions with Harriet, prepared with snappish questions that denied the grandeur of abstract theory by dragging the subject down to the personal. "Have Ulbricht and Adenauer drunk a toast yet?"

Harriet was at first bewildered, then angered, then almost inarticulate with fury. She was perfectly willing to believe her mother jealous, and thus hostile to a beautiful, intelligent daughter whose company was preferred by her husband to her own. What she could not accept was that her mother—who, after all, was quite beautiful and rather intelligent herself—was not clever enough to hide her jealousy. Harriet, for quite some time, did not like her mother very much, but, sensibly remembering, or reminded by Sorge of the source of her own genes, would have liked to respect her. Her standards, as she told Sorge, were obviously higher than her mother's, but she would like to think she had a mother who knew how to pretend. Pretense, of course, was hardly scientific, but one would be aware of motives and of one's mother's limitations, acceptable in that sense. So her voice would be choked with anger and the attempt at cool superiority when she answered, "They could, if certain principles were applied . . ." and Sorge, caught between an involuntary smile and impatience with Trudi, would glance quickly at his wife and then away, dismayed by the difficulty of reconciliation.

What confused them was the erratic course that accompanied the children's growth, a trail marked by guideposts from Gesell and Sleeping Beauty. As parents they were conscious of their careful practicality and frequently convinced they were failures. They often reached for an elusive cause and effect to no avail; nothing automatically followed its predecessor. They would drop one approach in favor of another, reluctant to discuss, admit, lapses in their children. Yet, with all their care, and pretense of an orderly world, Nathan often stunned them with easy, innocence-laden lies, David with his sullen conviction of innate evil everywhere but in his own glorified home, and Harriet with that intensity that alternately charmed and repelled Sorge while bewildering Trudi because she could neither sympathize with nor comprehend it.

But it hardly mattered what faults were in their offspring as in any case Trudi felt she did not know her own children. She vacillated: sometimes she argued with them as if they were all of an age, or she would withdraw, intoning from the remote heights of motherhood rules and regulations, strictures of behavior, requirements that brooked no alternative. Or, carefully enunciated, she would be Wise and Kind and Understanding. And, in her wild arcs from fairy tale to expert advice, always she sensed failure—some phrase neglected, some approach, some gesture that would have worked, drawing her and the children together in an approximation of the remembered magic circle of mother and nursing child. "I feel like a slut longing for virginity. The good old days."

But Sorge, fresh from an evening session with Harriet,

would not be drawn; it was easier, on those nights when he stayed at home, and he could tell himself it balanced the scales, to caress his wife with affection—sympathy? remorse?—until desire made definition meaningless.

So it was to me that Harriet came when she was in trouble—or rather, for me that she set the stage for confidences. Even then, when she was in college, she turned to me, seeking order and an impossible priest-like discipline of the eye and mind. For her sake, then, I tried to pretend, who had prided myself always on an avoidance of pretense with her—and he became painfully aware of his wife, and wasted years, at precisely the moment his daughter exacted his pledge of secrecy.

He went upstairs to say goodnight; it was spring vacation of Harriet's senior year and there were certain rites pertaining to the last child at home, a clinging to the known and trusted when all else changed: the boys married, the house echoing, Trudi showing more and more overtly her disillusionment with the products of her womb. He walked upstairs and found the bedroom empty, a half-finished letter displayed prominently on an otherwise bare desk. He read it; he was meant to.

"Dear rabbi

"Dear Ann Landers. My lover has not made love to me for five weeks. I don't think I would mind so much, but I seem to be pregnant and while I'd rather not tell him, there doesn't seem to be anyone else I can"

He read it once, then again and yet again, for here he was, the someone else: her father. Her father, he roared silently through the red and black elegant femininity Trudi and Harriet had created. Damn her! As damn all children for daring to make mockery of their parents' illusions, those dreams that multiply as the cells of the fetus and grow, nurtured, as the infants grow to encompass all the ifs and glorious fantasies of one's own compromised life. He had never guessed. That radiant, fresh body had been mounted—how many times—by how many gross, pimply, unworshipful cocks who use the penis as small men wield big cigars, to puff their potency to an unimpressed world? He had bathed her, disinfected her wounds, held the smooth arms and tiny waist while she skated, swam, rode a bike—preparation for what arrogant son of a bitch to pump against the taut muscles of her spread legs? Even after his brief period of effacement when she woke to find her sheets spotted, he had returned at her desire, to teach, to guide, to kiss pursed lips that, since then, had smeared and sucked—where? with whom?

His rage swelled and hardened and when he heard water running from the tub in the bathroom, and pictured his daughter, bathed, glistening, curved to dry supple, loving limbs, the swelling and rigidity reached his groin, and he stared at his engorged slacks, retching in the silent room.

It was to salvage something of himself as Harriet obviously wished him to be that he sat in the armchair before the dressing table, covered his lap with a large book, and rehearsed his expression in the mirror. His face, he noted with some satisfaction, was his father's face, a map of bewilderment. There was a kind of justice in that, but he would examine it later. For now, there was the letter, and he tested his nausea by rereading it from where he sat. And took in, for the first time, the discarded salutation: Dear rabbi.

He heard Harriet brushing her teeth (how well they had implanted in their children the rules of cleanliness) and rushed his thoughts. Dear rabbi. Negating, by its having occurred to her at all, the flippancy of the following phrases, the attitudinizing for pulp consumption; shouting an agony not only real, solitary, of some duration, but very nearly desperate: his daughter had contemplated, if only briefly, labeling her dilemma a religious one.

But in what context? He had ill-prepared his children to expect salvation from religious posturing, indeed, had made no real attempt to distinguish the posturing from the genuinely felt or experienced. If, from his own youth, he had moaned, like Dmitri, that too many riddles weigh men down on earth, he had sought answers in fields of his own choosing and making, rejecting the depth and possible solution of Dmitri's cry. And perhaps that is what we all do, we who flaunt our methodology: for all our pretensions of profundity and depth, we only skim the surface with an incredible arrogance. But that brought him back to the justice of his face being his father's (Dear rabbi; dear father) without explaining Harriet's reasoning: why bring her orgasms and hungers and pregnancy to the Temple?

There was an unpleasant image of scarved and barefoot women creeping to church doors late at night to lay a bundle on the step, ring a bell, and scurry away; a sour taste of the confessional, of surrogate fathers and mothers—sisters—who lovingly and loudly bore the sins, failures of others. His sister Yetta took pride in every sociological study showing the infinitesimal rate of illegitimacy among Jews; she would not listen to the possible and logical reason: that Jews were smart enough to practice contraception. What would Yetta say of Harriet? And why, incidentally, hadn't Harriet, twentieth-century Jewess, practiced contraception? It would be soothing to say it was all irrelevant: there would be no illegitimate child; he would see that his private, excruciating knowledge of failure would not be available to the rest of the world in the form of a squalling bastard with the name—what else could it have?—of Sorge. But that would come later. Meanwhile, Harriet's choice of confidante. The child was peripheral to what he so readily described as his own failure. And, of course, Trudi's. While Harriet had been prepared to relieve her parents of responsibility and consult the Torah through its interpreter. I cannot follow her thoughts. She never knew her grandfather; she had no formal training; when she was ten she began to read the books we put before her: Sacher, Graetz, Marcus, Tcherikover, Baron, Peretz, Aleichem, Singer—but that was history and mythology and belief once removed: religion without religion.

At ten—nearly ten—he had been studying with his father, attending Hebrew school, and bringing into his home the vulgarisms of public school messily scrambled with his own, tentative, first rebel yells. "I find the whole fucking world rather amusing."

His father slapped his face—so hard my head whipped to one side and I found myself staring from the corners of my eyes at this mild, worried man, the rabbi, who had struck me for the first time.

"You will not be amused by a world that needs your compassion," said the rabbi.

"Amused!" screamed mama. "He can be amused from here to Michigan Avenue but he will not use such words in this house. Or anywhere," she added and began to cry.

I was awestruck at my power to rouse them.

"The words will follow the person he is," said papa.

"You and your philosophy," sobbed mama. "While my son uses words from the gutter you talk philosophy."

"No, mama," said papa. "You misunderstand. He must be the kind of person the world needs. With faith and compassion and love. Then the language will be the same."

"If he talks well, at least he'll be a gentleman," said mama fiercely. "What would the neighbors say if they could hear him?"

"The neighbors," sighed papa. "While I talk of the whole world. Solomon will move away from the neighbors."

"And until then?" cried mama.

"Until then we will teach him how to behave."

"We will teach him how to talk."

"That will follow." Papa looked at his hands. "Listen to me. Solomon will live in a world I cannot predict. At night I mourn for him as if he had already failed, as I did. As if he had been defeated by the unknown, as I have been defeated by the known. He will need the little we can give him, and much more, because we were wrong in thinking simple answers awaited us; or perhaps the world changes so quickly that the simple answers we once sought would no longer be enough even if we found them. Solomon, I ask you not to use that word again. But I also tell you that it is unimportant next to the other, the person you must be, the person who is not remote and amused but involved and compassionate, the person who is free because he decides to tie himself to others. If we can teach him that, mama, it will be all right. In the end it will be the same."

"The end," said mama. "I can't wait fifty years for my son to learn to talk like a gentleman."

It did not take that long, but papa never knew. He died two months later, having introduced me to a concept of freedom nearly unintelligible to a ten-year-old boy but one, somehow, that has remained in my memory the longest of all. He never had time to go into it with me; he never had time to tell me that his religion and his idea of freedom were the same, that Judaism was responsibility and the ultimate necessity to choose. Because he himself could not choose, he could never use the precise phrases to teach me; because he himself could not serve Judaism and mankind with the certainty of firm belief, he could not point the way to me. I had to discover my own way. And, once discovered, I passed over the rabbi's tentative beliefs, gave them a popular, current philosophical-scientific name, as had others before me, and almost as quickly forgot it. Or forgot to use it, which is the same thing. Have I ever talked to Harriet as my father talked to me?

''You're waiting for me,'' said Harriet coming into the room with one quick glance at the letter on the desk.

''I came up to say goodnight,'' he said from his chair, the book covering his lap. She was one of the most beautiful women he had ever seen; he wondered that he recognized her. She could not be of him; how could he have created such radiant beauty, from his own fumblings, and Trudi's?

''And stayed to lecture,'' she said.

''No,'' he said heavily. ''I'd like to understand.''

Harriet's eyebrows rose. ''The zoology of contemporary society.''

''God damn it!'' he roared. ''Don't quote others to me. It is both pretentious and childish. This isn't a research project.''

''I'm sorry. I'm sorry, Daddy.'' She lay on the bed, on her back, hands at her sides. She wore a blue quilted robe; her stomach was flat. ''I wanted to say the right things.''

''To handle me.''

''No. Advice, perhaps. Suggestions.''

''Who was it?''

''No one you know. Does it matter?''

''How many have there been?''

''Does that matter?''

''I want to know.''

She sighed. ''Six.''

''My God,'' he moaned. ''My God. My God.''

''Aunt Yetta would say I'm atypical,'' she said and their eyes met in an involuntary smile.

''I was thinking of Yetta,'' he said. But then the echo of her voice saying the number returned to him and he jerked in his chair. ''You can't be serious. Fantasy. Magnification. Are you trying to impress me?''

She was angry, as if her integrity—her integrity!—had been

questioned. "You've had that many," she said. "More. And you're married. I'm not."

He stared at her. "What did you say?"

"You get a look on your face when you talk about them. We've known for a long time. At breakfast or dinner you'll casually mention so-and-so who was at a party or visited a seminar or worked on a committee and this look would be on your face and mother would always leave the table—"

"Be quiet," he said. "You don't know what you're saying."

"I know. Does it matter?"

There were no rules to follow, no guideposts, and he floundered. He had planned no approach, no specific scolding or anger or false sympathy, but whatever he might have had in mind when he read the letter was shattered by the cool objectivity of his daughter. The whole damn thing is out of hand; the bitch has made us equals. "*Are* you atypical?" he asked.

"So we are going to talk about zoology," she said. "The compleat scientist." He could even hear the way she spelled it.

"For someone who wants help, you're being pretty careless," he said.

"You mean I'm alienating my father." She looked thoughtfully at the ceiling. "I imagine I did that the first time I went to bed with someone who wasn't you."

Bitch. Using a mind he had trained. "Then why didn't you leave that sophomoric letter under your mother's nose?"

"Because I love her very much and she doesn't know it."

Unanswerable. For a moment he envied his wife, who had somehow inspired a protective love, while he, over the years, had kindled only a kind of equality. He brooded at the elegant room. I suppose there is solace in the fact that she came to me, even if only to flaunt what it seems I have flaunted to her.

Revenge. Basic, simple, final. But she did come to me and now I have to talk to her. Her anger had faded, her face was calm, and he looked at her with some of the awe he had felt when he saw his parents quarreling over his language: people he thought he knew and understood; predictable, comfortable, almost—at ten he would not have used the word—statistical. But already he had forgotten, or was forgetting, just what it was he had expected of Harriet, as, having found himself wrong about his parents, he had lost all assumptions and saw them as strangers, unclassified. He would have thought he had few assumptions about Harriet; he had educated, trained her, and given her his analysis of times, events, people, expecting her to use it wisely—in other words, as he would. And hadn't she done just that? She had built her life and was it so different from his? It gagged him now to formulate phrases about virginity or fidelity with what would be normative intolerance, having trained her in a different school. (Although there was, perhaps, the idea of perpetual virginity-fidelity in scientists: the need for innocence, openness, renewed trust in ultimate answers, loyalty, pride—he would have to think about this; it might make an amusing article.) Nor could he laugh with Harriet over empiricism: that banner seemed tattered when it flew over his own home. He could retreat: Harriet had given him that option by quoting Balzac on the social sciences. He could make his daughter the basis of a research project, discuss effects and implications of a society destroying itself with empiricism, rejecting the normative as somehow tainted, snickering at a morality it claimed was beyond its budget. But would Harriet agree with him? It did not matter; he could not fit her into a scene of deterioration. She was his daughter; no exception; like his parents, unclassified. And if that, too, was retreat, it was the best he could do.

Harriet stirred on the bed; the silence was lengthening and

as if she felt his inability to break it, she offered another option. "I should have been born in a different time."

But by now he was suspicious of her gifts; he waited.

"I mean," she said, "I'd like to have lived at a time when I didn't have choices, alternatives. When I would have been forced to accept the rules."

In spite of himself, he was amused. "Chaperones?"

"Partly."

"You would have run away from them."

"Nice girls didn't. Jane Austen."

"Nice girls then were identical with nice girls now. Elizabeth didn't need a chaperone."

She drew in a sharp breath; he was pleased to see he had hurt her. "Anyway," he added kindly. "What is this sudden faith in the past? There were as many illegitimate babies—" he paused, then went on "—then as now. The biggest difference is that now there's a chance of a girl's being taken by surprise. In those days, with all the clothes they wore . . ."

Harriet smiled. "By the time they got them off, desire had disappeared or hardened into determination."

"Precisely. They had no excuses. Even in Jane Austen. Wasn't there a girl named Lydia?"

Harriet shook her head. "An exception. Unclassifiable."

"Nonsense," he said. He repeated the word silently, wondering at his erratic course, and the possibility that his daughter—not memories of his parents, not the war, not even Trudi—would be the one to undermine his cause. For it was nonsense: no matter what he might have thought, everything was classifiable: that was the cornerstone of his belief, his life. Classification, statistical ranking, and predictability. It would take more than Harriet to destroy that. And yet. And yet he was the one who had set her apart. He considered adding naiveté to his list of the attributes of the virgin scientist. No, not yet.

He stood; the book, unneeded now, slipped to the floor. "Why did you think of writing to the rabbi?"

"I like him."

"That's all?"

"I think I trust him."

"But not as much as Ann Landers."

"I never would have mailed that letter."

"What, then? Back to the rabbi?"

"No. My father."

He looked down at her, his bulk a shadow across the bed and his small, beautiful daughter. "Not after the first, or the second, or even the third. Only after the sixth when you come home carrying a bastard."

She closed her eyes.

"Well?" he asked tightly. "Have you enjoyed yourself?"

"Yes. At least part of the time." She opened her eyes and looked up at him, at the twisted lines of his face. "Do you want me to lie? Would it make you happier if I gave you a list—guilt, fear, misery, shame—even though none of it was true? I did enjoy myself, I love being in bed with someone: I like the warmth and the closeness and the silence of the room. Especially the silence. I like an act that makes talk superfluous, that ridicules analysis." She moved quickly to sit crosslegged on the bed. "But something always went wrong. And then later they all seemed grubby, all the affairs, because they were genuine."

He hurt, all over, and began to twist his head from side to side to ease the muscles. Her words no longer interested him, but he wanted her to talk, to bridge the gap between now and the time one of them mentioned abortion. "Genuine?"

"I really loved them."

"All of them."

"All of them. I was a clown—I lived each show as if it were the real world. So it became real, at least for awhile. In the beginning I could see myself prancing and performing and saying the clever, provocative lines that always led to the same place, and I could tell the tinsel from the real: I wanted to be with someone when the nights were empty. But I always ended up caring as much about his pleasure as mine. More, sometimes. I couldn't have cared less about the tinsel; I'd coated it over. And then when it was ended, for one reason or another, all I could see was the dirt on the circus floor and I felt grubby. All I really wanted was to find someone I could love. And I did. Six times. I fell in love the way kids have best friends, without reason or permanence, or the need to be sure of either. All my passion, my attention to detail, my subservience became ludicrous. It was all so badly done, and so untrustworthy. It would have been better if I'd done it for money."

He was silent, unprepared for pity. "Who ended them?"

"They did."

"Every time?"

"Every time."

"Do you know why?"

"I suppose I gave too much, took them too seriously; every affair became a marriage in miniature."

"Why don't you get married?"

"I think I will. There's a boy, a Catholic on his way out of the Church, who seems to need me."

"You can't do things the easy way?"

"You mean a nice Jewish boy?"

"Partly."

"I've known six nice Jewish boys."

He did not know what he wanted of her, for her. He had no clear answers, no scientifically-formulated advice. And he was finding his love insufficient, diluted and scattered. Where was the core on which they both could settle?

"You didn't think of me?"

"Frequently. Constant betrayal."

"And it didn't bother you?"

"Of course it did. I dreamt about you."

"After you'd been in bed with one of them."

"Usually."

"You didn't dream of your mother?"

"No."

"Never?"

"Once. She took me away with her for a walk along a beach."

"And?"

"And I loved her."

Trudi was the core. Too late to discover that; he felt, of a sudden, lonely and himself a traitor. Poor Harriet: to love only in bed, and in dreams. I have given her neither tradition, nor love, nor freedom.

The next day he took her to a doctor in Chicago who gave them the name of a man on the west side and shot Harriet full of penicillin. Without an appointment, they waited in the converted living room of a large frame house indistinguishable from other frame houses on the block, save for a neat, quiet plaque on the porch announcing the doctor's name and office hours. The waiting room was full; the doctor, when they finally saw him, obese and curt. They were to come back at 8:30 and not before; none of the regular patients was to see them. What Sorge remembered most clearly, when he let himself recall that day, was the moment the doctor looked at him and growled, "You the father?" Without thinking, he answered yes. "Whyn't you marry her, then?" asked the doctor but not as if expecting a serious answer. And he got none; Sorge, caught in the pathetic humor of the moment, held the door for Harriet and they left.

They went to a movie and then to a bar where they ordered

hamburgers and left them untouched on chipped plates. Sorge called Trudi to say they would be late; the only lie that came to him was to say they were going to a concert at Orchestra Hall. Then he had to call to find out the program of the evening; by the time he returned to Harriet, crouched in the booth staring at the drink in front of her, he was too exhausted to be angry or apprehensive; he wanted only to finish and return to Evanston where such things should never be allowed to happen.

When they returned, the doctor was watching a televised baseball game. A nurse took Harriet upstairs and only when she called him (preparations, Sorge supposed, complete) did the doctor reluctantly haul himself from his chair and up the stairs. Sorge waited. The volume of the television set was turned up (if there were a home run or a triple play would that fat son of a bitch let his knife slip?) and the sound roared through Sorge's head as he tried to leaf through a brochure on the steady erosion of American freedoms and the liberals-socialists-communists who were trying to end the valued relationship between doctor and patient by bringing socialized medicine to the U.S.A.

Harriet returned, her face white and pinched, helped down the stairs by the soothing nurse. Sorge, having paid his hundred and fifty dollars in advance, took her out of the house and into his car and home to Evanston without asking a question, without saying a word. He thought of telling her about the brochure but this was not the time, nor would the time ever come. What did come was a strange, sad tie between them, obstacle as well as bond. They never spoke of that day, or of Harriet's half-finished letter. Sorge supposed she burned it or, perhaps, saved it as one saves a corsage: remembrance of past errors as well as triumphs. For himself, it was a while before he could look at her with the inexhaustible faith of a parent: he felt that between them they had killed his child.

8

YETTA, in her virtuous moment, had not told the whole story. When Sorge had finally cleared them all out—his efficient sons, his coldly solicitous daughters-in-law, a still-crying Harriet, and a protesting Yetta with her silent husband—he walked through the quiet house, as if to give Trudi one last chance to appear, and then sat down in his bedroom to call the police.

"This is Solomon Sorge. My sister—"

"Well, *Mr.* Sorge. We wondered when you'd get around to calling."

He was jarred by the hostility of the voice. His dislike of the telephone was a sour taste in his mouth. Who the devil does the fellow think he is to talk to me like that? Who does he think I am? Whose tragedy is this, anyway? He asked carefully, "To whom am I speaking?"

"Lieutenant Milton," came the heavy voice and Sorge sighed at the small beauties of life that he could not share with Trudi. "And you're calling about your wife."

"My sister—"

"Your sister called. I talked to her. I told her we always wait twenty-fours."

"For what?"

"For putting out an APB."

"An APB?"

"All points bulletin. Description, license of car—"

"She didn't take the car."

"She walked? At two o'clock in the morning?"

"It seems so."

"She alone?"

"Of course."

"You're sure of that."

"No." What can I be sure of except for Harriet's tears and the empty house? "But she didn't take the car."

"So where've you been?"

"I beg your pardon?"

"Why didn't you call?"

"My sister—"

"I know, I know. Your sister called. This morning. Monday. Your wife disappeared Saturday night. Where you been?"

"Thinking. And waiting."

"For what?"

"For Trudi to come home, of course."

"Or for somebody to get curious. You told them she went to Hawaii."

"That was a joke."

"Some joke."

"Not a good one, no. But I wanted to be left alone."

"For what? To destroy evidence?"

"Evidence of what?"

"Of what, he says. Of foul play."

Of course. How ridiculously slow he had been to see what was coming. He heard, in Milton's voice, the same anticipatory excitement of the day clerk's voice in that dingy hotel of last night: something could be about to happen, a moment of anger or violence in a dull routine, a chance, finally, to show oneself fit for one's job, alert, capable, unafraid, a man.

What, after all, did suburban police do with most of their time? They were swamped with calls on roaming dogs, children playing on railroad tracks, strange noises in the night magnified by fearful women whose husbands were on the road. Occasionally they had a burglary, a high speed chase down Sheridan or Green Bay Road; more often, automobile accidents on Edens Expressway or busy intersections near shopping centers where housewives drove with the same sure arrogance with which they pushed carts through grocery store aisles. Or where men drove recklessly in an attempt to prove themselves part of this world, suddenly almost totally feminine. Or, better yet, where those same men drove frantically from call to sales call to make enough money to maintain the little woman and her car. None of which made much sense, and wasn't this animus toward women of recent vintage? And, hopefully, of short duration. It was hardly in his style and tended to display some pettiness, a shallow . . . "What?" he asked.

"I said we'll be out there tomorrow," said Milton wearily, used to being ignored while respondents floated into fantasy.

"Who will be out?"

"Couple of detectives. Maybe me. Just to check."

"But the APB?"

"That too."

"Couldn't we wait?"

"Wait for what?"

"You don't understand. She'll come back by herself."

"Sure of that?"

Was it typical of the law that everyone had to be sure at all times of everything? "Of course not. I just think so. I should know my own wife."

"Did you know she'd run out on you?"

"No."

"So you didn't know her."

Be grateful for the smallest favor; foul play seemed to have been ruled out. "Perhaps not."

"Or you knew her too well and decided there was somebody you liked better."

No favors after all. "No."

"No other women?"

"Of course not." A natural disclaimer; I'll have to talk to Susan before they do.

"What's of course about it? Evanston's no better than any other place."

He hopes. If it were he might be out of a job. "I won't be home tomorrow."

"You'll be there. Have you called her friends?"

"No."

"Haven't tried very hard, have you?"

"I was . . . stunned."

"I'll bet. We'll be there at nine-thirty."

"I have conferences tomorrow. With my students."

"Not in much shape to counsel others, are you? Cancel 'em."

"I don't counsel them on marital problems."

"I don't give a damn what you tell 'em, I've got a job to do. Nine-thirty tomorrow."

"Now look," he began. By God, I'm getting angry; a good sign of innocence; I should have realized that. "I'm not a criminal and I have some rights granted to all. If you want to talk to me—and I have no objections—you'll have to fit me in when I say you can. Unless you're prepared to arrest me. And I seriously doubt you have anything like that in mind, or evidence for such action."

"Wait a minute . . ."

"If you want me to explain myself to you, I'll be glad to try, given some sympathy and an open mind. If you can achieve that. I have some doubts about that, too, given your performance today. As you put it, you have a job to do, but you also play a role which I have studied at some length and if you had a gram of intelligence you would try to conform to it." This is nonsense, he thought. All backwards. But he was in full flight and Milton's surprised silence pushed him on. "There is an element of the psychologist in an officer of the law; he is a careful mediator between the known and the unknown, or, better still, the approachable and the unapproachable. You are an Orpheus traveling from the familiar world to a region heard of but never fully seen—the vast area of law and law enforcement we know of but touch usually only on the fringes, as in a parking ticket . . ."

"I'm a what?"

"An Orpheus. Never mind. Your role is to be friend, father and messenger and when you fail in one you fail in all, leaving yourself no more nor less adequate than a chained watchdog terrifying the trespasser without showing him the existence of another way around or convincing him of the need for that alternate route. Your own needs in this instance must be sublimated, as are a doctor's, or anyone else who serves, so that your role becomes positive rather than negative. As in my case, where I have had a shock, not of my own making . . ." He faltered, plummeting after his flight. Could he disclaim responsibility for anything that happened directly to him, foolishly prattling to this ignorant police officer of responsibility while refusing it himself? Trudi had not acted without some cause; however fabricated, her reasons would have sprung from something in him, in their life together, in the creativity, or lack of it, with which they built, so that now, after so many years, he would have to say, I did such and such at this or that time and should have done otherwise. Or been otherwise. Damn Trudi. To force him into awareness and belated contrition while, by her absence, denying him the luxury of atonement, and all this at a time when, nearing sixty, he had expected to relax.

"Who's Orpheus?" asked Milton.

Sorge wished for Trudi, for Harriet, for anyone. He had always been swept by the need to share man's foibles. "A searcher. He traveled across the river Styx into Hell."

"What for?"

"To find his wife."

"And I'm Orpheus."

"Symbolically; you traverse two . . ."

"And it'll be hell when you find your wife."

"I didn't—"

"I don't need no symbols, Mr. Sorge. In my business we get to know what people mean, even when they don't know it. What time will you be through with your conferences?"

"At noon," said Sorge helplessly.

"We'll be there then. You might let us know if you hear anything."

He replaced the telephone, wondering at his farcical helplessness before men whose education—intelligence?—was a fraction of his own. The hotel clerk, Lieutenant Milton. And others in the past whose limited vocabularies had frisked about his heavy thoughts, leaving him rooted and dull. He sparkled, if at all, and gave as good as he got, only with those whose language was his own, whose contexts were velvet curtains against which he could rub in comfort. The others—the ones whose vernacular and outlook were sandpaper, abrasive to his touch—frightened and confused him and, when he accidentally came close enough, defeated him. I have lost touch with common man. Whoever he is. Recognizable, manipulable in behavioral hypotheses; foreign and terrifying in his fleshly independence.

"I cannot force you to love them," said his father of their neighbors. "Love—abstract, generalized love—is an art cultivated out of the desire to understand or tie oneself to something so large and noisy and active it cannot help but have some meaning. And the meaning many look for in people, the mass of them from the rich on Prairie Avenue to our poor neighbors, is that they are the past and the future: how many are willing to see the present in them? Climbing or falling: either way is movement. That is America. In the old country, we stayed still, surviving. What were we talking about?"

"Love, papa," said Solomon, aged nine, possessive of his father's wisdom which only he could understand.

"Well, love. It is the most important of all. But difficult. In many cases impossible and it may seem that the more we try the more ridiculous we become. So we turn to compassion—"

"Pity," said Solomon wisely.

"No," snapped the rabbi. "Who are we to pity others? To pity is to stand above, to look upon others as does God, to comprehend with a mixture of love and contempt a creation somehow fouled. But compassion is the sharing of suffering—something the Jews know better than anyone else; a position forced on us by our history. The world that molded us now needs its product. This terrible war, the revolution in Russia . . ."

"Papa?"

"Yes, my son."

"I thought rabbis were supposed to love everybody and make us all love everybody else."

The rabbi spread his thin fingers and flexed them slowly. "I cannot speak for all rabbis. Listen, Solomon. Once I thought I could, when I was young and filled with glorious delusions. Then I thought, yes, we were there to teach love and understanding, and a melding of disparities. But partly that was Odessa, the most exciting city in the world when I was young. Every day was a debate, a revolution in thinking.

The Haskalah, the enlightenment, centered in Odessa; we woke up and found there was a world and modern man, beyond the Torah and the synagogue.''

''But the rabbis,'' said Solomon.

Yes, the rabbis. They fought the enlightenment, most of them. And I was caught. But I thought there was a way out if we loved and talked together. I went from one to another, arguing, pleading, shouting. And I lost. Do you know why?''

''Yes, papa,'' said Solomon, who had heard the story.

''Because the tsar decided Jews weren't good enough to live in the interior and chased them all into the Pale. All those who had been allowed to move into the interior under Alexander II, all of them and their children and their children's children were shoved into the Pale. And our little excitements were drowned in the mass of people who poured in and milled around and clustered in groups: the Maccabees, the Zionists, the Bundists, the Radicals. Love! Who could love them? They forgot tradition, they lost the meaning of Judaism, they argued abolition of everything that had ever been important to us. So I lost, because not only could I not love them, I didn't want to have anything to do with them. It wasn't the tsar who drove me from Russia, it was the Bundists and the Radicals.''

''But you were going to be arrested,'' said Solomon, suddenly terrified he was going to lose the most thrilling part of the story; he had never heard this version.

''Your mama needed a reason to leave,'' said the rabbi gently, apologetically.

''Mama!'' cried Solomon. ''But you said—''

''I would have been arrested. Yes. Undoubtedly I would have, sooner or later. I was letting the Bund use the synagogue for strike rallies. I still thought I could find a way to mediate between the Zionists who were illegal in Russia, and the Bundists, the revolutionaries who spent their time hiding from the tsar's troops, all the while hurling insults at the Zionists, calling them bourgeois Utopians. Odessa had become a Tower of Babel and I, in my arrogance, tried to play God and resolve the many tongues into one. I was as mad as they. In the end I had no love for them, no compassion, no feeling of belonging. I wanted to be needed by frightened people who had nowhere to turn and knew it. So I came to America."

"You lied to mama," said Solomon. "And to me."

"Have you listened?" asked the rabbi quietly.

"Yes, papa, but—"

"Your mama loved everyone. She whipped them with her tongue, she cursed them, she screamed and shouted, but she loved them. I could not, so I wept."

"And you lied!"

"I had to leave, Solomon."

"But mama would have left. She wanted to go to Palestine."

"Your mama wanted to put all the Jews of Russia on a ship and go to Palestine with them. Her desire was never more real than that."

"You still could have gone."

"If we could have gotten permits . . . perhaps. But I was not sure of Palestine, of the need for me there, or of the Jewish state as a possibility."

"You weren't sure of anything," accused Solomon, parroting his mother.

"No," said the rabbi. He gestured helplessly. "Listen! I want you to understand. In those days everything sounded equally good and equally bad, equally possible and impossible: Zionism and socialism. Leave Russia or rebuild Russia. Russians first or Jews first, or neither, simply bourgeois. I wanted, at least for awhile, to be a rabbi again, not a confused mass of politics. I wanted to be with people I could understand, people with simple problems of survival, and the need to comprehend their religion as a force in their lives. Why else was I a rabbi?"

"But how do I know," cried Solomon. "How do I know when you're right and when you're wrong?"

The rabbi leaned back and closed his eyes.

"And when you're lying!" cried Solomon desperately.

The rabbi's head moved from side to side. "It takes time," he said, "for a man to decide. All he can give his son is his struggle."

Solomon drew an angry breath. And waited for something else moving inside him. "Poor man," he said softly.

"Don't," said the rabbi. "You are too young for that."

"It's all right, papa. I'm not pitying you. I'm feeling compassion for you." And he burst into tears as his father shrank back, clasping his hands until the veins stood out in the humped blue ridges of old age.

I have always been pleased to hurt or astonish others.

And isn't it possible, given my propensity for harsh impressions, that I knew where Milton was going and led him on, allowing, even encouraging, him to consider foul play? Do I discover myself only in direct proportion to my shock value? Or retain myself: I wound after being hurt, I astound when attacked. In another age, I would have been a money lender.

Violence borders our lives: the difference between a criminal and an innocent is the difference in the size of their pastures, the extent of their maneuverability. My father was a gentle man who wept easily, but there was violence in his voice when he spoke of the babel of Odessa: not only did he not love the people, he felt the borders closing in—and knew he had to escape to enlarge his arena. It was enough, then, to achieve the negative: not to do violence by word or deed. He lost something in Odessa, and for all his talk of compassion, he never regained what he lost: he never again loved people. He became a terrified old man.

And what of Solomon Alexei Sorge, who saw in science not, perhaps, the hope of Man, but of himself, and toyed with hypotheses with something of the amusement for which his father once slapped his face? American optimism demanded that each generation progress so far beyond the previous one—how far depending on individual initiative, guts, and faith in the risk-taking, profit-potential of capitalism. By those lights, he had progressed: a satisfactory and assured income generously padded with book royalties, foundation grants, expense-paid trips to conferences around the world; a tidy collection of stocks and bonds; a substantial home in a comfortably stuffy suburb—a long way from the noisy openness of Chicago's west side. But Sorge saw, with all, an element of regression. The American dream did not require love of, or even interest in, one's fellow man. On the contrary. There was a kind of glorious battle hymn to the American Way: the land is rich, raw and waiting; those who make it can make it big; given freedom and raw materials, it is inconceivable that anyone should fail; thus, he who fails wasn't willing to work or simply didn't have it in him to make that magnificent all-out push. Leave him behind; he's not our kind; we need doers, and those are the ones we reward.

There was a breathtaking simplicity behind it all. The grandeur of a straight road bulldozed out of the desire for wealth and power, smoothed by the marching feet of the successful. The thrilling excitement of the chase, the race, the contest. And the magnificence of the visible carrots hanging before each quivering nose: comfort, indulgence, influence, fame. Who could resist? No wonder they flocked by the millions to partake of man's oldest, most enduring fantasy.

But those who failed? They had a way of multiplying and, perforce, of huddling together. Of what use to them the carrots pulling ever farther away? Of what use, in fact, the mythology surrounding the carrots, ever more remote from their own lives? Little wonder that Rabbi Boris Sorge, seeking simplicity, should have been confused by the actuality of the American dream.

Would he have been satisfied if he knew that his people would partake of that dream in the years after his death? Would he have been content to know that the Jewish immigrant did make it, did rise from the west side to break barriers in Chicago and the suburbs, to establish flourishing businesses or become wealthy doctors, dentists, lawyers, to live out, for themselves and their children, the essentials of the Dream (save the presidency, but even that, someday . . .)? Or would he have remained querulously impatient because there were still the Negroes and the Puerto Ricans and, if all else were finally swept into the stream, the American Indian?

Utopia would have broken his heart. He, his people, had been chosen to serve, and such service was not needed in Utopia. One could say, and the rabbi sometimes implied, that the Jew who believes he has been chosen for service thrives on chaos and inequality, on all the neatly chosen concepts strung together to limn that which needs to be changed, that which calls for service to create the Utopia which will make the servant irrelevant, except, perhaps, as a reminder. And the Jew, it had been said, was one who could not sleep and kept others awake, too.

Yet the rabbi fled Russia. Perhaps he suspected what he would find in America. Or, perhaps, America was a way station and he was, indeed, planning on Palestine as his resting place. I never had a chance to put it to him that way. Instead, we talked of abstracts and he hid from me. "Pity leads to charity balls; compassion to social work." Yes, of course, but what was he really thinking? That his compassion could change the world or sustain the Jew who was balancing cultures? Or that his version of compassion, driven into me as a doctrine, would be the necessary force? Or that we would both fail, but plant the seed in the next generation? In whom? In my eminent sons? In Harriet? We've made a mess of it, rabbi. I couldn't begin to explain it to you.

And so this sense of retrogression, of having failed, personally and directly, his father as well as the image he and the rabbi together had created. It might be amusing or, in some contexts, pathetic to recall the rabbi's earnest injunctions to the men of his synagogue that in America their task was to participate—not to hide behind the lassitude of despair that wrapped their Russian villages, nor to exhaust themselves in the constant readiness to flee before the hooves of the Cossacks or the drunken revelry of the peasants—but to play a part in the everyday commercial and political life of their new country. It took some getting used to, but they would have succeeded, these wildly dreaming immigrants, even without the exhortations of their rabbi. They were probably far ahead of him, if not in articulation, at least in their fierce acceptance of work and accumulation as necessary to their sons' elevation. They were quite willing, even prepared, to do without loving the goyim—did the goyim ask for their love?—and so had leaped the first hurdle of the competitive system. They were less sure of the desirability of their children's Americanization—that problem they brought to the rabbi. Who, still concentrating on the freedom to participate, was barely prepared for the newer questions. "It is not possible that freedom should succeed in destroying Judaism when every manner of oppression has failed," he said, but, trying to read the future, he was not sure and fell back, again, on the need of the Jew to serve; the need of others to have the Jew to serve, to change, to remake, to suffer.

The issues he dodged in 1918, the year of his death, would persist in his son's lifetime, to be avoided more subtly than by the father: they would become sociological hypotheses. Political and social participation, compassion, love, acculturation, Zionism, socialism—all would feed into the scientist's mill and come out as neat loaves of yeasty clichés, while the central issue, What Is A Jew? would become a variation of What Pressures Coexist in Potentially Mutually Exclusive Roles? and because no one could define the terms would never get to the mill at all.

And now, forty-six years later, querying his inability to cope with so-called common man, was it quibbling or retreating for Sorge to recall his father's loss of innocence? Would he have recalled it at all if, nearly buried, had not lurked the idea that Trudi might be of the genus common man and therein lay his failure? The thought was arresting: he began to consider what quality of arrogance he had brought to his marriage and how much, if at all, Trudi had fought. In twenty-nine years, their quarrels had been few, but had she fought it would not have been through quarrels: he was not a satisfactory opponent and she wearied quickly of defining terms and delimiting frames of reference. Nor would she, had she, fought him in bed. He had once tried to justify his experiments elsewhere by some sexual lack in his wife, but it was no good: Trudi was a joyous partner whose exertions, matching his in the silence he decreed, became the antiphony to daylight separation: his absorption with Harriet, Trudi's rehearsed companionship with David and Nathan. Well, then, that was where she fought: in the daytime, and not only through the children, but in the ordinary, everyday activities she piled ever higher to counter his attempts to create something unusual, meaningful, and (hail, rabbi, I have not forgotten you) prophetic.

He began to scrape and stack the dishes from the family lunch, wondering at the ease with which he accepted himself as a failure. He had not doubted his culpability when Harriet brought him her pregnancy and numerical history of lovers; he could think of Trudi as sister to the common man he could not comprehend; and he could think of at least one other notable example, with his sons, when without hesitation he had chosen to berate himself. It was not, he felt, a matter of humility, but of weakness in a lifetime's façade, and as he ran hot water over the dishes it came to him, with some satisfaction, that a man's strength or weakness, even if once his own, became, over the years, a function of his wife's behavior and attitudes so that finally he could say, She sustained me, or She broke me, and never know for sure whether he would have been the same with another wife or none at all. That, too, was weakness, but he thought it inherent in his sex. Or would have liked to think so. (Could a questionnaire be constructed to prove the hypothesis? He would have to ask the psychologists. Or would it be a question of chemistry? Or of ethnomethodology? Sociology of the family? Criminology? There were no limits really, to a thorough study.) He doubted that the question would have arisen, had Trudi been present to walk into the kitchen with a comment whose wit gave him proprietary pleasure or whose banality lent him the superiority of exasperation.

Trudi as lender, himself as recipient, was a concept increasingly familiar, increasingly a component of the idea of failure. If it was natural, even desirable in the scheme of human continuity, to see one's parent as donor and oneself as grateful receiver, it was most emphatically unnatural to wait with outstretched hands for one's wife to bestow godly gifts of self-esteem, confidence, pride, even superiority. Even if one had recently decided a wife could be the instrument of making or breaking a man. What have I given her? Where is that scientific middle ground where we crouch with relief before springing to one fatal side or another? Where were my offers, my donations, my shared delights, exclusive of the everyday provisions that the dullest give their mates: food, clothing, shelter? Now I want her to share Milton with me. What would I have done with Milton a month ago? Labeled him, marked him down for a hypothesis, fitted him into a questionnaire. Hoarded him.

He began to rebel. It was too easy, with Trudi gone, to fix blame entirely on himself, the abandoned failure doing dishes in his wife's kitchen. He had a role, roles to fill: duties to perform. If he could not communicate with common man, he could study him; if he studied (took from) his wife, he had only been fulfilling himself and from that Trudi could not help but benefit.

He liked to keep his study door open to hear her as she worked. At first he had been disturbed to discover she talked to herself while vacuuming, ironing, dusting: any time she was alone, isolated within her shell of unthinking activity. Later he was amused, even pleased, his thoughts tender as toward a convalescent or young child.

''What have I in common with those immigrants?'' she asked as she pushed the vacuum cleaner beneath the couch. ''All those who came here when I was a baby. Nothing. Not background, not attitudes, not feelings, not the world I live in. But there is something. There must be or I wouldn't ask the question. It would never occur to me unless somehow I were connected with them. Continuation. Is that what they call tradition? Not the songs and the prayers and the services, but being a part of those people and the way they behaved and thought. I feel I must accept them. Must I?''

Sometimes she sang, sometimes she quoted bits of poetry or novels she was reading, or became a modern Joan. She was dusting the foyer bench the morning she rattled off the fifth amendment and berated Senator McCarthy in terms certain to put her in contempt of congress. While polishing the banister she spoke to Nasser of the rights of the Israelis. On her knees, scrubbing the kitchen floor, she argued with Stalin over the fate of poets and novelists. Ironing Sorge's shirts, she debated, angrily, the return of seized industries to Germans. "I keep coming back to my Jewishness. Can't I forget it? Or bypass it? How would I see the world if I were a Gentile? Would I hate the Germans so much? Would I have wept for those doctors in Russia?" And later, "Would I have been so terrified at what I thought were implications of the Rosenberg trial? Or is it me? No one else seems worried." And later still, "I'm too aware of myself. And what I am. I can't write a book or paint a picture and stand aside to see what I'm thinking. There are too many things I don't understand."

Then Sorge's fondness rose in him until he could no longer contain it and he left his study to kiss her. "Taking a break," he said. "Let's have a cup of coffee."

But what most pleased him was her love of language. Whatever her activity, she would murmur words at random, picking them from her reading, or casual conversation, to roll on her tongue like a child with a bubble gum ball, stretching, exaggerating syllables, repeating them in sing-song, sensual caress. "Somnolent. Sommmmmmm-no-lent. Al-ci-bi-a-des. Con-*tem*-pla-tive. Atavistic. Aaaaa-ta-vis-tic. Rodomontade. Misogyny. Amanuensis. Uxorious. Ux-ooo-rious. Gallimaufry. Har-mo-ni-um. In-taaag-li-o. You-ghiogeny." (The name of a pullman car on—was it the Pennsylvania? Sorge barely remembered her pointing it out, gleefully, from the window of their bedroom as they traveled to New York.) "Dzig-get-tai." (Good God, has she been reading the Bible?) "Li-quid-ate. Peg-o-man-cy. Ob-si-dian. Ex-tra-ne-ous."

But Sorge had stopped listening after pegomancy, feeling as if a favorite pupil had been sitting at the feet of someone else. Her reading was no longer obvious, her directions no longer predictable. What year was that? I can't remember.

Probably about ten years ago. And I became suspicious. Not of the commonplace: a man or men; but of words. A word. So that where once he left the study door open to listen and smile and work to the murmur of her charming inanities, now he began to spy on her, to creep about the house, listening and watching, noting the unusual, the unpredictable. Her actions took on a mysterious cast: what thoughts was she hiding as she hummed Beethoven's *Les Adieux* sonata while making chicken soup, or quoted Edwin Arlington Robinson while darning socks, or posed questions for Rabbi Akiba while polishing silver? And where the hell had pegomancy come from? What had she read, what had she thought? What direction was she taking?

I never asked her, for it had come to me suddenly that not once, in all her monologues, did she mention me. I never asked her. Instead, I refined my techniques to spy on my wife as, once, I spied on my sons.

9

DAVID AND NATHAN had never met Max Rosenthal—he died before they were born—but they heard enough about him to know he had saved their grandmother and their father, and made their grandfather's reputation. For the little grocer who had once questioned Rabbi Sorge on the role of the Jews in America, married the rabbi's widow when his own wife died, educated the rabbi's children, and by endless embroidered recollection, created a memory in west side Chicago of the rabbi as a firm, principled, brave, wise and compassionate leader who had, alas, fallen before he could see the ascent of his people to the heights of American life—an ascent for which he had paved the way, on whose road he had set his fellow Jews' feet, whose glories and pitfalls he had foreseen, predicted, and for which he had prepared Russian Jewry in America. What Max Rosenthal gained from his mythology Sorge was never sure—he could not talk to his stepfather as he had talked to the rabbi (and even if he could, how could he say Why are you making up these beautiful lies about my father?). What Sorge's mother gained was clear enough: a second husband who did obeisance to the first while providing the widow and children with more comforts than they had ever known. While Sorge was left without weapons. He could not resent the man who so diligently apotheosized his father and who, moreover, was giving his mother a good life and a softer tongue. He could not be angry with a man who was taking his father's place when this man made that place inaccessible to mortals. He could only sit in the silent loneliness of memories while his stepfather, his mother, his sister and brothers and the whole west side memorialized a man who had never lived, forcing a confusion of memory and recall upon the boy who wanted only to continue and complete the snatches of conversation that had made up his first ten years.

But this David and Nathan never knew. Harriet knew some of it, from her evening sessions with her father, but even she knew only a part. Sorge never shared those lonely years with anyone, least of all the sons he felt he lost when they were children. They grew up with their grandmother's tales ringing them and their grandfather with glory, limning Max Rosenthal as a peripheral figure who, from that outside position, had managed to influence all those in the magic inner circle while, incidentally, feeding and clothing them and sending the four children through college. Thus, it was a double honor to be David and Nathan: grandsons of the immortal rabbi, stepgrandsons of the grocer Max Rosenthal. It could be said, then, that if the boys grew up largely without the conventional father, they were constantly shadowed by two grandfathers, exacting, lovable, all-embracing in the one's spirituality and the other's satisfaction of material needs.

There was nothing subtle about the lessons, no sugarcoating to make example palatable. It was, surely, an honor—a double honor—to be David and Nathan, but it was also heavy responsibility, a burden to be borne with dignity and unfailing awareness of the heritage, the mold, the greatness which was theirs.

But in all the talk, the memorializing, the quoting, there was left unspecified exactly how the heirs were to carry their burden: was it better to be prophet or disciple? Sarah Sorge departed for Israel when David was ten, Nathan nine years old, without resolving the dilemma or leaving clues for the solution. She left echoes of persistent, emphatic, positive nagging that set the boys chasing shadows of greatness and goodness while their father, standing at the living room blackboard, tried to build reality through sociological solidity.

Bits and pieces of Max Rosenthal and Rabbi Sorge clung to Sarah's letters from Israel in exclamatory phrases, parenthetical injunctions, wistful recollections. Like jagged fragments of colored glass stuck randomly through news of British, Arabs, Irgun, the Negev, new apartments, old hovels, and—always—immigrants to the promised land, the rabbi and his biographer were increasingly atomized, eluding the most diligent search for meaning. What remained was amorphous anxiety: *something* was not being fulfilled, *some* figures stood tall and found others wanting, *some* example was not being followed. In the end, contemporary heroes were more easily comprehended by teenagers.

For a brief time the heroes were real: their uncles who had died two years apart—Leon in the Normandy landing, Daniel shot by the British in Israel. But their grandmother's and father's grief had humanized the heroes, reducing their stature. Nothing was left but literature.

They discovered the library and made it their preserve, resisting Sorge's short-lived attempt to guide their reading, as well as Trudi's more persistent efforts to join them in browsing, to select for them on the basis of the magic number at the bottom of each blurb that blandly stated the age level for which the book was written. They chose together and read together with a wild catholicity that bemused their teachers and startled Sorge when he chanced to see the stacks of books on their night-tables.

And it was a combination of factors—that same catholicity, Trudi's hurt withdrawal after her offers had been refused, Sorge's growing absorption with Harriet, the acknowledged sanctity of the boys' bedroom—that delayed Sorge's discovery of their crammed bookshelves: evidence that more books were coming out of the library than were going in.

He should not have been in the bedroom. There had been a pact between boys and parents: David and Nathan would make their beds, dust, vacuum, wash windows; and in return, the room was theirs, the door need not be locked for the family would honor privacy. They were in high school, mature, capable, trustworthy—their privacy was honored. So I should not have been there in the first place. What made me go? Something in the air, a kind of silent giggling connivance, a piratical incense that led me, when they were at a movie, to climb the stairs and acquaint myself with the robbers' den.

The room was large, divided into sections by a bookshelf running almost the length, crossed like a T at the window wall by a twelve foot desk. Fossils of discarded projects dotted walls and shelves: ship and airplane models, soap carvings, liquid aluminum statues, football helmets, baseball trophies, a can of marbles, kiln-dried ashtrays from school, a framed, scientifically-aged Gettysburg address and second inaugural from their trip to New Salem, posters proclaiming the eighth-grade play in which they both had small parts, and oddly, fragments of religion: a quotation from Hillel, a menorah on the desk, a book about Sabbatai Zevi, a print of Theodore Herzl, a map of Israel and—astonishingly, to Sorge who had not known they read the book—lines from the Bible written in flamboyant red magic marker on old shirt cardboards tacked to the wall. "Ecclesiastes: Whatsoever mine eyes desired I kept not from them." "Ecclesiastes: Go thy way, eat thy bread with joy, And drink thy wine with a merry heart; For God hath already accepted thy works." "Haggai: He that earneth wages earneth wages for a bag with holes." "Joel: Your old men shall dream dreams, Your young men shall see visions." "Micah: A man's enemies are the men of his own house."

It was neither religion nor philosophy; it was adolescent selectivity—sardonic, rebellious, nearsighted, perverted and demeaning. But each phrase, as a graphic line on rebellion and faulty eyesight, held him: each meant something to his sons, therefore to himself, the victim of Micah's insight that mocked him from above Nathan's bed. And the other victims: Rabbi Boris Sorge and the grocer Max Rosenthal. Clever. I have clever sons. More clever than their father who did not know how to thumb his nose when he was young, who, perhaps, was not aware of the desire until he became older and chose political science as his field. And by then both his fathers were dead.

David and Nathan had gone to Sunday school and had been confirmed. Over Trudi's objections, there had been no bar mitzvah—I thumbed my nose that way, too. But the secularized Judaism on their walls came not from Sunday school, or confirmation, or Sorge's careful chalk talks, but some private source of anger and calculated distrust that had to be manifested in some other way. He found it in the bookshelves.

Not a specific book, or category of books, but simply books as objects: a surfeit of them, some with the name of the Temple library stamped inside, most with the markings of the Evanston public library—and in the closet, neatly stacked, he found the plastic dust jackets carefully removed from each stolen book.

He always shied away from direct confrontation. Without waiting for the shock to subside, or clear thought to follow, he obeyed a blind impulse and descended to the basement to collect empty cartons. He filled two, weeding out the library-stamped books from those inscribed with loving birthday or Hannukah comments "from mother and dad," or Aunt Yetta or, some years back, Uncle Leon and Uncle Daniel. Then he lugged them down the back stairs and out to the garage, making a return trip to the living room to tell Trudi he was going out to mail a letter, and finally, in the private night, he drove to the library.

He stood in the shadow of the building, shoving the books, one at a time, through the night return slot. They should be doing this, he thought, shrinking back as a car's headlights swept him. But it's so much easier this way. At least for now. When the cartons were empty, he tossed them into the back seat of the car and turned north, to drive home.

I followed none of the tragic scenarios that might have been written for me. I did not drive around all night trying to calm frantic nerves. I did not rush home and blame Trudi for what she had done to our boys; I did not even tell Trudi what had happened. I did not go to a bar to order a drink in whose depths I might cogitate the future. I did not weep or wail or mutter imprecations, nor moan nor cry nor murmur that all was lost. I simply knew, with a certainty most scientists would envy, that I had failed, and that was when I began to spy on my sons.

They were privileged teenagers: having come to adolescence without fear or want or doubt as to a home base, they took for granted not so much the grand, sweeping myths of democracy and capitalism as the little, overlooked details of a good life—lightbulbs and toothpaste, new shoes and afternoon snacks, ball point pens and ice skates, rainproof roofs and erasable typing paper, books in translation and transistor radios, contour chairs and contraceptives. They took for granted a wealth and variety that bewildered more than half the world, accepting it as, if not their due, at least their lot because their parents not only had come to accept it as well, but behaved as if all turned upon a well-fed, well-clothed, well-educated, well-satisfied younger generation.

(That had been his hypothesis in 1952 when his sons were sixteen and fifteen years old, thieves on whom he spied. Sitting in his half-empty bedroom fourteen years later, minus a wife, recalling that earlier time, he knew he was only partly right. There were plenty of them who, like his sons, accepted and toyed with what the past had built, but there were also the kids who trained in Ohio for the battlefields of Mississippi and, in 1964, when their numbers were growing on campus after campus, they could not be discounted as a weird minority. He had projected, before, from his sons in whom he had lost all pride, or right to pride. He had fed them too well, from the wrong cup.)

We gave them everything but awareness of what they had and how they got it, an appreciation of how rare, in the world, those little details are. And because of our failure—and for God knows what other reasons besides—they crammed their bookshelves and (a spy learns much that he would rather not know) their closets and dressers as well.

His next discovery. Somehow—a lapse in spying—he missed the conversation over the denuded bookshelves; there was a wary period of careful talk and sidelong glances, of waiting for a confrontation that never took place; then life returned to normal. Except that Sorge had refined his techniques and could walk down the hall without creaking the floor boards, could pause outside a closed door long enough to catch movements and intelligible sounds, could even follow his sons on an excursion to Marshall Field's where, working together with a smoothness that aroused his reluctant admiration, they stole a cashmere sweater and a silk shirt.

He was not a man of desperate, unthinking action. When he went through his sons' closets and dressers the next day he made a careful list of all the items he found and for three months he compared his list with the contents he recounted each week. Everytime the telephone rang he expected it to be the police from Chicago or whatever suburb his sons were looting that day; he waited for the police and they never called. The three months stretched into four and he had proof, he had his facts, but still he waited. In the fourth month, seeking final, definitive proof, he went through the department store bills. He knew Trudi had not bought those expensive hairbrushes, shirts, socks, ties, gloves, but he wanted to make sure. And he did. And still the police did not call.

So, without caring whether the boards creaked or he bumped against the banister, he climbed the stairs to his sons' room, for there was no one else to do it. The jig is up, he thought; cheese it, the cops; oh officer my boys never done nothing wrong before this, they was good boys, I brought them up good, strict and all, why did this happen to me?

To me, not to Trudi. She tried—strict and all—while I abdicated: my father's son. Was I so determined to be a failure? And what do I do now—redeem myself or my sons? Or do we kneel together in supplication for forgiveness before Trudi's sorrowful countenance? Forgive me mother, for I have sinned.

He walked into his sons' room without knocking and hulked over them in the shadows beyond their illuminated desks. Then he turned back to close the door. "I don't want your mother to hear this," he said as David and Nathan raised curious eyes from their homework.

"All that stuff has to go back," he said. "All of it. Including anything I've missed here." And he slapped down the list he had made, written in neat columns in his tall, angular handwriting.

David scanned the items. "We were going to give you the silver hairbrush for Father's Day."

Damn it, this was no time to smile. "The smoking jacket for my birthday . . . ?"

Nathan nodded. "VL and A. We always like to go there. We almost got caught that day."

The surrealism of the exchange threatened to fascinate him, draw him in, away from the reality he had come to reinstate between himself and his sons. But if that reality, to match minimum expectations, should include guilt, a certain amount of fear, some eagerness to atone or, at least, seek atonement, how instill that in one's sons whose eyes held only mild curiosity and some amusement over the time they almost got caught? Well, for a start, make them talk.

He sat on one of the beds. "How did you work it?"

Nathan—or was it David? It was odd; just as years later he would have difficulty distinguishing their wives one from the other, now he was not sure he could tell his sons apart—shrugged contemptuously. "It didn't take much brains. They're watching for the snatch and run kind. We always stayed in the store for awhile after we took something."

His other son grinned. "Sometimes we exchanged one thing we took for another one with the clerk helping us find the right size."

"How?" He did not tell them he had followed them once; he wanted to hear them talk; could this contribute to Szold's study of the criminal mind?

"Look, dad," said one of the monsters before him, claiming kinship. "You pick up something, like a sweater—"

"With delicate fingers," said the other monster. "Discriminating, sophisticated fingers."

"Sophisticated fingers," echoed the first and it became a chant. "You caress the sweater, you examine it—"

"Knowingly."

"Knowingly. You wander gaily, trippingly down the counter, looking at other sweaters, comparing—"

"Man of distinction."

"Notably. You wander. After a while, you've wandered way the hell the other side of the store—"

"And casually, insouciantly up the escalator—"

"And with friendly charm you chat with an old bag next to you while your busy little fingers take the price tag off the sweater."

"Naughty little fingers."

"Clever little fingers. Where were we?"

"Still wandering with gay abandon."

"But now we're upstairs. And up again as many floors as we can find or feel necessary. *Then*."

"The evilly smiling cohort awaits in the men's room with one of the store's sacks brought from home."

"And in pops our innocent sweater, now forever ours."

"Ravished and raped."

"Innocence lost forever."

"Of course there are other diabolical methods."

"Like return and exchange."

"Return and exchange."

"With a slightly hangdog, help-me-out expression. Oh dear Mr. Salesman or kind Saleslady as the case may be—oh dear, my darling mother picked out this sweater for me but it's just not my color."

"It clashes with my razor."

"The one I use to shave my legs."

"So can't you help me find a better color, more suited to my sensitive temperament?"

"And damned if they don't."

"With expressions of endearment if it's a bag—"

"And man-to-man sympathy if otherwise."

"And I—or we—walk out, pillars of society—"

"Keeping the economy flourishing by spreading our purchasing power from store to store."

"Busy stores."

"Of a certainty. It wouldn't work in a quiet store."

"Or a little one."

"Or Saks. They're careful as hell at Saks."

"But if you follow the rules—"

"Strictly, like good, law-abiding citizens—"

"You're safe."

"Except from the wrath of your father," said Trudi from the doorway. She looked ill. "Show your wrath, Sol."

"Christ," muttered one of the boys, for the first time reacting normally and Sorge, while resenting the reaction, silently echoed the complaint. It had not occurred to him that if he could listen at closed doors so could Trudi. He was disappointed in her. And his wrath? He felt as sick as she looked but wrath was what he was trying to avoid, though she could not understand if he told her. He could admire the elemental in Trudi at certain chosen times; at this time he wanted none of it. "I'll handle this," he said.

She nodded. "I'll just listen."

But he could not help himself. "How long have you known?"

"About five minutes. Our clever sons raised their voices in enthusiasm as I passed the door. What were you going to do with your haul?" she asked them. "Whatever you took, I would have noticed you wearing things I didn't buy."

"The shirt I said my girl bought for my birthday," began one of the boys.

"And the sweater I said I bought out of my allowance," said the other.

Trudi nodded again. "And the rest you were going to hoard, using them one at a time until you left for college and wowed your friends with your affluence."

"Well . . ." said David or Nathan.

"We knew it couldn't go on forever," said Nathan or David.

"Oh?" asked Trudi quietly. "Why not? You weren't doing anything wrong, were you?"

"Wait a minute," began Sorge, frustrated and alarmed, set back only momentarily as Trudi threw him a look of staggering fury. "Wait," he repeated. "I said I'd handle this."

"What's to handle?" asked one of the thieves. "It's all over. We always knew we'd have to quit as soon as you found out."

"And the library books?" asked Sorge. "I found out about those."

"Whatever happened to them?"

"I returned them."

"Yeh, we thought so. But, well, you didn't say anything about them."

"And we hadn't got it out of our system yet."

"You brats!" cried Trudi. "Sol, don't sit there and discuss this reasonably. They're not reasonable people."

"On the contrary," said Sorge, his temper beginning to rise, not at his sons, but at his wife. "They are most reasonable. And must be dealt with accordingly."

"Then deal with!" she cried. "You're a father, not a scientist. You should be dispensing justice, not discussing."

"God damn it!" he roared. "Will you let me take care of this in my own way?"

"How can I?" she cried. "You've got a couple of insolent, amoral, smirking criminals on your hands and I won't let you help them sneak out with a discussion on the role and function of shoplifters in an expanding economy."

That stopped him. Where had she learned to use his language as a weapon against him? Where had she learned to probe the sensitive, because vulnerable, areas of his concerns? I.e.: He might admit, occasionally and briefly, that the glorious convoluted jargon of the social sciences satisfied the same hunger as an eight-year-old's coded letter to a friend or the giggling jive talk of teenagers, but it was a private admission. He might concede, occasionally and in passing, the delighted, collective snobbery of his inner circle, but that was a personal concession. There was just enough validity for just enough of the jargon to make his admissions and concessions easily discarded, as long as he was spared ridicule. Particularly from his wife. Particularly and especially from his wife in the presence of his sons. Thank God Harriet was not there.

A stifled giggle from one of his sons roused him: he had no time to consider or chastise his wife. It was absurd to suppose parents could lash each other before their children with impunity. If nothing else, it blurred the socially adapted roles of mother and father, and diluted the wrong they were there to discuss. And as Trudi had indicated when she interfered, they were discussing a wrong.

"Let's get this over with," he muttered, turning his back on Trudi. His anger had risen, then turned against himself. He knew he would much prefer Trudi to take over: it was no longer a question of socially adapted roles, but of his own failure. In the uncomfortable silence of the room, with his wife staring at his back, his sons at their large, capable, thieving hands, he began to see himself as the thief, his sons as his heirs. Long ago he had taken (a kinder word) a convenient view of religion from Max Rosenthal: it is easier to praise the piety—real or imagined—of another than to attain piety oneself. Was the dictum really that simple? Did he mean piety, or perhaps conscience, responsibility, awareness, self-esteem, the strength of being one's own mirror? These were the terms, the ideas, the goals he might have taken from his father; but I was too busy tossing him in the garbage to rot forgotten. I wanted no part of his struggle; I wanted neatly packaged rules. I wanted no heritage from Odessa or the west side of Chicago or even my mother's radiant vision of the promised land. My past was each day's yesterday: Max Rosenthal's cushioned method for being both Jew and Gentile, Russian and American, a man and a pretense at what we are pleased to call a rational animal. And so I stole again, by choosing a field that borrowed (a much kinder word) from other disciplines, ignoring the horrendous fact that the logical end of my chosen life's work was the manipulation of my fellow man, prattling, instead, of making the bastard science legitimate, of knowledge for its own sake, of politics as the proper study of man, religious man, cultural man, economic man, family man—all of whom have disappeared though we cling to the distinctions so as not to rub ourselves out. The rabbi was a whole man; his heirs were fragmented: they could not even bring up their own children.

"Let's get this over with," he said again, but he could not, the sense of failure was choking him. He had not failed because he was a political scientist; he had chosen his field because of prior, or contemporary, failure. Unlike his father, he had found a haven. Not in geography, not in God, but in an ill-defined netherworld of adopted jargon, borrowed clichés, and half-baked philosophizing. Not all of it, oh no, but enough to make him feel comfortable, enough to make him almost rich, enough to allow him to forget his father. He was lucky his sons were not murderers.

"Let's get this over with," he said again, but a strange thing happened; his sons were huddled together on one of the beds and Trudi had risen, was holding his arm, was leading him out of the door.

"We'll talk about it again tomorrow," she said, and led him downstairs to the kitchen where he sat and watched as she put on a pot of coffee. He could still see his sons huddled on the bed; somehow he had gotten across to them. Did I say anything while I was thinking? Perhaps I was talking to them the whole time. Perhaps it's settled. But if not, it was all right; Trudi would finish it. She would take care of them. She might put them to work to earn enough to pay for what they stole. He should have mentioned that. Maybe he did. She might make them take everything back; that would take as much skill as the original thefts. He should have mentioned that, too. But maybe I did. Maybe I did.

When Trudi brought him the coffee, his head was down; he was trying not to weep. But even the tears would have been borrowed; they were, at least in part, the result of what he knew he *should* be feeling. And he knew, too, that the other part—the genuine tears that had begun to streak his face—would disappear, that man recovered from a sense of failure almost as quickly as he did from an illness.

10

LIEUTENANT MILTON was short and stout, with a jolly, bulbous nose, cold, flat eyes, and a hoarse voice punctuated by rasps as he rhythmically cleared his throat. He was not in uniform but the two men flanking him were.

"Now tell us all about it," he said, sitting in the living room while his men stood by the door. Sorge, having risen at six to clean the house, waited for a comment, some remark, lodged in surprise, that a man bereft of housewifely comforts could so maintain his home in neatness, cleanliness, order. None came. Milton sat, stocky and solid, in a creased leather chair Sorge had wiped with a treated rag; his eyes wandered about the comfortable, well-worn room Sorge had dusted and vacuumed; his mouth worked only to take in air. "All about it. From the beginning," Milton said.

Sorge thought, We were married in 1935 but that isn't what you mean. And it would be arrogant to assume that as the beginning.

"Sit down," said Milton, the host, and Sorge, to recapture status, countered by offering coffee. "No. Thanks."

"You don't drink while on duty?"

"Something like that."

Or with a potential murderer, thought Sorge, swept again, hungrily, by the desire to share with Trudi this absurdity, this

Marx brothers nonsense, this foolish man with the Santa nose and the power of the state at his back. He was aware, with pained amusement, that the desire to share with his wife was increasing in direct proportion to the length of her absence, and that, if the proposition was valid, such desire had been minimal (muted? squelched?) when she was present. But her absence, vague and unreal the past few days, was made so definite, such a palpable *thing* to be examined, by Milton's heavy body and wandering eyes (did he expect to find a corpse in the living room?), the thought came to Sorge that it might be too late, not only to desire Trudi's presence, but to study his desire or lack of it.

"Well?" said Milton.

Sorge sat down. "My wife has disappeared," he said and saying it felt naked, ashamed, as if confessing a serious illness he had brought on himself by failing to take precautions; confessing, moreover, to a doctor clinically but not emotionally interested. "Saturday night," he added and that was just as bad because today was Tuesday and he had not yet said, Trudi, I miss you.

"Okay," said Milton, setting machinery in motion: he slid down in his chair, looked to see that his cohorts were taking notes, cleared his throat. "Description."

Sorge was startled. "Didn't my sister—?"

"Sure. Sisters-in-law and husbands see a woman different."

How did I see my wife? How did Yetta see her? As too tiny for me. "Tiny," he said. "Five-one. Brown hair. Greenish eyes."

There was a pause. "Distinguishing marks?" asked Milton patiently.

Sorge was reluctant. "A mole on her left thigh. A scar on the first finger of her right hand; she cut herself slicing something in the kitchen."

"She's left-handed?"

"Yes. There's a small spot high up on her back—a white spot—no pigment. She was—she is quite beautiful."

"She wear glasses?"

"No."

"Not even for reading?"

"No."

"You got a picture?"

Sorge went to the secretary in the corner of the room; he had anticipated this and the night before had selected two of his favorites: Trudi pensive at Starved Rock, Trudi laughing in the doorway of Sayat Nova in New York. "Christ," said Milton softly, reverently, staring at them. "She must of had to fight 'em off."

"Everyone liked—likes her," said Sorge warily; if Yetta had prattled of Trudi's alleged lover to this stalwart of the law what could he answer? That Trudi was not the type? Every woman is the type, given certain factors in conjunction. And I no longer have the fine certainty that allowed me to throw Yetta out.

"And she liked them," Milton hazarded.

"She liked people, yes."

"One in particular?"

"Yes. Her husband."

"Doesn't look like it, does it? Anyone besides her loving husband?"

"No."

"Not to your knowledge."

"No."

"Find any love letters around?"

"I haven't looked."

"You haven't looked. No farewell note, I take it."

"No."

"Why haven't you looked?"

"I didn't think of it."

"You didn't think of it. Mind if we do?"

"Do what?"

"Look around."

"Yes. Yes, I do mind."

"You afraid we'll find something?"

"It isn't that."

"Then what is it?"

"This is my house. Mine and Trudi's. I should look first."

"But you didn't think of it before."

"No."

"You sure you haven't looked?"

"I've said I haven't."

"Mind if we look for Trudi?"

"Don't call her that!"

"Sorry. May we have your permission to conduct a search for Mrs. Sorge on the premises?"

Sorge's hatred was a great bird, flapping its wings, setting up currents of air about his head, its claws scraping along his skin, its feathers enfolding, smothering him. He gasped. The amusement, the slapstick was gone; this stupid man with the sloppy grammar and narrow mind was quite serious and meant to invade his life. He had never known such hatred, such virulent, helpless hatred. "You need a search warrant," he managed to say, but he had been outflanked and he knew it.

"I can get one," said Milton gently. "But I had a feeling you'd cooperate."

Sorge moved his hand. "Just stay out of the drawers."

Milton nodded to the two uniformed men. "Stay out of the drawers." And stayed in his chair as they left the room. "Tell me about her," he said confidingly, man to man.

Sorge shook his head. "An ordinary housewife. There's nothing to tell."

"She help you in your work?"

"No."

"Just what is your work?"

"I'm a professor of political science."

"And what's that? Just pretend I'm ignorant and tell me what you do."

Pretend. He can't be serious. But, as noted, he is serious; he sits in my living room with a cheerful nose and cold eyes and dares call my wife by her first name as if she has gone beyond the human into the statistical world of the news story. My God, I could kill him. But that, he reflected, was precisely the kind of action for which Milton waited while his men scoured the house. "I study, and teach, the political system."

"Means nothing to me," said Milton cheerfully.

"I'm not surprised."

"Well, how about explaining it? We've got lots of time."

True. The afternoon stretched before them. And if Milton stayed long enough, what a fitting climax to have him and his minions there when Trudi walked in, her arms loaded with groceries, or bags from Field's and Saks and Bramsons, or oddly-wrapped packages from the antique shops of Long Grove, to raise her heavy, dark eyebrows and ask him if he and his visitor wouldn't like some coffee. So, then, talk. Spin out the day. This stupid bastard might even learn something in the process.

"Politics has been defined variously. My favorites include Oakeshott's 'activity of attending to the general arrangements of a collection of people who, in respect of their common recognition of a manner of attending to its arrangements, compose a single community.' He also says that political activity takes the form of the 'amendment of existing arrangements by exploring and pursuing what is intimated in them.' Lasswell speaks of arenas in which participants are striving to accomplish their purposes by influencing outcomes; these purposes directed toward preferred events, or values and interpretations of values in terms of institutional practices. Participants are seeking to maximize power and other values by influencing outcomes. In the decision process, participants with various value perspectives employing base values by various strategies interact in an arena to influence outcomes and effects. Easton describes political science as a study of authoritative allocation of values for a society as it is influenced by the distribution and use of power. Of course Easton simplifies. There is quite an argument on the importance of power in the political arena, whether it is central or peripheral. Van Dyke speaks of human needs and wants or associated desires and purposes. Naturally power could be one of these; one may assume those who attain power desire to do so. In light of these factors Lasswell has formulated an equation for political man: private motives transformed into displacement onto public objects transformed into rationalization in terms of public interest equals Political Man. Rather neat, I think. It encompasses almost everything I've said. I assume you would agree.''

There was a short, heavy silence. ''Was that really necessary, professor?'' asked Milton sadly.

Necessary? Of course not. He was back to the eight-year-old with his coded letters. One of Brecht's definitions of science was its delineation of means and ends to help one gain clarity. Brecht would have been wiser with a man like Milton; he would have led Milton gently, spoon-fed him to an awareness of his field's significance, applied another of his definitions of science—that it helps or forces the individual to account for the ultimate meaning of his own life—to bring Milton into the fold. But then Brecht did not have Sorge's weakness; Brecht's wife, one had to assume, did not disappear one Saturday night leaving him to his furies. Nor would

Brecht—assuming again—be asked to define his life's work while, as background, his home was being searched for the corpse of his wife. Sorge was cramped by sudden fear: what if they should find her? It? Impossible. He had searched on Saturday night. But surely, in his anguish and haste, he had overlooked a corner, a crevice, a dark hiding place behind a door or beneath a table. Ridiculous. A fairy tale. But what, then? Trudi, where are you? What am I going to do?

He felt the house tremble beneath the clods of the police—they were in the attic now—and began to understand, for the first time, the Moscow trials: the frantic confessions to heinous crimes never committed. Fear and uncertainty nullified the past, made anything possible, even probable; multiplied guilt and responsibility, turned fleeting fantasy into a reality executed in minute detail with victims and villains, made thought a crime—guilty, guilty, guilty!

(It might make a good, solid study: the use of fear to distort the past; though the methodology would be difficult. Might try content analysis—tie in the Spanish Inquisition, other periods of hysteria when guilt was clasped like an infant to be nurtured as the only permanent fact of existence. Too fanciful, that: he was forgetting his role in the study. Wilson would be upset; his leftist ideology had permitted him only one conclusion: those who confess are guilty. But I won't worry about Wilson. He beat me out on the grant to study Cuban refugees; there's probably a grant somewhere for a good, solid study of the Moscow trials.)

"What are you thinking?" asked Milton.

"About the Moscow trials."

Footsteps on the attic stairs. The policemen were descending.

"You're not on trial, professor. I thought you might be thinking about your wife."

Guilty. I was not thinking about my wife. And what's it to

you, anyway, Lieutenant? But I won't ask him that. We won't talk about Trudi in this house. We'll talk inanities. "You don't approve of me, do you?"

"Oh, I don't know." Milton stretched out his stubby legs, cocked his head to listen to the footsteps, now on the cellar stairs, then gazed benevolently at Sorge. "I've never been able to make up my mind about you people."

"You mean you don't like Jews."

"Now who said anything like that? Jews are just as rotten as anybody else. I look at everybody the same. But, as a matter of fact, I wasn't talking about Jews. I was talking about this crew of professors up here."

"Sorry," Sorge mumbled.

"Think nothing of it. You people jump too fast."

"Professors?"

"No, Jews."

Damn the man. "Sorry again."

"You always so sorry about everything?"

"Not usually."

"No, I think you are. I bet you are. I've watched you professors. Every time you get a goddam parking ticket you apologize. What makes you think you're so much better than everybody else?"

"It doesn't logically follow—"

"I'm not talking about logic; I'm talking about what happens. Anybody who's always sorry is acting like Jesus, like he's responsible for everything."

"Your perception amazes me."

"Well, you learn a lot when you're a cop. Have to. Otherwise you'd go crazy."

"And you're very good at it."

"Well, I've been at it a long time. Look, what's with you people? Why are you always coming around? Like we're a bunch of animals in a zoo. We oughta charge admission, for Christ's sake."

"We don't always come around, surely?"

"Three times in the last ten months." His voice rose to a falsetto. "Lieutenant Milton, we're doing a study of the effects of the Summerdale police scandal on morale and overall performance of your force. Lieutenant Milton, we're trying to determine the significant variables in the relationship of Evanston Negroes to the police. Lieutenant Milton, how would you describe your role, and that of your fellow police, in a metropolitan government such as is envisaged for the north and northwest suburbs?"

Even in the childish falsetto, the projects had a solid, comfortable ring; Sorge was proud of his department, and said so.

"Important to who?" asked Milton. "Not to me. I got a job to do and your boys keep interrupting me."

"Your job could be affected by our studies."

"How? Name me one study that's ever affected me. Or the police."

"There was one in Chicago in the late forties. Lohman and Reitzes did a study of police behavior toward minority groups. An educational program was formulated and the police were restudied after they had been through the program. It was found that, while attitudes remained stable, performance changed. You can read it in the *American Journal of Sociology,* either 1951 or 1952; I'll check on the exact date if you're interested."

"You changed the way the police behaved?"

"I didn't. Lohman and Reitzes—"

"You know what I mean. You honest to God changed the way they behaved?"

"Yes."

"But you didn't change the way they thought."

''No. That, of course, is far more difficult. The educational program was a fairly short one.''

''But you changed the way they acted.''

''Yes.''

''I'll be damned. And that's what your boys are trying to do here?''

''I haven't seen their studies. Not too many projects are action projects, but it's possible—''

''Nobody's going to change my boys but me.''

''That's nonsense.''

''The hell it is. You guys sneak around and think you can change the world. What the hell, you can't even keep your own houses in order.''

''My own problems have nothing to do with—''

''The hell they haven't. Jesus H. Christ, if you think I'm going to take that crap from a bunch of fancy thinkers with fancy words, you've got another think coming. Look, you want to know about me? I'm a simple guy with a job to do. I've got a wife who hasn't run out on me, and five kids, and I don't have a big house like this: we're crowded. But we don't have any big ideas about changing anything, we just want to live the best we can the way things are. I do my job and the kids go to school and my wife acts like a wife. It's not so easy to live a good life but we try. We live by the rules and we don't want any half-assed professors coming around trying to mix us up. We got enough problems as it is. We do our job—that's the best we can do. Or should have to do. And no matter what you professors do, that's the way things are gonna stay. Who the hell do you think you are to tell us we oughta change? We like the way we are. We're as good as anybody. Matter of fact, we're a lot better than you—we *work.* We keep the wheels turning. We don't hafta apologize to nobody.''

In the defiant, half-whined words, Sorge heard the defensiveness: somehow roles had been reversed and the policeman was pleading with the professor. He was delighted with the evident dichotomy: his work, and that of his colleagues, dealt with these men, lumped them together under the convenient category of layman; this was the first time he had heard expressed, so clearly, the gulf which separated them. His fingers itched for a pencil; he could do a study of policemen that would equal Sutherland's of a thief for depth and significance. It could be generalized; it could be grand theory that would equal anything Parsons had tried to do. This dichotomy, this defensiveness, this resistance, could be part of the biggest thing he had ever . . .

The policemen were back, leaning over Milton, whispering. Milton's back straightened; there was no defensiveness now; he was an officer of the Law, conscious of his power. "You have a cellar, professor."

Sorge nodded.

"With a dirt floor covered with tar paper."

He nodded again.

"We have to dig it up."

"You have to what?"

"Dig it up. Okay with you?"

"Of course it's not okay with me. What do you think I am?"

"That's what I'm trying to find out. With your help. I can get a warrant, you know. It's just a matter of time. And not much time, at that."

"But what for?"

"Come on, professor, you're not that dumb."

"But you can't honestly believe—"

"You're damned right I believe. I believe anything. What makes you think you're sacred in my book? Look, professor, I told you: I go by the rules. One of the rules says Investigate. None of the rules says trust professors. There isn't a rule in the book that says trust anybody. Even if there was, after you've been a cop for awhile, you'd learn to take it with a couple grains of salt. You don't think I could look at a man and say he wouldn't do such and such because he's doing a study of metropolitan government, do you? One thing I've learned, and it's the most important thing a cop can learn: don't trust nobody, underneath they're all criminals."

"How pleasant."

"Oh, it's all right," said Milton cheerfully. "It's part of the job. It's not up to me to make the world better, like you try to do. All I have to do is keep it from getting worse."

"Do you have friends?"

"Of course I have friends."

"But you'd dig up their cellar."

"Damned right I would. Now do we dig up yours or not? If we don't do it today, we do it tomorrow or the next day."

"I did not murder my wife."

"Then you won't mind our digging up the cellar."

"I have no idea where she is."

"Then where's the problem?"

"This is invasion of privacy."

"Not if you give us permission."

"I don't know what has happened to her!"

"By God," said Milton to his men. "The professor is afraid." He looked at Sorge. "What are you afraid of, professor?"

Sorge shook his head. He could see Trudi curled up beneath the hard-packed dirt of the cellar floor, eyes shut tight, fists clenched, smooth skin moldering in the damp, tiny bones crushed beneath the tromping feet of policemen. Coffinless, prayerless, cold and alone. He shook his head. "Leave me alone."

"I can't do that, professor," said Milton gently. "Do we start digging?"

Sorge's hands moved in his lap. Trudi used to sit in his lap, long ago. They would read together, or listen to music, until his hands began wandering and it would be time to go to bed. But it was many years since Trudi had sat in his lap. "All right. Get it over with."

Milton gestured to the policemen who went out quietly, but he did not move; he stayed in his chair, watching Sorge. "We found shovels in the garage."

Sorge nodded. "Is there anything else I can give you?"

"Just cooperation, professor. I'd like to talk about your wife."

"No."

"Why not? It might help us find her."

"You've already decided where she is."

"Have a heart, professor. I don't like digging up your cellar. And I haven't decided anything. I just investigate." His voice became soothing. "It might help you to talk about her."

"No."

"Like that party Saturday night. What happened at the party? If she really did walk out on you, something must have happened at the party."

"Nothing."

"You're not cooperating, professor. Why didn't she leave on Friday or Sunday? Why Saturday? What kind of party was it?"

"Just a party. Some of the faculty and their wives. Nothing special. We have them or go to them all the time. You'd find them dull."

"Oh, I don't know. Did she spend any time with somebody in one of the bedrooms?"

"Of course not." He should have sounded more indignant; he should have shouted. But, my God, I am so tired. I've been tired since Trudi left. I don't think clearly anymore. He could hear the shovels ringing against the hard dirt of the cellar floor.

"Not that you know of."

"She was the hostess. She didn't leave the room."

"Not even to go to the kitchen?"

"All right. She went to the kitchen."

"And the bathroom?"

"I suppose so."

"Was she drinking much?"

"Trudi never drank much."

"Not even on Saturday night?"

"Not even then. There was no reason to."

"Who was here?"

"I don't even remember."

"Maybe you'd better try. I'd like a list."

"You're not going to talk to them?"

"If the investigation continues."

"You mean if you don't find anything in the cellar."

"Right."

"But why talk to my friends? They had all left before . . ."

"You sure of that?"

"I said goodnight to all of them at the door."

"And nobody came back? You stayed with her while she cleaned up?"

What had he done? He'd gone to bed. That damned form he'd filled out in bed. "No."

"You went upstairs?"

"I went up to bed and waited for her."

"And she didn't come?"

"No."

"Many nights she didn't come?"

"That's none of your damn business."

"Everything is my business. Did you sleep together every night?"

"Yes."

"She never slept with anybody else?"

"No."

"That's what you said before."

"It hasn't changed."

"That you know of."

"All right. That I know of."

"Let's go back to the party. Who was here?"

"I'll try to remember."

"Do that."

"Barry Rosenthal and his wife; he's in comparative religion. Frank Spiros, political science. Roy and Susan—"

"What about Mrs. Spiros?"

"They're divorced. She's in California, or somewhere west. Roy and Susan Hazlitt; he's in the law school. Joe Dicks and his wife; he's in sociology. Mike Granch and his wife; he's in political science. Frank O'Connell and his wife; he's in economics. Eugene Eisen and his wife; they both teach Russian. Harry Fox and his wife; he's in economics. I think that's all."

"Fifteen," said Milton, writing in a notebook. "A nice group. And you did what?"

"It was just an ordinary party. We ate; we talked; Barry burned some incense; he was giving a lecture on some kind of religion, I remember. Joe Dicks played some jazzed up Bach on the piano; we were having a wild discussion on how to get through to the less motivated kids; and Eugene Eisen acted out parts of Pushkin's *Captain's Daughter* mixing up Russian and English words; it was quite amusing. Frank Spiros got drunk—he's still in love with his wife, the one in California—but he never gets obnoxious; he did a marvelous imitation of an imaginary dinner party with Eisenhower and Mao sitting next to each other. That's about all; it was nothing special; just a good party."

"Sounds like fun," said Milton, and Sorge caught the wistful note before it was erased by official tones. "What about your wife?"

"What about her? She talked and laughed with the rest of us. She served food. She had a good time."

"Nobody got her angry? Or embarrassed? Or even off in a corner for a quiet talk?"

"No."

"Was she being blackmailed?"

"Trudi? What for?"

"How do I know what for? There could be a dozen reasons."

"Well, she wasn't."

"Did she ever get violent?"

"Never."

"Pretty sure of yourself."

"Of Trudi."

"Uh-huh. Now tell me about Susan Hazlitt."

"What?"

"Susan Hazlitt. One of your guests."

"But why in particular . . ." Why in particular the one guest he did not want to talk about, the only woman, of the six who were there, he had made love to. He was not proud of Susan Hazlitt, or of himself: she thought she was climbing the academic ladder by spreading her legs for him; he allowed himself to agree with her and even hint at acquiescence when she implied she would have made him a better wife than Trudi, helped him to go farther, faster, ending up—the two of them, triumphantly—in Washington. All those professors Kennedy had brought in—why wasn't Sorge among them? His knowledge was as great; his published works as numerous, as well-received; his reputation as secure. The variable was his wife. Wasn't it something of a pity . . . And he, by silence or renewed lovemaking, agreed, abandoning Trudi in a maelstrom of lies, lust, and his own ambitions, never formulated until put into words by Susan Hazlitt. "Why that one in particular?"

Milton leaned back, listening to the shovels, the rhythmic tossing of dirt. "It's a funny thing, professor. The dumb ones like me can always tell when the smart ones give themselves away. Ever notice that? We don't know the long words, we don't have the big houses or the fancy parties, but we can always spot somebody who's hiding something. You think that's a gift, maybe, to make up for the things we don't have? What do you think?"

"I haven't the faintest idea what you're talking about."

Milton shrugged. "You named everybody who came to your party and you listed the wives. One of them had a name. Susan Hazlitt. So what about her?"

"Nothing. She and Roy have been friends of ours for ten years. Ever since they came here from Michigan."

"No extra-curricular activities between you and your good friend?"

Sorge searched for wit, for lightness, for unconcern. He found nothing. He could not talk to this man. "What difference could it possibly make?"

"Come now, professor. Ever hear of motive?"

"I did not kill my wife."

"I believe you. Now tell me about your girl friend."

He was beginning to feel anger. The relief spread through him, over his aching fatigue. "If I had a girl friend I would not tell you about her. I won't tell you a damn thing. This has gone far enough, too far. I want you to get out, and take your men with you."

"Professor," said Milton sorrowfully. "I can't go now. You gave us permission to dig."

"I withdraw the permission." He stood up. "Get out of my house."

"Too late," said Milton. "We've started to dig. Why don't you sit down? It shouldn't take too much longer."

"No longer. Get out."

"You're a big man, professor. But you're acting like a little boy. Don't you think it's interesting that you wouldn't get mad about your wife, but you get mad about your girl friend? I find things like that interesting."

"Get out!" he roared.

"Sit down," said Milton with quiet patience. "We'll go when we're finished. You don't have to talk about Susan if you don't want to."

"Mrs. Hazlitt, to you."

"Can't I call any of your women by their first names?" asked Milton plaintively.

Sorge strode to the window. The quiet street rested in the sunlight: a collection of suburban houses and trees and gardens peacefully far from the noise and filth of the city. He had worked hard to get here; he worked hard to stay here. Milton did not belong; Sorge did. "As soon as your men are through, you'll leave."

"Probably. Why don't you sit down?"

"I don't feel like sitting down."

Milton stretched out his legs, looking at his shoes as he tapped them together in a little dance. Sorge stood at the window. The silence lasted until the sound of shoveling ceased and the footsteps of the policemen were heard again on the cellar steps.

They leaned over to report in little bursts of hisses and whispers. "Nothing, huh?" said Milton loudly. "Well, you can't win 'em all. We'll try something else for awhile. Let's go."

The three of them paused at the front door. "Professor," said Milton happily. "You haven't seen the last of us. Don't go on a trip anywhere, huh?"

"I hadn't planned on it," said Sorge from his place at the window.

"Well, don't plan on it. I don't like mysteries, professor. I try not to leave them lying around. I try to solve them. If there's anything you can think of, anything you forgot to tell me, you might give me a ring." He waited. "Okay?"

"Of course. But there won't be anything."

"You never can tell. Late at night people think of the damnedest things. You'd be amazed. You really don't know much, do you, professor?" and waving his hand, he left, flanked by his men, to pop in again a second later. "I'm keeping her picture. You don't mind? You must have plenty. Such a loving husband." And finally left for good.

Sorge, at the window, watched them walking single-file down the walk. They didn't find her. They didn't find her. They didn't find her. He was trembling, exalted: she was not buried beneath the cellar floor. He grasped the window sill. How did they know? They weren't down there long enough to dig up the whole cellar. He pushed off from the window and walked to the back stairs, turning on the light as he descended. The tar paper was rolled back, the floor marked off like a checkerboard. At five-foot intervals, neat pock-like holes stared emptily at the light, a pile of dirt beside each hole. They hadn't even filled in the holes. He picked up a shovel. They had looked not directly for a body, but for signs that the dirt had been disturbed. And they had found none. They didn't find her, he thought, tossing dirt into each hole, packing it down with the back of the shovel. They didn't find her. She is not here.

When he was finished, he re-spread the tar paper, smoothing it to the four corners of the room. The shelves along one wall were filled with preserves and jams and canned fruit Trudi had put up the previous summer and he stood, resting, looking at the jars: peach jam, plum jam, grape jelly, chili sauce, canned peaches, minted pears, watermelon pickle, spiced quince, strawberry and blueberry jam, applesauce. Very domestic was Trudi. He was the envy of his friends for his jewel of a wife. His missing jewel. "She ever sleep with anybody else?" How the hell do I know anymore? How do I know what she did between cleaning house and putting up jellies now that she's shown me she wants all her time to herself, not just the odd hours when I'm away and her work is done? "She go into one of the bedrooms with anybody?" No, she hadn't, but the question, and the questioner, were as ugly as if she had.

He was suddenly furious with Trudi: if she had not left him he never would have had to meet that bastard; their paths, in all likelihood, never would have crossed. Damn Trudi. What right had she to subject him to such encounters? And such doubts? Such unknowns? How did she know, wherever she was, what she had done to him? She didn't care enough to find out. Not a letter, not a telephone call, not a postcard. Nothing.

But there was Milton. With his list. And before he could call Sorge's friends, there was a call Sorge had to make. Susan loved to drop innuendoes like sparkling nuggets in the path of anyone who followed her meandering conversations. It was not enough to make love to a man; someone, anyone, had to know about it; someone, anyone, had to be surprised or shocked or, preferably, envious. He had to do that, then, and right away. He took a jar of peaches from the shelf, to eat with his dinner, and went upstairs to call Susan Hazlitt.

11

"JOEY ROTHSTEIN has a girl," Solomon, aged eight, announced to his parents. "He put his hand up her skirt."

Mama's hand flashed out to slap his face. "You don't talk like that to your mama and papa!"

"Like what?" Solomon cried. "I just told what happened."

"What happened, what happened," sputtered mama. "In Palestine it wouldn't be what happened."

"No, mama?" asked the rabbi. "In Palestine boys don't put their hands up girls' skirts?"

"Not good Jewish boys," said mama firmly.

"Joey is Jewish," said Solomon.

"He's becoming an American," said mama with contempt.

"He is growing up," said papa.

"He's twelve," said Solomon.

"Twelve," sighed mama. "Acting like a *goyishe kopf* and he's not even bar mitzvah yet."

"What's not Jewish about a feel?" asked Solomon.

"A what?" said mama.

Papa, reluctantly but with a lurking animation, explained in rapid Yiddish. Mama screeched faintly and began to rock from side to side.

"Where did you hear that, Solomon?" asked papa.

"From Joey," said Solomon, becoming frightened. "What did I say wrong?"

Mama was crying. "This is where you bring us to live! Where my son grows up with animals!"

"What did I say?" Solomon repeated.

"You talk like a gangster!" sobbed mama.

"What did I say?" shouted Solomon.

"Come," said papa, rising from his chair. "We will take a walk."

They rode a streetcar to the lakefront and walked near the water. The day was warm, a summer Sunday; families were picnicking and playing catch, young couples strolled past, engrossed in each other, bumping into other couples, apologizing with mutual, knowing smiles. Sunbathers and swimmers were at the water's edge, calling to each other, shouting at the waves that tumbled them, tossing balls of seaweed to squealing girls. Solomon, hot and self-conscious in his black suit, walking beside his father, erect and solemn, looked at the girls in their bathing outfits, trying to see them with Joey Rothstein's eyes; then looked away, vaguely ashamed. He should not have mentioned Joey. But he was curious and excited; it wasn't often papa went for a walk with him; something mysterious hovered in the hazy air.

"You can look at them, Solomon," said the rabbi with an amused smile. "Attractive women are meant to be looked at. They are most content when being looked at. But they are fragile; easily demeaned."

"How?" asked Solomon, looking at the brightly-dressed, laughing girls. He was already as tall as some of them.

"By being treated crudely, without respect. Even by thinking of a woman disrespectfully you bruise her, you harm her, you do her damage from which she cannot always recover. A woman is delicate and dependent."

"*Mama?*" asked Solomon incredulously.

Papa chuckled. "Your mama is strong and proud and determined. But what would happen to mama if she was being spoken of in whispers, talked of as if any man could touch her, put his hand up her skirt?"

"*Mama?*" Solomon repeated. "Nobody would believe that."

"For awhile they would doubt. But most people are all too ready to believe stories and after a time your mama would not be able to walk down the street: others would be smirking and whispering, cutting her. And that damage would be irrevocable, at least in this neighborhood. So little it takes to diminish a fine woman."

"Nobody," said Solomon firmly, "would dare touch mama."

Papa hesitated, then sighed. "A Joey Rothstein can talk about a feel with anyone."

"But Joey . . . that was with a *girl.* Anyway, why can't a man feel a girl with respect?"

"There is no respect when he is twelve and experimenting. Not when he is any age and experimenting."

"Experimenting with what?"

The rabbi sighed again. "I would like to wait until you are older. But I do not think I have much time. Sit down, Solomon."

They sat on a bench beneath an elm tree and Solomon waited, wishing he was Joey Rothstein and knew what was coming, whatever it was, but still excited, still curious before his father's solemnity and the tag ends of his mother's exaggerated concern. Perhaps he preferred the half-heard whispers, half-seen leers at school and on the street, but it was too late to make the choice and it was his fault; he had been dumb enough to mention Joey Rothstein.

The rabbi clasped his hands and bowed his head; Solomon

had to lean forward to hear him. ''When a man and woman love each other and marry, their new closeness takes many forms. One of these is sexual intercourse.''

''But—''

''Don't interrupt me, Solomon. You may ask questions later. Sexual intercourse is a form of communication between man and wife in which they become one physically as they are already one spiritually.''

''But—''

''Solomon!''

''Yes, papa. I'm sorry.''

''In sexual intercourse, the penis of the husband, which has become firm, enters the vagina of the wife. The vagina is a passage in the woman's body—''

''A hole?''

''An entrance, a passage. In its movement within the wife's body, the penis discharges a fluid which carries thousands of sperms. One of these sperms, traveling to the wife's womb, joins an egg which is waiting for it. The two unite to form a new life—a child is created and grows in the womb of the wife.''

The rabbi paused. Solomon, struggling with a vague picture, looked at his hands; he was ashamed to look at his father. ''How does the penis get in?''

''The husband puts it in.''

''He pushes it in?''

''Very gently.''

''He just shoves it in?''

''He pushes it in gently.''

''But it would hurt the . . . the woman.''

''No, it does not hurt. The vagina becomes enlarged and lubricated to receive it.''

''How big is it?''

Papa held his hands apart. ''About this big.''

"That big?"

"When it is firm, yes."

"And that goes inside a woman?"

"Yes. When—"

"But you never did that to mama."

"Not *to* mama; with mama. I told you, that is how children are created."

"Mama wouldn't let you do that to her."

"With her, Solomon. And she wanted me to."

"Why?"

"For the children and—"

"And you had to do it four times to get me and Leon and Daniel and Yetta?"

The rabbi cleared his throat. "A man and his wife have intercourse so that they may have children, but also because they want to."

"Why?"

"Because it is pleasurable."

"You didn't say that before; you said—"

"I know what I said. There are nerves in the vagina and in the penis which respond in a pleasurable way."

"You mean it feels good?"

"Yes, that is what I mean."

"But how can it?"

"That is part of the mystery. Sexual intercourse is a mysterious, beautiful—"

"It doesn't sound very beautiful."

"When you are older and have a wife you love you will understand."

"But I don't understand. What does that have to do with Joey Rothstein and whispers about mama that harm her?"

"Whispers have to do with a man and woman having intercourse when they are not married."

"But that's impossible."

''No.''

''But you said when a man and woman marry they have sexual intercourse.''

''They do.'' The rabbi paused. ''But intercourse is a physical act as well as an emotional form of communication. Any man and woman can have intercourse.''

''Why should they?''

''I told you: it is pleasurable.''

''Even if they're not married?''

''Even then.''

''And that's bad?''

''It is wrong. It lacks love, beauty, respect, and awareness of the needs of the partner.''

''And that's wrong?''

''The meaning disappears. The meaning of intercourse is in the love, the permanence, two people feel for each other and in the spirituality of the act, as well as its culmination in the creation of a child. If intercourse is reduced to physical pleasure, without the presence of the spirit, it is as if two beasts met for nothing but temporary satisfaction, as if you were scratching an itch. You might as well—forgive me—have a bowel movement: it relieves an urge and gives satisfaction. That is all wanton intercourse is. There is no meaning, no scheme, no higher beauty. Just some muscles rubbing against each other.''

''But mama would never do that.''

''No, your mama would not.''

''Would Mrs. Cohen?''

''No.''

''Or Mrs. Burstein?''

''No.''

''Or Mrs. Kassel?''

''No, but these women—''

''Our neighbors wouldn't but other women would?''

"Some women."

"And they would be wrong?"

"Yes."

"Don't they know that?"

"Most of them know that."

"And they do it anyway?"

"They forget or ignore what they know in the excitement of the moment."

"Intercourse is exciting?"

"The emotions that lead to intercourse are exciting. The desire to touch another, to be touched, to find satisfaction for a physical desire. It is as if you are thirsty and know that tea is not good for you but you are so thirsty and the tea is there and tempting and you drink it anyway."

"Intercourse isn't good for you?"

"Not if you are not married. It harms you inside where beauty takes form, where pleasure is given meaning, where the world must make sense. Inside is where you must have innocence if you are to understand value. Jacob did not recognize Leah in his dark bed—he could believe it was Rachel—because he had never known Rachel. He had loved her for seven years but never learned the shape and substance of her body. His simple acceptance of the veiled Leah was pure innocence; his awakening, as that of all innocents, was harsh, but he was learning value and meaning. He was becoming a man. And he was then willing to wait another seven years for Rachel. The other, the haste to touch and use without love, without feelings, without value, but only for momentary excitement, is the sign of a child."

"And that was Joey Rothstein's experiment?"

"Yes."

"Could he have intercourse? He's only twelve."

"He could. I hope he will not."

"Has his father told him it's wrong?"

"I would hope so."

"Then why did he put his hand up the girl's skirt?"

"Because he wanted to experiment with his feelings and with hers. He wanted to feel excited and make her feel excited."

"Was his penis hard?"

"It may have been."

"Did he feel excited?"

"How can I know? He probably felt brave and a little afraid. Twelve is a fumbling age. But in a few years—"

"Then will he ever get married?"

"Why not?"

"I don't know. I just thought, maybe if he's done a lot of wrong things he wouldn't be able to get married."

"He would, if he could find a woman who would take him."

"Most of them wouldn't want him, huh?"

"If he has spent years experimenting, no good girl would want him."

"Papa?"

"Yes, Solomon."

"Do you have to do it twice in a row to get twins?"

Well, all that was long ago. Papa was dead and I was seventeen before I followed Joey Rothstein's example; eighteen before I drank the tea that was not good for me. I found it, as papa had said, pleasurable; and I recognized no harm in that inner region where pleasure is given meaning and the world must make sense. It was as if papa had never spoken. His voice was silent. All that remained, lingering where I could not touch or erase it, was the feeling that he had discovered something forever hidden from me.

12

SUSAN HAZLITT, aged forty, had been married twenty years. Her husband was a lesser luminary in the law school, publishing infrequently, but establishing a casual rapport with his students that the administration termed valuable. He spoke at regular intervals of leaving the university to join a firm in Chicago or New York—"but I'd probably die of a heart attack in five years and Susan wouldn't want to be a rich widow, she's not cut out for it."

"What is she cut out for?" asked Sorge.

"Devoted housewifery," said Hazlitt. "Spiced by an occasional fling with a horny professor."

Sorge looked grave, thoughtfully unprovoked, waiting. He had never been fond of Roy Hazlitt and thus, as is usually the case, had underestimated him. But the range of a cuckold's feelings were limited by the experience and the elemental reactions it called forth: as a man he was insulted, as a child he was furious that something he thought his was being shared, as a creature he feared for his comforts. And Roy Hazlitt, who blended into a cocktail crowd or an empty Sunday morning campus with equal ease, no doubt would blend into the role of cuckold with the same self-effacing skill. Except for his brief flare, his comment on horny professors. That came as something of a surprise.

"That's why I'm not leaving the university. The pace of a legal practice would kill me. And I can't rob Susan of the quiet home life, something to come back to, a place for her to rest and recover. It's part of my husbandly responsibilities."

Sorge listened for irony and heard none. He looked for anger and saw none. He waited for a sense of guilt and felt none. He shrugged and moved to another part of the room.

And a few days later, watching Susan undress in her bedroom, he listened for echoes of Roy Hazlitt's non-ironic, unangry pain and heard none. Hazlitt, loving his wife, was too easily understood: that was his cross.

But Susan, if it came to that, was hardly a mystery. The only question, arising occasionally from her commitment to him, her readiness, her careful blend of submission and coy independence, was whether she had serious expectations of his leaving Trudi for a new life with her. He had never indicated that he would. Nor had she asked for a declaration. But there was that gentle aura of expectation, of hope deferred each time they parted, that caused him to tread warily and advanced the day when he would be forced to call a halt.

In the meantime, she was attractive, she was pleasant, she came when he called. Even when he would give no reason over the telephone, as he refused to do on Tuesday afternoon, three A.E.—the third day after the disappearance of his wife; but, then, she would have her own interpretation of his call: why did they usually meet?

She tossed a silent kiss as she came through the door. "Where's Trudi?"

"She's not here."

"Convenient. Where is she?"

"Gone. Do you want a drink?"

"Of course, darling. Jack Daniels. Gone where?"

He filled two glasses. "I don't know."

"Well, it's not important. Did she say how long she'd be?"

"You don't understand." He handed her the drink and sat opposite her. "She's left me."

"Trudi?"

"Well of course Trudi. Who else are we talking about?"

"But Trudi? Sweet, quiet, deadly—"

"That's enough. I didn't call you here to discuss my wife."

"No, I suppose not. Why did she leave?"

"I don't know."

"I doubt that. But I suppose it's irrelevant now." She rose to sit on the arm of his chair. "Poor darling. Abandoned to the wiles of other women."

"I didn't call you to discuss that, either."

"Didn't you?" He heard the first tremors of excitement in her voice, the preliminary to planning, the cautious, careful calculation of a driver who has suddenly discovered a fork in what she thought was a straight road. But there was more: a proprietary note, a warning to those other women of a claim staked out and filed—prior knowledge. And if I ever again slide into bed with this woman I justify that claim, I raise her hopes—no, I don't give a damn about her hopes, only my own anonymity. So: get her pledge of silence and get rid of her. Send her back to her husband to rest and recover.

"I called you because I wanted to talk to you before the police do."

"The police? Why the police?"

"They think I murdered her."

She laughed, a long peal of genuine amusement with a jagged toll, here and there, of disappointment. "You're making it up." Then, a little angrily. "It's a lousy joke, Sol."

"I'm not making it up and it's not a joke. She left Saturday night after the party, she's been gone since and no one has heard from her. I assume no one has heard from her, I haven't checked. . . . She hasn't called you?''

''No. Saturday night? When all your lights were on and I called you?''

''I was looking for her. The police think I killed her. They dug up the cellar this morning.''

''But why didn't you tell me Saturday night? Why did you wait until today to call me? Does it take the police to make you call me?''

''You're whining.'' Did hope, bringing fear, always make women unpleasant? Their selfishness was always acceptable, a necessary, even amusing concomitant, until they began to hope, and had to clutch at the pretense they had worn so elegantly until then. It was a miracle, or a sign of the inherent loneliness and insecurity of men, that so many of them actually got married. ''This has nothing to do with you. We're talking about my wife, my problem, and the police are after me, not you.''

''Then why call me?''

''Because I need your help.''

''You just told me this had nothing to do with me.''

''Peripherally. There's an ass of a lieutenant who's looking for a motive for my crime.''

''And I'm the motive?''

''He might think so.''

''But of course you and I know better.''

''Susan.'' He put an arm about her waist and when she resisted pulled her to his lap. Her perfume was a transparent cape about her shoulders; Trudi never used perfume. He put his hands on her breasts and pulled her back to rest against his shoulder. She was bigger than Trudi, not as beautiful, more of a child. ''Would you want to be a motive for murder?''

''Don't be an idiot, Sol. You know I would.''

''For Trudi's murder?''

"I never liked Trudi."

"You acted as if—"

"I acted."

His fingers, independent, were following remembered patterns on her breasts; he felt the nipples harden and called himself a fool. He shifted and spread his thighs beneath her, felt her warmth settle, heard her catch her breath, and called himself a bigger fool than he had thought possible. But it was not the first time he had advanced reasons to deny reason (Trudi had been gone since Saturday and the week before that she had had her period and the week before that she had always been too tired and that week Susan had been out of town and so on) and he was too exhausted to do even much of that. It's the fatigue that makes me vulnerable, he thought as he turned Susan's head to his and kissed her.

He had always been bored with the part about getting upstairs to the bedroom. Love-making should proceed smoothly, rhythmically, without hiatus, from approach to culmination. It should set its own pace, make its own rules, dominate the participants. There should be no talking or distractions. ("You try not to swallow when we make love," Trudi had said.) There should be nothing, not thought, activity, gesture or sound extraneous to the act.

But he was too big for the couch and too old for the floor. So he had to stop in the middle, hold back his busy hands, stumble to his feet and manipulate a panting, unzipped, unbuttoned woman who refused to open her eyes up the stairs, through the bedroom door and onto his bed. The rhythm was broken; he was set back fifteen minutes after he had stripped her and himself, after she had indicated she wanted the covers pulled back so they could slip between the sheets. Either they had to pretend marriage or neither of them was so swept away as to forget the basic comforts of life and love.

But as soon as he lay full length with Susan he knew something was wrong; he had been set back by more than fifteen minutes. The delay had given him time to think—an activity he forbade himself during lovemaking—and to compare Susan and his wife. He knew he was being absurd. It was a basic rule that a man in bed with a woman other than his wife does not make comparisons: the exercise is both futile and dangerous. For if the woman came off better, imagination would see her superior in other respects and thus, potentially, a better wife. Therein lay the seeds of discontent. But if his wife came off better, what was he doing in bed with another woman? Therein lay the seeds of fidelity. And on this warm afternoon, his legs entwined with Susan Hazlitt's in a bed he had shared for twenty-nine years with his wife, that same wife took all the prizes in his reluctant comparison. But what plant could grow from the seeds of fidelity if sown now? A dirty trick had been played on him: he was about to mount a woman who couldn't begin to compare with his wife at a time when it would do no good to display nobility and climb out of the bed, unsatisfied but faithful.

So he went on, but with a last-minute change—it was preferable, somehow, to be mounted rather than to mount—slipping an arm beneath Susan to lift her astride him. And then, finally, he stopped thinking so that when she again lay next to him, on her stomach, her head on his arm, and smugly chanted "Susan and Sol. Sol and Susan. It has a nice sound," he was reluctant to talk, to make conversation, and he was angry.

"Like a comic strip." He wanted to be rid of her, to fall asleep and sleep until Trudi returned, to have Trudi lie next to him in the indentation left by Susan's body and to promise her, secretly and silently, that Susan would never lie there again. Nor anyone else? Probably. In his weakened state the promise came easily. More easily than the admission that this was what he had to look forward to with Trudi gone: Susan and more Susans each aware, as he would be, that he was no longer acting from choice but from necessity. Which was what this Susan—linking their names in mystic incantation—already knew and was prepared to use. She would offer her body, no innovation anymore but offered now and in the future on his terms, crouched over him if necessary though he knew she preferred to be flat, her strong legs pullings his hips down to hers. She would lie next to him, drawing a magic circle around another woman's bed, to convince him that there would be no empty transition period: I am here; I belong here. She would deny, by the simple means of ignoring, her husband, her home, her daughter at Lawrence, her son at Grinnell, her miniature poodle and elaborate aquarium, even, though this might take some explaining later on, her escapades with various professors. She would make definite her casual offer of some time back to convert to Judaism if that would please him. In short, her coy submissiveness would harden to determined submission in the newly-cleared field and she could do it without guilt; she had not lifted a finger to force Trudi to leave; she was, happily, the passive bystander who was willing to pick up the pieces. Eager to pick up the pieces.

None of which he wanted. If Trudi made her madness permanent, he had one responsibility: to sift the pieces himself. Let Susan pick them up, let Susan act out the Jewish housewife, let Susan push him to Washington and a different life from the one he had made his own, let Susan remove the traces of his marriage, and he would justify Trudi's leaving. The only way he could remain innocent was to suffer. And he would not give up his innocence for Susan Hazlitt. She was hardly worth it.

He moved to get out of the bed but she restrained him. "I don't want to go home yet."

"But I want you to go."

"But what about me? What I want? Don't you care at all what I want? Don't you ever think about what I want?"

"Susan—"

"Don't give me a lecture, Sol. I'm not in the mood for a lecture. I don't like you when you lecture. Anyway, I can't go home. You haven't told me why you called me. I didn't call you, you know. You called me."

Her use of repetition was sexual; she only employed it after intercourse, as if recreating the rhythm of her climax or building to another one. He found it disturbing; it was the reason he was always the first to leave the bed, to dress, to depart. But of course this time he had called her. "All right." He propped the pillow and sat against it. "I don't want you talking to the police."

"Well, I won't," she said doubtfully. "If you don't want me to. I won't do anything you don't want me to do. Only—why don't you want me to?"

"Because the lieutenant has a small world he wants to inflate. Because he's a fool who envies and scorns what he is incapable of having. Because he is dangerous."

"To us?"

"To me. He is the kind of official who tampers with statistics to make himself look important. He's the kind who uses teenagers on vacation to inflate the unemployment figures. He enters assault with intent to kill in his books as a fist fight to make his force more impressive as keepers of the peace. But he will call a disappearance a murder to fill his time and perhaps give himself material for a dreary autobiography. Murder in Evanston or How I Trapped the Wily Professor. He plays with statistics and no one—*no one*—has a right to do that. Particularly if the fraud extends to someone who uses them everyday. Then it becomes intolerable. I won't allow it."

"You won't allow what?"

"I won't allow him to use my tools to trap me."

"But I'm not a tool. He couldn't use me as a tool. How could he make me a tool?"

"Why do you argue with me? You would become a statistic: Other Woman: Subhead A—mistress; Subhead B—motive. Subhead B-1: Willing to leave her husband for suspect. Subhead B-2: Urged suspect to leave Evanston and move to Washington. Tabulate how many times this has been cause for murder. Probability: .56. Or .71. Or .82. I have no idea what the probability is. But he would find it. Even I could, if I had to. That's why he's dangerous. He's playing with another man's life blood without the proper training or respect for it."

She laughed. "Sol, you're jealous!"

He shoved his legs over the side of the bed and stood up, towering over her, forcing the lines of his face to patience. "This is not jealousy. I fear that man. Can't you see that? Just once would you look at me and not see yourself?"

"But *I* don't fear him," she said. "I don't see why I shouldn't talk to him if he calls. I can't ignore him if he calls. I can't say no if he calls."

"You will say no!" he bellowed. "You'll do just as I say!"

"I might," she said softly. "Now come back to bed; you look silly standing there naked."

There had been a time when, in bed and out, their talks had been monologues by Sorge, based on his books and lectures, spiced with approving or questioning commentary by Susan. She had accepted him as master and based her supposed adoration on being chosen by him. Whatever her failings, she must be remarkable for a remarkable man's having chosen her. It was simple, direct, and satisfying: so most wives and mistresses of famous men, themselves quite ordinary, lord it over others not so fortunate.

Now she was either assured or desperate or resigned to failure. It was his weakness that he could attribute almost any behavior to almost any cause: he had the respect for probability that Milton lacked. And thus had none of Milton's sureness.

For if he could not be certain which cause was operative, how could he organize his own response? Organization depended on tradition and none of his liaisons lasted long enough to create such a foundation; only his marriage had provided one and, having it, he seemingly had misread it.

He turned his back on the bed and began to dress. He could analyze Milton as long as Milton was away. He could meditate on Trudi as long as Trudi was absent. He could understand Susan as long as she was silent, behind him. But with the first spoken word, the first interchange of personalities, he was lost, without footings. I don't know the ground rules. I never learned them.

"I don't want so much," Susan said. "Just the chance to feel alive and interested. That's not much to want, is it? Is that too much to want?"

"I can't give it to you," he said, buttoning his shirt, his back to her.

"But if I think you can, then you can. I'm so bored, Sol! I've done all the things I was supposed to do—I've gone to college and gotten married and had children and brought them up. Now what am I supposed to do? Society gave me an education and God gave me a body and who's to say I shouldn't use them both? I could be your partner."

"And Roy? You can't be a partner to him?"

"I'm trying to tell you. He isn't interested in my education or my body."

He turned around. "Recently?"

"Five years recently." She smiled. "Grounds for divorce, darling?"

"But you don't want a divorce."

"Oh, I do, Sol, you don't know how I do. But not until I have someone to go to. I won't be alone. One of those frantic searching women who laugh too much. I won't be one of them. I have certain desires and I intend to fulfill them if possible. I have a terrible hunger for money, for the lack of concern in the posture of every rich woman. I want the world as my playground—I'm tired of once-a-year vacations in some idyllic spot—I want Argentina and Italy and Switzerland and Africa to be as accessible as Yellowstone. And I want to be important. Money is part of it, fame is the rest. You could be famous; I wouldn't mind hanging on. There are so many possibilities open to people today; it's a damn shame to accept mediocrity and ignore what could be. The masses are hungry for someone to adore; why couldn't it be me?''

''Because you adore so much yourself?''

''All right, I read the society pages. I read the women's magazines. And I've learned the rules. But I can't follow them alone. I won't get a divorce and be even more on the fringes than I am now. I couldn't stand that.''

''Not with your conditioning.''

''Would you call it that? I just respond to the world as I see it. And it's no place for a woman alone. I'll never face that.''

''It's better to play around with professors.''

''But, darling, I'd do that anyway. Who else do I know? What else can I do? Unless you'll marry me.''

''But I don't want to marry you.''

''It's not as if I'm having all that good a time. I get tired of playing the little girl. Everyone says professors want aggressive wives and maybe that's true but they want little-girl mistresses. They want their students in bed with them is what they want, without the scandal. So they look for women who act like students—all sweet and giggly and aren't-you-the-great-man. Lord, I get tired of it.''

So he was wrong again. Possibly. She could have been pretending with all the others but not with him. It would be simple to ask her, but he would not; why, after all, should he, since he was trying to avoid anything permanent with her, even the suggestion of permanence?

Anyway, he was sick of the whole affair: Susan and Milton and his own fears. His fears were groundless: there was nothing for Milton to find and nothing he could fabricate. Milton himself was a cog, and for that reason frightening, but his higher-ups would be amenable to reason if it came to that. As for Susan, she had turned out to be quite ordinary and as always when discovering this in his acquaintances he felt cheated and a little relieved: some responsibility had been lifted from him. Every time he heard an intelligent remark, however minor, every time he saw the glimmer of a mind at work, however faint, he became excited and anticipatory; he created a personality to which he could respond. He accepted the responsibility of an interchange, of giving as well as taking. And almost every time he found he had overrated, he had invested another person with exaggerated ability. Almost always he felt cheated. And a little relieved, for he could pass on to another recipient with no guilt. An exhausting process, the search for the uncommon, but I don't know any other; like Susan, what else would I do?

But Susan was perhaps the worst, for there had always been, because she decreed it, the possibility that they could move together to something permanent. He could deny it, he did deny it, but the possibility sparked their meetings and made her more than a little special. To discover, then, her mediocrity, was a severe blow. For whether Roy had dismissed her from his attentions five years ago because of her affairs, or she had begun the affairs because of his dismissal, in either case it was a short story out of a woman's magazine. As was her complaint that she was bored. Everyone who could hold a pencil in this mid-twentieth century enlightenment wrote of the plight of women, moaned of wasted minds (though no one had found cause to say that of their bodies), created college scholarships or home education programs or weaving classes to give them something to do, castigated employers for not admiring the special qualities femininity could bring to an executive position. It had become the everyday occupation of everyone but the civil rights workers and they, too, occasionally, spoke of second-class citizens as including women. It was, of course, significant that most of these articles appeared in women's magazines: men were tired of reading and hearing the complaints. Men had never been as impressed with women as women were; men had always recognized the core of conformity, the ordinary, common streak that ran through women. And they had used it, for how else could they be sure of a stable home? Used it, but not been impressed by it; one could as well be impressed by height or weight, or any other biological factor. So why be disappointed in Susan? She is like all the rest: convinced—and doing her share of the convincing—of dissatisfaction, incapable of finding her own way in the grooves of mediocrity.

I have become an anti-feminist. Trudi had no idea what she was doing when she left me.

But Trudi, though ordinary, had never voiced unhappiness. She would retreat into silence when faced with offspring she no longer liked; she would go for hours, sometimes days, without responding to his conversational gambits; she took some courses at Northwestern and the University of Chicago Downtown Center and she worked at volunteer jobs with an orphanage, selling UNICEF cards at Christmas time, running a community lecture series. But she knew these were not the marks of an uncommon person, but a woman who had too much time on her hands because of the scientific gadgets that filled her home. She accepted herself, and the life she created.

But she left.

"What shall I tell the lieutenant?" asked Susan. She was making the bed, her bare buttocks taut as she reached across to fluff the pillows.

"Tell him I have no desire to marry you and have never had the desire."

"Is that the truth?"

"Of course it is."

She dressed quickly, turning in silence to let him pull the zipper up the back of her dress. "And now that Trudi is gone?"

"She'll be back."

"But if she isn't?"

"She will be."

"But *if.*"

"Then I need time to think."

"I can wait, Sol. I've waited a long time already."

"No." He preceded her downstairs and picked up her sweater. "It may be that I don't make a good husband."

"With the right wife—"

"No."

"But you'll call me soon."

"No. I said I needed time to think."

"But what about me?"

"You'll find someone who wants to be in the president's cabinet. You're bound to. Anyone who looks as hard, and as willingly, as you do, is bound to find something."

"Is that a hypothesis?"

"A guess."

"What happened to the bold scientist?"

"He's looking for his wife."

He watched her walk to her house half a block away. Her shoulders were back and she looked carefully at Frank Spiros' house across the street. Frank was already divorced, and lonely. Sorge did not think it would be long before Susan and Frank called him to join them for a drink. And he would refuse. Because he was looking for his wife.

13

ON WEDNESDAY MORNING he did not shave. The night before he had begun to look through desk and dresser drawers; he was anxious to finish. Not that he had found so much of interest. Trudi saved bills and receipted checks, invitations and thank-you notes, unusual Christmas and New Year cards, picture postcards sent by friends abroad, the children's early attempts at poetry, arithmetic and drawing, photographs never mounted, ball point pens that no longer wrote, broken rulers, crumbling erasers, ink-spattered blotters, bent paper clips—all shoved in splendid confusion to the corners of her desk drawers. But nothing that was Trudi. No diaries, no ruled pads with jotted thoughts or ideas, not even a note to herself to remember a phone call or letter or job to be done. Nothing but the minutiae of a dreary round of everyday activities, plodding, as she had once said of an acquaintance, through the years from youth to old age. He was horrified, and saddened, and mixed a drink.

The glasses he and Susan had used the day before were still where they had left them, their reflection dulled by the dust on the table. His urgent need to clean house had dissipated; it was a chore he dreaded. He considered hiring someone, but not yet; he could not replace Trudi yet. The house smelled musty and had a drab, second-hand look—dishes on the kitchen counter, sunken pillows and wrinkled rugs in the living room, an unmade bed upstairs—but he would not bring another woman into the house. He discounted Susan: she had come and gone and would not come again.

He drained his glass and refilled it. If Trudi were irreplaceable, at least for now, she could not have been as dreary as her collection would indicate. What he had been reading was not her reflection—not all of it—he knew that, but it was becoming difficult for him to picture her. He could remember her beauty but not facial expressions; he could recall her words but not the sound of her voice. Which was nonsense; she had been gone only four days. Except that already he had put a stamp of finality on her disappearance; the four days had seemed four years because he could envision four years, and eight, and sixteen with no word from his wife. As often as he might predicate his actions on the possibility that Trudi would walk through the door at any moment, groceries or packages or library books in her arms, he could not really credit it: belief had turned to forlorn hope in only four days. In eight days he might come to accept his aloneness; in sixteen he might doubt that he had been married at all.

There was something monstrous in his ready acceptance, as if he had been preparing for it a long time, as if he had arranged the disappearance and the steady progression of his reactions like a novice playwright or a scientist. Trudi deserved better than that. If only because she was his wife, freely chosen by him, she deserved better than that.

She had been chosen at a time when there were others from whom he could choose. He was twenty-seven years old, teaching at a small, enclosed college in New Jersey; he had already published his first article and was a favorite of the department chairman and his daughter. The year was 1935—a good time for professors who cherished their small paychecks and the enormous opportunities for research inherent in the depression. Sorge roomed alone in a boarding house near the college; he had friends and, chiefly because of a kind of abandonment in those years—a job, a home, a community in the midst of despair—he had women. Not, of course, the chairman's daughter. She was young, plain, and eager to talk of the significance of life. He found her pathetic and charming; he was just discovering—and she became its representative—the insularity of a campus, and as he questioned its value once the depression was over, so he questioned hers when his apprenticeship ended.

But the questioning, like so much in those years—affairs, conversations, studies—was superficial; no one could pinpoint exact significance. The depression was so overwhelming, yet still removed, that Sorge and his fellows were afraid of emphasizing the wrong things. They moved cautiously, then wondered if they should have been bold. They loved, and thought perhaps they were playing games in the midst of disaster. They argued, and felt guilty at inflating their importance. And so nothing was allowed to become deep or lasting and it was as if the mythology of the previous decade was repeated over and over in their beautiful little world.

Until, on a visit to Chicago, he met Trudi Loeffler and saw for the first time that he might have an antidote to the campus.

She was sixteen years old, a senior in high school, a lovely girl who was not allowed to be alone with a man. Sorge courted her in her living room for eight consecutive weekends, while her father talked of Germany and her mother of their plans for Trudi to go to college. She was their only child.

Joseph Loeffler owned two toy shops, one near the University of Chicago, the other on the Gold Coast. He imported toys from Europe, multiplied his price ten times, and sold to Americans who were willing to eat less as long as their children were happy. "Why not? I should feel guilty? Don't I use the money to bring Jews over here? How else will the Americans help the Jews in Germany? Do they do anything for them now?''

''We don't really know,'' said Sorge, ''what is happening in Germany.''

''We don't know? We can't listen to the stories people tell? We can't see what the new laws mean? We are fools and blind as well?''

Sorge had learned, previously, that Joseph Loeffler's questions were to be taken as declarative sentences. He no longer tried to answer them. ''There are many who come back and say there is no problem for the Jews.''

''It's your scientists who say that? Your smart men who see what they want to see? I should believe them?''

''They see what there is to see.''

''Then why do they tell lies? If I, Joseph Loeffler, know what is happening, why don't they, the educated ones? Why do they cover it up? So no one will get too excited about Jews? Because no one cares about Jews anyway?''

''I haven't been there. I don't know what is happening.''

''You don't know? You, a big scientist and professor, can't read the signs? The Jew is being destroyed in Germany!''

And because it was not a question, but a shouted statement, it carried the force of prophecy; Sorge saw it as possible, probable, for the first time.

As a Jew, he felt a moment of terror. As a young man opening his career, in love with the silent girl opposite him, he felt impatience and some contempt for an old man who would not take the word of eyewitnesses. Jews always exaggerated events and imaginings; no doubt there was some anti-semitism in Germany, as everywhere, but until reliable observers reported it as systematic and ruthless as Loeffler's refugees would have them believe, why not leave it alone? He did not want the world to feel responsible for him as a Jew; he could make his own way if they would leave him alone. Besides, the world had never lifted its collective finger to help the Russian Jews; why should he—an American now —get involved if the German Jews cried out? He wanted only to be left alone and not to symbolize anything.

It was not the reasoning his father would have adopted, but then, his father was dead.

"What about you, Trudi?" he asked. "What do you think?"

"I think," she said, "American scientists should import all of German Jewry for a massive research project on anti-semitism as a function of government and its effect on a nation-oriented religious group."

There was a long silence, broken finally by Trudi's mother. "You'll stay to dinner, Solomon?"

Joseph Loeffler said, "Is it a college education this girl needs, or to be taught some manners?"

"I made a brisket," said Hannah Loeffler.

"We brought her up wrong, maybe? To insult our guests?"'

"And a kugel. You'll stay?"

Sorge and Trudi looked at each other while her parents' apologies flowed over them. "Mr. Loeffler," he said, his eyes on Trudi's, "I want to marry your daughter."

Trudi smiled. Her father said, "This rude child?" Her mother said, "She is going to college next year."

Joseph Loeffler said, "You want to marry her?" Hannah Loeffler said, "Maybe in four years . . ."

"You think you love her?"

"After she graduates . . ."

"You think she loves you?"

"If you still want to."

"You think she's ready to be a wife? A mother?"

"Let's talk about it at dinner."

"You think you're ready to be a husband and a father?"

"We could eat right now."

"You think you're good enough for her?"

"Come to the table, Joseph."

"I'm hungry because you don't like the discussion?"

"We can talk at the table. It's easier."

"With a full mouth it's easier?"

"All right, friendlier. Trudi is going to college. I will not change my mind about that."

"*You* will not change *your* mind?"

Trudi stood up, tiny, beautiful, suddenly very gay. "Come to dinner, Solomon. Brisket and kugel. Our engagement supper."

He stood, towering above her, very sure that she would have her way and they would be married, very sure that that satisfied him. He would tame her mockery while treasuring her wit; he would escape the campus in coming home to her, but bring her the college for her education; he would rescue her from an eternally questioning father to bring her to a world of facts, statistics, reality. And, of course, he loved her. He loved best that which he wanted to change—his own occasional unsureness with her—but that very unsureness convinced him there was much in her he did not yet know: enough to support his love after he became sure and secure.

They sat at the table, eating in silence, waiting for the second round of a bout they knew already settled; Trudi almost always got her way, larded with questions from Joseph and commentary from Hannah, but still her way. And they could not find anything seriously wrong with Sorge, though Joseph, protectively, probed, "You think you're good enough for her?"

"That is not the problem," said Hannah. "Solomon is a fine boy. But Trudi is going to college. It was decided long ago."

"Who decided?" said Joseph. "Did I decide?"

"We decided," said Hannah. "Together."

"Together?" said Joseph. "So why didn't somebody tell me we decided together? Did we decide the same way we decided on the toy shops?"

Hannah shrugged narrow shoulders, her strong features, not as lovely as her daughter's but more elegant, held in firm lines. "We've done well with them."

"So who is arguing? Didn't I agree it was a good idea? Aren't all your ideas good?"

"And I know what is best for Trudi."

"You don't have enough yet? You don't have a home and furniture and clothes and a husband who makes money even in the depression? You still want more? You want to decide for your daughter she should be a credit to you just like your Joseph? You don't have enough? *Mein kind?*"

The endearment, tacked on, without a shade of irony, was an insult; both Sorge and Trudi looked up in surprise. Hannah's mouth tightened. "I do not intend to let my daughter be dependent on a husband all her life."

"That is a bad thing?" asked Joseph.

"It is unnecessary. She has a good mind. She should have a choice as to how she uses it, not be trapped in one place."

"Trapped? Trapped? What does that mean?"

"It means," said Trudi, "being a good Jewish housewife, passing the menorah like a torch from one generation to another. Mama is not a keeper of the menorah."

Joseph pushed his plate away. "Who said you could talk about your mama that way? Apologize! Now!"

"I'm sorry, mama."

Hannah bowed her head. "I accept your apology. You are too young to understand. Religion has nothing to do with it, and your sarcasm only shows how young you are. But I can bear sarcasm and your father's insults, because I know I am right. Someday you will understand."

"Understand?" cried Joseph. "Understand what? That her mother all of a sudden after thirty years doesn't want to be a wife anymore?"

"That is not what I am saying."

"Then what are you saying? Shouldn't I know? Don't I have a part in this play you are writing? Do I sit back and say nothing while you teach Trudi a husband is—what? Unnecessary?"

"Hush, Joseph. Finish your dinner."

"I should finish my dinner so I can't ask you what you mean?"

"What do you mean, mama?" asked Trudi.

"I mean that we live in a new world, a new age. It is too late for me, but I don't complain; I accept my years as I accept every burden I must bear. But I will not have my daughter live as if nothing had changed. I will not have her bound by meaningless traditions. She will have an education and learn how to use her mind as well as her face. She will marry, of course, someday, but she will have the choice, even then, of staying with her husband or leaving him if she is disappointed."

"I'm right here, mama," said Trudi. "You don't have to talk over my head."

"My God," whispered Joseph. "This is a choice my daughter should make?" As if he had forgotten Hannah was his wife.

"Why not?" demanded Hannah. "Finally, now, women can be free of tradition—"

"No!" shouted Joseph. He stood next to the table and hunched his shoulders, head down, fists clenched. "What nonsense is this you talk? Is a Jewish woman ever free of her history? Can she throw it away as if it has no meaning? Can she deny that it has created her, that it guides her when she marries and has children? You would deny that?"

"This is not a ghetto, Joseph. I will not have my daughter act from necessity. She will have choices and be completely free to choose. She will not be bound."

"What's this?" cried Joseph. "What's this? What's this? Who is not bound? Who does not have duties and responsibilities that bind him? Who does not have traditions that bind him? You would have Trudi forget that she is Jewish and a woman and our daughter? What choices should she have? To make a home and then destroy it?"

"Mama," said Trudi. "Talk to me. I've made up my mind."

"Sixteen years old," Hannah said tightly. "And you've made up your mind. You think you want to marry Solomon and have some children and help the Sisterhood give a tea and collect money for *Bicker Cholim.* This is your romance. It won't be enough for you. It will not be enough for a child of mine."

"You mean," said Trudi softly, "you're afraid I'll outdo you at being an ordinary housewife."

"Trudi," said Joseph.

Trudi shrugged. "I'm too young to be president."

"You're too young for many things," Hannah snapped. "And too young to appreciate what you are. Your father talks of the past. What of my past?" And she talked of her past, a story Sorge had not heard before, though he should have suspected that her peculiar, tense elegance hid more than a few complaints. She came from one of the best Jewish families in Austria, a family that produced rabbis, teachers, businessmen. They were wealthy and lived in great comfort, traveling and entertaining noted Jews from all Europe. Hannah and her brother had been educated in Switzerland, her cousins in Germany. Joseph Loeffler, son of a hotelkeeper, was several cuts beneath her, but she had dreamed of hotels throughout Europe, in all the major cities. She had seen her connections and Joseph's acumen as a powerful partnership that would make of their home a salon for Europe's scholars and bankers, businessmen and politicians. And not just Jews: Hannah saw herself drawing together all the powers of Europe in amity and a new harmony: a rebirth of the Jews as central to the cultural, political and economic life of the continent. It would all happen in her living room. She would be the force that made Europe one.

But Joseph was more concerned with shadows on the horizon than with a chain of hotels. Some of his relatives had already gone to Palestine; shortly after they were married he presented Hannah with a choice of two homes, both repugnant to her: America or Palestine. She wanted to stay in Austria; Europe was the center of the world; the Jews would survive, would do better than that when her salon became the heart of European consciousness. Joseph did not scorn; he sympathized; but he was determined and finally, three years after Trudi was born, made the choice himself and moved his family to America, to Chicago where he had an uncle in the furniture business.

"We knew no one! Everything was beginning new: the language, the customs, even how to buy something. We were so little, we were nobody. And what are we now? We have not met one author, one painter, one banker, one politician. We have friends who come to talk from ignorance, what they read or what they hear. No one knows anything, we are too far from the center. This my husband did for me! So what did I have? I had my child and my hopes for her, that is what I had. How can you do this to me now?"

"You didn't plan well, mama," said Trudi coldly. "You should have had a son."

"I could have had three sons!" cried Hannah. "I lost three children before you were born!"

Trudi looked up quickly. "You never told me."

"Why should I? These problems are my own. The pain and the heartache and the loneliness—they are my own. You don't hear me complain. But what are you doing to me? Sixteen years old and you want to get married. This is not the ghetto! And you are something better than the granddaughter of a hotelkeeper. But you won't believe it. Oh, no, my daughter won't believe it or act like it. She wants to get married so by the time she's twenty she'll be a *yente* and who will know or care what she could have been? Well, I will know. And I won't let you do it. My Trudi will be something better than the daughter of a toy shop owner and the wife of a teacher in a little college somewhere in New Jersey."

"But that's all I am, mama, and all I will be or want to be."

"I will not allow it."

"Papa?"

Joseph stood by the table, head down.

"Don't ask him!" cried Hannah. "What does he care? If I didn't put the money away each week there would be nothing for you to go to college. Not your father; he saves nothing. He spends everything on the *juden.* As if they are not rich enough to come here and get settled by themselves—those smug Germans with all their money. *We* came by ourselves; no one helped us. But no, your father has to take care of them here with your money—money you should have for college. What does he care for his family? Strangers from Germany he cares about, but not his own family."

"Enough," said Joseph. "When have I not taken care of my own before taking care of others? When have you gone hungry? Or been cold? Or badly dressed? Didn't I say Trudi could go to college? Didn't I tell you there would be enough money for that? What are you denied because I bring these people from Germany? Don't we have enough to be comfortable, enough to spare something to save the lives of Jews?

Don't I share 5000 years with these people, aren't they my own as much as you and Trudi; must I squeeze everything I have into these rooms and on your backs instead of sharing it to save a little of Israel? Don't you understand how this would spread if it is successful in Germany, how country after country would destroy the Jews because it serves one purpose or another? Don't you understand that this is my duty, that there is nothing else I can do as a Jew and as a man? What do you want from me? That I break myself into little pieces and be a businessman always and a father sometimes, and a Jew whenever it is convenient? That would please you?"

"No one ever helped the Jews," said Hannah. "They have always had to do everything for themselves."

"*Nu?* What can you say to such a woman? The Jews have helped the Jews! This you cannot understand?"

"And do they thank you, these Jews?"

"Do I do it for thanks? Does a man do his duty so someone will kiss him for it? What should I do? Send them a bill?"

"When they get settled, I do not think it is too much to ask that they repay you."

"Vayes Mere." He walked to Trudi and put his hand on her shoulder. "You want to marry this man? You love him?"

"Yes, papa."

"You want to make him a good wife and help him?"

"Yes, papa."

"Then, why not? You could still go to college if you want to?"

"Not at first, papa. Maybe later."

"Later!" screamed Hannah. "Later you'll have a baby! And then another one! And when will you go to college?"

"When I'm forty," said Trudi quietly.

"Then marry him," said Joseph. "I say marry him."

"I warn you," said Hannah. "I warn you, if you marry

now I will not give you recipes and baby clothes and advice. You do this on your own.''

''Mama is of the new school,'' Trudi said to Sorge. ''Teach your children self-reliance.''

''You try your sarcasm on somebody else, young lady. You have disappointed me.''

Trudi nodded. ''Your whip. All my life I've been afraid of disappointing you. It would have been easier for all of us if you had been angry occasionally, instead of disappointed. I might have loved you more.''

Hannah screamed, a short, piercing scream, her hand clutching at her breast.

''What is it?'' cried Joseph.

''My heart,'' Hannah gasped. ''Oh, what pain. What pain.'' Her fingers clawed in the general area of her heart and her head fell back.

''Mein kind!'' cried Joseph. ''Trudi, Solomon, help me. The couch? Her bed? Where?''

''The couch, papa,'' said Trudi with steady coolness. ''I'll call Doctor Stein.''

''Wait,'' croaked Hannah. ''No doctor. Just rest. And my family near me.''

''Of course a doctor, mama,'' said Trudi. ''A heart attack is a serious matter. I'll be right back.''

''No,'' said Hannah, her voice stronger. ''I'll be better. Just stay near me. I'll lie down for awhile.''

Sorge carried her to the couch and looked down at her, smiling. Since he was sure of the outcome, he could admire her, even like her.

''Water?'' asked Joseph. ''Or wine?''

''A little wine, papa,'' said Trudi. ''Where does it hurt, mama?''

Hannah's fingers moved in vague circles. ''Here. And here. It's hard to breathe.''

Joseph held the wine glass to Hannah's lips. "Why not the doctor, *mein kind?"*

Hannah drank, and sighed. "My family is the best doctor I could have."

Joseph looked helplessly at Trudi. "Should we call him?"

"I don't think so, papa. I don't think mama is very sick. Are you, mama?"

Hannah sighed again. "I don't complain. I suppose that with time I'll be all right."

"Of course you will, mama. And it won't take so long. I'd be unhappy if you couldn't come to my wedding."

Hannah's fingers flew to her breast, resting there protectively.

"Maybe you should wait?" said Joseph. "If your mother isn't well . . . ?"

"But why, papa? If I went away to college, I wouldn't be here to take care of mama."

"Well, maybe college could wait a year—?"

"No," said Hannah. "College in Chicago. Near home."

"I don't think so," said Trudi. "I would prefer to marry Solomon."

"You would prefer!" screamed Hannah, sitting up. "You would prefer! What about your parents?"

"A miraculous recovery, mama," said Trudi.

"What's this?" cried Joseph. "You're well now?"

Hannah closed her eyes. "If I died this minute, my own daughter wouldn't care."

"Are you sick or well?" demanded Joseph.

"I'm better," said Hannah through narrow lips.

"She's all right, papa," said Trudi coldly. "She was never anything else."

"I was in pain!" cried Hannah.

"Papa," said Trudi. "Will you come to my wedding?"

"She pretended?" said Joseph. "She frightened us like that and it was pretending?"

"Papa," said Trudi. "Will you help me plan my wedding?"

Joseph waited, but the silence lengthened and Hannah said nothing. "That is a mother's task," he said finally.

"Don't worry, papa," said Trudi. "I'll send her an invitation."

"Trudi," said Joseph. "Haven't you got what you wanted?"

"Yes, papa," she said. "Have you?"

"Enough," he said, but gently, sadly, acknowledging the peculiar status of a girl who was about to be a married woman, and thus able to question his happiness, but who was also his daughter, and thus forbidden to do so. His face was lined and shrunken, pulled into itself, rejecting those around him. And the withdrawal lasted. Even at the wedding, in the rabbi's office, he was aloof, as if the struggle to reach this point had destroyed too much to make possible his participation. He was a quiet little man who kissed his daughter formally, as carefully shook hands with Sorge, and stared silently at his wife until she, too, kissed Trudi and reached up to pat Sorge's cheek. The ceremony was simple: there were no tears, no laughter, no further recriminations. Sorge's mother and stepfather, his sister and brothers all stood by, aware, somehow, of Hannah's fragility and Joseph's remoteness; they moved carefully and spoke softly so as not to break anything. Only Yetta pitched her voice with its normal shrillness: "We'll be friends, won't we?" and Trudi smiled gratefully. "We'll have secrets, like sisters." And Sorge's mother enveloped the bride, whispering, "He's a good boy," making sure Trudi knew what before she might only have guessed. The rest was silence and courtesy.

And six months later, when Max Rosenthal died and

Sorge's mother moved in with them—in Evanston where Sorge had become an assistant professor—Joseph Loeffler drifted each week and then each day to their house, ostensibly to join forces with Sarah Sorge who was working with the Council of Jewish Women to settle German Jewish refugees, but also to sit with his daughter and justify his life through her contentment. Yetta, newly married to her insurance agent, came often to keep her promise of friendship. Sorge's brothers, away at college, visited on holidays, to flirt with Trudi and question Sorge on the vagaries of professors. And finally, a year before she died of cancer, Hannah came, to admire the three babies and proffer advice on their college education. It was a time of family, when they drew from each other as the news from Germany gave their warmth and solidity a magic, temporal charm they were to remember later with nostalgia and some disbelief.

And now what do I believe? That after twenty-nine years she decided her mother was right after all? Unlikely that she would ever admit her mother was right. That her father was wrong? Still unlikely; she adored him; she came close to a breakdown when he died. It was, perhaps, these papers, this minutiae that fill her desk drawers. But she made her life; I tried to help her and she refused. The causes she could have supported, the studies she could have made, the organizations that cried out for someone with her energy and ability—but she wouldn't take on any of them. In the end I probably sounded like Hannah . . . my God, did she listen to me and hear Hannah?

The telephone rang and he answered it to spend ten minutes telling David nothing had changed. Each day David called, as did Nathan and Harriet and Yetta, and each day he had the same message. Today he spent weary minutes explaining Milton until finally, worn out with David's legal advice, he hung up and looked at the telephone with distaste.

He was not ready to talk to anyone about Trudi—that was the real reason he had not called her friends or tried to track her down in any systematic fashion. He gagged at the idea of mouthing, over and over, the question—is she there?—and, given a negative answer, fielding the other questions, explanations, conjectures. He could not face it. Not even with the faint hope of finding his wife.

He took the receiver off the hook, covering the telephone with a pillow to shut off protesting buzzes or tones an outraged system might send his way. And then, having finished with the desk, went upstairs to search Trudi's dressers.

Her clothes were very good: expensive, quiet, elegant. She followed fashion only insofar as it suited her; because of the difficulty of finding good clothes small enough for her figure she had had many dresses made to her design. She could have made a career there; she had real style and a flair for fabric and line. How often did I tell her that? Dozens of times, at least. I tried everything except faking a heart attack.

He found sketches of skirts, blouses, dresses, robes, coats—no slacks: she thought them unflattering and self-defeating for any woman who laid claim to femininity; except for gardening she never wore them. He found a drawer of fabric swatches; at one time she had made many of her own clothes, but in the last few years had stopped sewing; he was not sure why. In fact, thinking of it, she had not been very busy the last few years: she had read more, or sat in reverie, or taken solitary walks, but the bustling activity of one household project following another in swift succession had slackened and almost ceased. He was not sure just when it had happened, or why. I suppose it could indicate unhappiness, but she never said anything, we rarely quarreled and then only over little things quickly forgotten; but then, thinking of *that,* they had not talked much at all the last few years: I always had a research project or papers to grade or lectures to prepare; she always had a book to read. And last year when I went to Argentina she didn't come along. And I let it pass: what did she do while I was gone?

In another drawer he found blouses, each in its plastic bag, as were the sweaters in the drawer beneath. The top drawer held underthings: white, blue, black, some with lace, some plain, all piled neatly, brassieres cupped into each other, girdles overlapping in a long row, each pair of nylons folded and tucked in an accordion-pleated plastic bag. A *balabosta,* he thought, and in the quiet, dead house smiled with brief tenderness.

A drawer in her jewelry box slid open when the lid was raised. Inside, in the drawer and the main compartment was every bracelet, necklace, pin, set of earrings she had owned from the time he met her. Here were the Austrian bracelet her grandmother had given her, the first watch Sorge had bought her, the cameo her father had imported for her wedding. Here were the simple chains and oval pins she had once liked and the heavier silver and gold pieces she had come to prefer of late. Sorge found the white velvet ribbon she wore around her neck at their first formal University dance; a Spanish pendant he had bought in a New York antique shop twenty years ago; two jeweled bracelets her mother had left her that she had never worn; a red and gold enamel flower David and Nathan had bought for her thirtieth birthday. It was a little like learning the history of England from a compilation of crown jewels; what atavistic impulse had caused her to save every piece of jewelry at the same time she was giving away old clothes, shoes, furniture—even money in generous checks to every cause collector who rang the bell or sent an importunate form letter?

In a recent study of juvenile delinquency, a colleague of Sorge's had departed from cool objectivism to declare with the enthusiasm of a discoverer: ''We are given clues every day, every minute; what we could accomplish could we but read and act upon those clues!'' But what, wondered Sorge as he lifted and let fall his wife's jewels, what happens when we cannot read the clues but act anyway? What happens to the clues themselves? Do they shrivel up and clutter what would be comprehension if the path were clear? Orphans of dead relationships. The role of a scientist is to isolate clues and to employ them and the questions or solutions to which they point in the agonizing task of ordering the universe. (''Divide and conquer,'' Trudi had once said.) But—have we ever asked this?—how many kinds of clues are there? And what happens to us and them if we misread or ignore them entirely in our serene arrogance? What happens to the ordered universe in the piddling example of one man's marriage? The vanity of a man who would save the world with game theory while his wife saved only jewelry. And if it was true that scientific method did not a marriage make, how far from the single to the general would one have to go to find validity in his chosen field?

He closed the jewelry box. He would give the stuff to Harriet; after a time she would appreciate it. As if that made an ending.

In the closet they no longer shared, since Sorge had begun using David and Nathan's, Trudi's dresses, skirts, suits hung in a martial row, winter things in garment bags, transition clothes off to one side. Winter shoes were boxed, summer ones side by side beneath the clothes; on the shelf were hats and purses lined up neatly, already looking unused and unattended. Sorge unzipped the garment bags, looked helplessly at the woolens and velvets and silks inside, then carefully zipped them closed. The odor of moth crystals stung his nose; that, and the sense of despair that swept him as he faced the sex in his wife's well-made, well-chosen garments, made him gag; he breathed deeply and swallowed hard again and again, rubbing his unshaven cheeks with both hands, forcing an evaluation: since the children were born she has never been this important to me. And her clothes: I paid for them, approved of them, and thought of them, if at all, as a rather extraordinary extension of an ordinary personality. They can have no meaning for me now. None.

But he went on with the closet, reaching up to search the shelved boxes—nested shoes wrapped in tissue paper, toes facing heels, tightly locked in a travesty of love. And then a lighter box, filled not with shoes but with folded paper—letters, envelopes, the jottings he had failed to find in the desk downstairs.

He became excited, anticipatory—the end and the beginning of the hunt—and sat on the bed to tumble out the papers and meet his wife.

At first he met only himself: early letters from New Jersey to Trudi Loeffler in Chicago. "We don't have test tubes and scales and vacuum tubes, but we have *people* and we can dispel chaos among them as surely as the chemists and physicists have done in the world of matter." Well, I was young and eager; it must be the prerogative of youth to sound like oligarchs. But he was uneasy, faintly guilty, the sentence had a contemporary ring and he wished he had an antidote—Trudi's answer, any of her gently taunting letters, but he had long since thrown them away.

He opened a brown leather diary with one entry, dated August 3, 1936: "Yetta gave me this for my birthday. I do not intend to keep it up. How dull for posterity to read, a hundred years from now, that I washed David's diapers, cleaned the living room, and made myself a new fall dress. Diaries should be microcosms of a period written with the wisdom of prophecy and hindsight. I have no profound thoughts to record." He read it over and over, trying to recapture the seventeen-year-old girl who had given up before she had begun. Why did I marry her?

A scribbled note on the reverse side of a grocery list: "Bertolt Brecht: 'I sit in the car watching the driver change the wheel. I do not like the place I am coming from; I do not much like the place I am going to. Then why do I watch impatiently as the driver changes the wheel?' Is that Solomon's cry or mine? Or, saddest of all, is it the two of us wailing in unison?" He waved the paper back and forth, as if to toss it away. The handwriting was more mature than that in the diary; if he tried, he could almost believe Trudi had not written it. The confusion, the misery, the hopelessness of a traveler who would as soon be stranded was more than he could bear: he considered throwing the rest of the papers away unread. But she was his wife, his responsibility, and he went on.

He picked up an envelope, blank except for two lines: "Who says we have to love our children? What if they are unlovable?"

The program of a concert at Orchestra Hall with a marginal comment: "I couldn't stand so much magnificence all at one time. I couldn't wait for it to end; I wanted to leave in the middle. Sol was furious and told me to grow up."

A copy of the invitation to Harriet's wedding: "I was the typical bride's mother. I wept. Was I crying for Harriet's future or my past or because my new girdle was too tight?"

A raggedly torn sheet from a scratch pad: "e.e. cummings:

> 'As long as you and I have lips for singing
> and to kiss with—
> Who cares if some one-eyed son of a bitch invents
> an instrument to measure spring with?' "

A list of book titles with three crossed off, and a line at the bottom: "I cannot read books about the rape of children."

A book jacket from a group biography of suffragettes with lines scrawled across the inner side: "Wouldn't Sol have loved to be married to Lucy Stone! The combination is irresistible. The phenomenology of the woman's vote. Affect and feminine participation in the political process. Marital feedback at election time. Together they could have gotten the vote for six-year-olds."

And then, after melancholy and wit, a carefully written page, fresh and unfaded. "He is rather short, and spare, as if all excess had been sloughed off or, rather, scraped away, for he gives the impression of being honed down to sharpness and angles. His nose is thin, narrow in a thin, narrow face that just escapes gauntness. His eyes are light blue, his hair sandy and straight, rather unattractive. His lips are thin and hard, when he kisses me mine are the ones that yield.

"He mocks his intelligence, and mine, which makes me almost his equal. He teases his own desire, to convince himself, and perhaps me, of mine. He is patient with me, but not as if I were a child; he has made it clear he sees me as a woman and wants me as a woman. There may be method to his conversation, his lovemaking, his reactions to me, but if so I cannot see it. He has the supreme virtue of spontaneity, or he is a superb actor. It does not really matter which. Well, perhaps it does, but everything is so precarious in its anarchy I don't want to probe too deeply. I will have to accept the surface, at least for now.

"It would be better, I think, if I had no idea of loving him. I could accept myself more easily if my actions did not imply an immature ease in loving, or a childish need to rationalize by manufacturing love. I shall have to ask him about that, unless that would be opening the gates to"

He turned over the page. Nothing. She had not finished it.

The smell of moth crystals was stronger, overpowering; he stumbled to the bathroom and stood over the open toilet, retching. He hunched there, propped on both hands gripping the bowl, breathing in short, harsh gasps. How had he once described the elemental reactions of a cuckold? As a man—insulted; as a child—furious that something he thought his was being shared; as a creature—fearing for his comforts. A fool's definition. He should have added: as a husband—stricken with the loss of freedom.

Worse: he knew the man from Trudi's explicit description: Felix Gold, writer, sometime radio commentator, foreign correspondent in World War II—and some action seemed called for. He could not even stay huddled in his bathroom; he was forced into a confrontation. She had no right to do that to him. Felix Gold. A nice guy. Twice divorced, skilled in ferreting out attractive widows and divorcées from the female hives of Chicago; he and Sorge had often gone for swims in the lake or the University pool, coming back home for a drink, for dinner, for long talks on the patio with Trudi sitting silently in the background. They had even planned to do a book together, a study of peasant elites in emerging nations. Instead they shared a woman. He bent over the toilet again, but his stomach was empty; he had forgotten to eat breakfast.

He straightened slowly. His back hurt and the terrible fatigue of the past days had returned. He rinsed his mouth at the washbowl, returned to the bedroom to pocket his wife's memorabilia, and went to the telephone to dial Gold's number. When there was no answer, he hung up, mixed a drink, and hunched back to the chair by the telephone, waiting five minutes before dialing again. And again and again, through the long, empty day, he dialed and waited before hanging up to measure five minutes and then try again.

14

"SOLLY WOLLY GOLLY I'm glad to see you! Rumors all over town and I haven't been able to get you on the phone. You all right?"

"I'm all right, Leonard. Sit down."

"I am down. Got a little drinky for a tired man?"

"Bourbon."

"Done. On an ice cube. Are the rumors true?"

"I haven't heard them."

"Your wife is in the Sierra Maestre plotting against Castro. She's in Tibet organizing guerrillas against Mao. She's in France sitting on De Gaulle's lap persuading him to allow the Germans to have nuclear weapons, God forbid. She's in Warsaw mimeographing copies of the Rapacki plan. Or she's buried under the forsythia bush in the back yard."

"Am I supposed to be amused?"

"I didn't make up the last one, Solly. I heard it."

"Milton's been busy."

"Well, he's calling people. He called me."

"And mentioned the forsythia bush."

"Nothing so crude. For a barbarian he's rather skillful. Even flattering. He asked me if I'd ever made Trudi."

"And you told him what?"

"For Christ's sake, Solly, nobody ever made Trudi. That's right, isn't it?"

"She's gone."

"Well, that doesn't mean . . . Does it? Sweet little Trudi was screwing around with some lucky bastard after she said no to me and a dozen others?"

"You asked her?"

"Well, carefully. Subtly. In a mature way. But Trudi was a bright girl, she understood these things. She's really gone?"

"That's what I said."

"No tearful goodbyes? No weepy farewell note? Just gone?"

"Why not?"

"Why not! Well, it's hardly common behavior, is it?"

"And Trudi was common?"

"What the hell's got into you, Solly? I've always known you were a careful bastard but I never thought you were a cold fish."

"I'm grief-stricken."

"No, you're not. And that's the hell of it. She was a nice girl. I liked her."

"So did I."

"Well, you're not acting like it."

"What day is this?"

"Thursday. You need a shave."

"I haven't had time."

"Did you meet your class yesterday?"

"My God, I forgot all about it."

"Well, didn't anyone call? I suppose they tried, though; your line was busy all day."

"I was trying to get someone."

"When did you eat last?"

"I don't remember."

"Come on. I'll scramble some eggs, or something. Maybe

you are grief-stricken. Peculiar way of showing it, though, the way you talk. What did you do to make her leave?''

''You're sure she's not under the forsythia bush.''

''You didn't kill her, Solly. I told Milton that. I know him like a brother, I said. He's not a murderer, I said. I told him we'd known each other for years, ever since I sold you your first insurance policy, and we've been friends, I said, and I understand Solly like he was my own self. A gentle man trying not to be confused about the world. That's a good line, isn't it? Wait a minute while I write it down.''

''You keep a notebook?''

''Have to. It's hellish, being a writer. These flashes come at the oddest times; have to write them down or I'd forget them. When I write my books it's like putting a puzzle together; all these phrases and sentences I've jotted down. Sometimes I wake up at night and write down a dream. The best books have dreams in them; it makes them valid psychologically. Very important, these days. You got any bread?''

''In the cupboard on your right.''

''Thanks. Trudi understood what I was doing, you know. That's why I loved her. Love in the sense of gratitude.''

''And bed.''

''Well, I tried once. But she said no. Nicely. So we could remain friends. I appreciated that because I really did like her. Is this all the butter you have?''

''I don't know. I suppose so.''

''It'll have to do. She'd listen to me talk about my books; once she even read a manuscript I gave her.''

''Did she like it?''

''She offered intelligent criticism. A real Writer—capital W, as opposed to technician, small t—doesn't want readers to 'like' his books—like in quotes, referring to the kind of thing you take out of the library and remember only in terms of the overdue fine you pay—he wants criticism, discussion, attack, defense. You couldn't understand that, Solly; you write your books for students, a captive audience that feeds the stuff back to you at exam time."

"That's not exactly . . ."

"Maybe not. Here, eat your toast and eggs. Any instant coffee? Never mind, I found it. Maybe not, but close. You don't face the problems of the novelist: the harnessing of the imagination, the creation of people who can worm their way into the reader's life, weaving psychology and philosophy into the plot so they take the reader unawares, teach him in the midst of his pleasure, so to speak. The excruciating responsibility of a novelist! A good, serious, dedicated novelist, that is, who isn't concerned with popularity and having a best seller. The awful responsibility! I often wonder if I'm big enough to accept it. Coffee?"

"Fine. How many novels have you written?"

"Seven. And learning all the time. This is my apprenticeship. One of these days I'll have a book published, but I'm in no hurry. No real hurry."

"The world can wait?"

"Well, it's got to, according to the publishers who read my manuscripts. But I understand; after all, I live with the problem. It's not easy to sell insurance all day and write at night. Once I publish and make some money I'll write full time."

"But you're not concerned with having a best seller."

"I don't write for the best seller market, no, but I wouldn't object to a modest reception. One that would provide me enough to live on."

"And Deborah? She agrees with this plan?"

"She's not as simpatico as Trudi was. A wife worries about the groceries. Trudi worried about my message to the world. She actually egged me on to talk to her, do you know that?

Hours and hours I'd talk and she'd sit there, listening, with that little smile on her face, and nodding her head with absolute comprehension. She was a marvel, that woman. I often thought of her as my inspiration. I'm dedicating my new book to her."

"Not your wife."

"Trudi was the one who listened. A novelist faces a terrible dilemma when it comes to talking about his work. He knows he should work in the agonizing isolation of the true artist but he needs a sounding board when he's trying something new. So he turns to the outside world. And what does he find? People are dull, uncomprehending, too interested in themselves. They want the final, polished product of a culture, not the raw ingredients groping for amalgamation. Trudi, darling Trudi, listened; she cared about what I was trying to do."

"And what were you trying to do?"

"Use an entirely new method, a scientific method in the writing of a novel. This should interest you, Solly. It's right up your alley. I am making an outline of key subjects that should be written about today, with subheads of how they should be handled."

"Today?"

"Mid twentieth century America, the time of psychic awareness, sexual flexibility—my own phrase—human rights, the quest for meaning in abundance and leisure. A new world, a new era! And I can write about it, Solly; I've got the power. I can feel it, surging through me, every time I read a book: the knowledge that I could do it better, that I can write! It's all I can do to stay away from the typewriter when I'm reading someone else's book, I'm so full of things to say, phrases, sentences, whole paragraphs, dialogue, narrative—the whole, beautiful thing."

"But you stay away."

"Well, there's a time to write and a time to read, as they say in Ecclesiastes. Or ought to. But I'll do it. The time will come."

"And your subjects and subheads? Where do they come from?"

"Solly, don't tell anyone about this. Only Trudi knew. It could revolutionize writing. I read the critics. Book reviews in newspapers and magazines, books of criticism, studies of modern authors. Critics are always saying what an author should have done to make his book a success. When I write my new book those are the things I will do. It won't be hit or miss; I'll know exactly what to look for, how to handle my subjects, how to round them off, how to make them significant. What are you smiling about?"

"Was I smiling? I was wondering why you don't leave the studies alone and read the authors instead. And the great works of the past, the landmarks of—"

"No, no, no; you of all people should know that science has made the past obsolete. I grant you it's amusing, occasionally instructive to the student of manners, even entertaining. But we can't build on a past that has no resemblance to the present; there's no point in it, no future, so to speak. Everything today is new, unsullied by precedent, fresh material for innocent eyes, newborn eyes in a newborn world. And born anew every day! Read the papers: weapons become obsolete before they get off the drawing board. My God, it's all we can do to keep up with today; why should we clutter up our lives with yesterday? This is what the novelist has to understand: his own time and his position as explicator of it. A kind of physician to the masses, if you like. I should write that down, too. It's damn good; I'll find a place to use it. Where was I?"

"Doctoring the world."

"No, you've misunderstood me. A physician diagnoses,

prescribes, soothes or warns. He communicates to his patients, clarifying symptoms they cannot understand without him. A novelist looks at the symptoms of love, hate, war, what have you, and out of the chaos creates an organized, cohesive work the layman can understand and use.''

''But if it is obsolete tomorrow?''

''Well, novels don't become obsolete as fast as weapons. But you're right; it's a good point. Only the historian, the student of manners, will be interested in our novels fifty years from now. It's part of the terrible burden of the artist, to know that he must write for his own time with no hope of immortality, that others will replace him, are waiting to replace him as soon as he falters. It's a little like selling insurance: as long as you satisfy the demands of your customers you're on top, but make a mistake, or slacken off in your attention to their changing needs, and you're sunk. They'll go somewhere else and in a month or two they won't even remember your name. You through eating? Let's have another drink. You?''

''No. But help yourself.''

''Thanks. There is one way I use other authors. Dead and alive. Trudi told me—and she was right, absolutely right—that a novel sounds better, more profound, more important if it's filled with quotations. It gives the reader confidence; he thinks the author is a learned man. Wisdom isn't enough; you have to show off your learning as well. So my characters are always quoting other people. And I, as the omnipotent narrator, throw in quotes here and there, to spice things up, so to speak. It's all part of putting the puzzle together: a phrase I wrote one night, a quote from Shakespeare or some other satisfactory source, a line from—''

''But if you haven't read Shakespeare?''

''My dear Solly, book reviews are filled with quotable lines. Critics are just as anxious to show off their learning as we poor novelists. However, my main sources are dictionaries of quotations; book stores are loaded with them, lovely little volumes with all the wit and cleverness of the ages bound between two hard covers. Not that I am dependent on that wit and cleverness—my age has its own and I can make up the rest—but the reader—oh, hallowed, pampered judge!—clasps the quotes eagerly to his bosom and believes he is in the land of giants, particularly—and this is most significant—particularly if the authors of the quotes are not identified. Then, when the reader sees only a line in single quotes, and knows he is face to face with one of the Greats—capital G—he feels that the author has made him an equal: we both know, don't we, dear reader, where *that* line came from, so I won't insult you by identifying it. The author has made the reader a partner, and together they rush to the end of the book, loving each other every step of the way. Beautiful! Trudi saw all that."

"And egged you on."

"Well, I wouldn't say there was a question of egging. She listened, she made suggestions, she comforted and sympathized. She had great insight into the soul of an artist, the pains of gestation and birth, the terrifying but necessary alienation from the masses, the *hell* of creation. She was a shining light in the dark of my most despairing moments, those times when I almost lost faith in my method and my powers. Thank God that doesn't happen often, but when it does Trudi is there, smiling, listening, suggesting, upholding my faith. Good Lord, how I'll miss her! But whatever made her leave, she'll miss me just as much; every woman wants to be the inspiration for a genius—it's built into their system, so to speak—and Trudi, for all she refused me as a lover, made it quite clear she recognized my genius. In fact, that's probably why she wouldn't go to bed with me, much as she wanted to; it would have destroyed our intellectual relationship. You don't mind my talking like this, do you,

Solly? We both loved her—Solly? Good God, Solly, are you *crying?*''

''A few tears, perhaps.''

''Christ, I *am* sorry. It's too soon for me to talk about her. I apologize, Solly. Please forgive me.''

''For what? For being a fool? For being Trudi's means of revenge on me? You poor ass, Leonard, don't you see what that dear sweet child was doing?''

''Doing? I've been telling you what she was doing.''

''You've been playing a recording of one man's fantasy. Trudi was my wife! Doesn't that suggest anything to you even in your befuddlement? There she sat, hour after hour, encouraging you in your nonsense because in it she could see resemblances to mine.''

''Nonsense? Hell, Solly, I thought you'd understand me at least as well as Trudi did.''

''Oh, I understand you, Leonard, and if I wanted to use you I could smile sweetly and give aid and comfort to you in your foolishness. My God, how she must have hated me! And how she must have gloated, knowing that sooner or later we would have this talk and I would see what she had done. But she didn't even care enough to hang around and wait for the results. How long has this intellectual coupling been going on?''

''Now just a minute—''

''How long?''

''Two or three years, but—''

''Two or three years. She was that angry, that contemptuous for two or three years and God knows how long before that. She mocked thirty years of my life and then walked out on me before I could defend either my work or my marriage. That's your shining light, Leonard: a bitch who used you to satisfy her contempt for her husband. Who may have deserved it, but that doesn't change—''

"Wait a minute. God damn it, wait a minute. It was *me* Trudi cared about, not you. She wasn't even thinking of you when she helped me. You're damn right she was my shining light and just because you're jealous . . . Hell, I told you I didn't make love to her, what more do you care about?"

"—doesn't change the fact that by attacking me directly, instead of retreating into silence, and using you as her instrument, she might have given us a chance to survive. *You'll* miss her! You have no idea how *I* will miss her, how every minute of every day I'll sit in this house wanting her, feeling her lovely neck between my hands."

"Feeling what?"

"Oh, you're thinking of the forsythia bush again. What would you tell Milton now, Leonard? That the gentle Solomon Sorge never harbored thoughts of doing damage to another human? Or that he can become enraged, like any other cuckold?"

"Solly . . . Solly, I told you . . . I swear to God . . ."

"It was *you* she was thinking of, was it? The hell she was. An unfaithful wife spends more time thinking of her husband than of her lover. That's solace of a kind, but hardly sufficient to restore harmony. You don't see that? You cling to Trudi as disciple and mentor wrapped in one worshipful package? Look at yourself, for God's sake. Hour after hour for two or three years—how unspecific you are, Leonard, about something as precious as Trudi, the poor man's flashlight—hour after hour my wife gave of herself unfounded arrogance and the perpetuation and glorification of stupidity, to a pathologic exaggeration of mankind's—and thus her husband's—foibles—and all this without an ulterior motive? Even you cannot accept that."

"You're not well, Solly; I should have known; I should have kept quiet. It takes a big man, a well-adjusted man, a mature man, to learn of his wife's interest, if only intellectual, in another man. This is all my fault and if you'll accept my sincere apology—"

"Damn it, don't apologize to me! I want nothing from you. We have too much in common already: we were both made fools of by the same woman. I won't be bound now by sniveling apologies and magnanimous fake acceptance. I will have nothing to do with you; take your fantasies and get out of here. And don't ever come back; you make me sick."

"You are sick, Solly. But I want you to know I understand—"

"You understand nothing."

"You've had a shock—"

"Not even that Trudi probably despised you."

"Now hold on, Solly. I'll excuse only so much in view of your bereavement. Trudi loved me. I know that hurts you, but it's true. That's the real reason she wouldn't let me make love to her; she was afraid she would get too involved emotionally and destroy what little she had left of her marriage. I was too strong for her. She was even afraid to talk to me about you."

"She never talked about me?"

"Never. She was obviously afraid she would break down."

"She was obviously a victim of her own decency, in spite of what she was doing to both of us. What a dilemma she made for herself! I could almost feel sorry for her."

"Are you yawning?"

"I'm tired, Leonard. I'm always tired these days. Why don't you go home?"

"I don't know. We ought to settle this thing."

"There's nothing to settle. Trudi despised us both, but that will bother me more than you because you will not believe it. Go home and keep your fantasies polished and shining; just don't come here again. You bore me."

"Why don't you take a nap, Solly? I'll stay here to make sure you're all right and when you wake up you'll feel better, we can talk like civilized people."

"Do I have to throw you out, Leonard? I don't want you here."

"You don't mean that. We've been friends for . . ."

"You needn't worry about the insurance. I won't cancel it."

"I wasn't—"

"Oh, yes, you were. You were afraid that in a month or two I wouldn't even remember your name. How can I ever forget you, Leonard? Whenever I pick up a book, I'll think of you, struggling not to go to your typewriter, or picking over quotations in one of your invaluable dictionaries. Someday I may even see your name on the cover of a book, though I most sincerely doubt it. Now get the hell out of here; I'm tired of you."

"You have no right . . . A minute ago you said you were just tired."

"That too."

"You're confused, Solly. I feel sorry for you."

"Get out!"

"If you really want me to go—"

"Out!"

"A friendship of fifteen years you're willing to end without another word?"

"We've said all the words we need to say. Get out."

"I'm going, Solly. If you want me—"

"I won't want you."

"—you have my phone number. And I'll come if you call. I know what friendship means to a man in trouble."

"Goodbye, Leonard."

"I'll always be available to you, whenever you need me. Solly, don't turn your back on me. Solly, I'll miss you. I have so few intelligent friends. So few people I can really talk to. No one understands the travail of an artist, the hunger for good talk and long words, the . . . All right, I'm going. But you'll call me, I know you will. You'll wake up one morning and think of me and understand that you need a good friend, someone who sympathizes with you and can recapture the old days when Trudi was here. Come to think of it, that's probably why she didn't want to go to bed with me; she didn't want to destroy the fine relationship you and I had built up. Solly? Are you listening to me?"

"No."

"All right. I'm leaving. Goodbye, Solly. Take care of yourself. Solly? You'll take care of yourself?"

"I've always taken care of myself. Goodbye, Leonard."

"Call me, Solly. I'll be waiting."

15

THE CHAIRMAN of Sorge's department at the University was small and hunched: a man forever seeking grants from foundations and the government and, when successful, presenting them to his professors as a lover gives jewelry to his mistress: look how much I care for you, for your fame and your beauty, for your comfort; you may repay me by putting out. And they did. Research was a glorious occupation; papers, articles, books, appeared with the efficiency of mass production while graduate students taught. There was a camaraderie among the professors: avoid teaching at all, if possible; if not, teach graduate students, under no conditions get caught with an undergraduate class. They smiled and chatted together, trading epigrams, upholstering their world of research with a stuffing called the layman and a fabric called theory. It was, as the chairman liked to say, a jolly department.

They did not like dissension among themselves, nor too much knowledge of the personal lives of their members. It was bad enough to know about their peers in other departments: Roy Hazlitt who watched his wife take half the campus as lovers; the geography professor who was drinking himself to an early retirement; the drama assistant who would be leaving at the end of the year because of his private coaching of would-be actors (not actresses: he did not find them interesting). The social scientists did not want to be privy to these secrets: they were occupied with altering humanity and it was painful to see their material in the raw, to realize how far they had to go. Most assuredly, then, they did not want to face Solomon Sorge in his misery or hear the details of enforced bachelorhood.

"They all send regards," said the chairman. "But this is a busy time of year . . . Exams coming up . . ."

Sorge nodded. It was not important. "You're wondering why I missed my class yesterday."

"Not wondering, my dear Solomon. We've all been on the telephone with that misnamed policeman. We understand what you're going through. As a matter of fact, I had a feeling you might not come—be able to come and I was there to meet your class."

Sorge nodded again. His head felt loose, wobbling on his neck in tired, passive acquiescence to any suggestion. He was confused by the demands on his attention: he should be calling Felix Gold but there had been no time today and the longer he waited the less sure he became of his own cause. I should not have talked to Leonard; he forced me to pity him and I cannot endure that now. There is no one I can afford to pity except myself. And it is becoming increasingly difficult to do that.

The chairman was looking let-down. "Don't you want to know what I taught your class?"

"What? Oh. Blake as a revolutionary, I suppose."

The chairman flushed; there was a look of fury in his eyes, then he shuttered it and gave a bark of laughter. "I do go on about him, don't I?"

"No. I'm sorry. It was a lucky guess." A stupid answer. A week ago he would have been more diplomatic; he would not have exposed the chairman's unimportant foible—that sort of thing was not done in the department—or, having inadvertently done so, he would have covered his tracks with more skill, more sophistication: the chairman admired sophistication and would have forgiven him with grace, passed over the incident with ease. But now he did not care: the chairman was fast becoming as remote as the department, as the University, his feelings and good will unimportant, his desires irrelevant. Sorge could not connect him with any vision of the future. He passed an exploratory hand over the contours of his face, fingertips scratching against the stubble of his beard, and tried to see a future empty of his wife, but crowded with echoes of his children, of Leonard's babbling, of Felix Gold's revelations still to come. Nothing: he could imagine nothing beyond a feeling, almost palpable, of isolation, of a muffled world just outside the reality of whatever he faced at the moment. Yetta, Susan, Leonard, Milton, his children, even Trudi no longer existed, because they were not in his line of sight. He felt helpless, muzzled, yet too tired, too lax, to be curious about his own helplessness.

"Well," said the chairman with a bravely self-deprecating chuckle, "*just for today* we won't discuss Blake." Pushing aside his own predilections as does a fellow mourner in a chapel. "We don't want you to feel alone, my dear Solomon. It is not as if you were a businessman: you are part of a community of scholars, an integral part, and we will all do what we can to help you through this difficult time. Would it help to talk about your—ah—Trudi? A lovely girl, I always thought. A devoted . . . Of course sometimes we cannot tell . . . Well. I thought if you needed someone to talk to, to listen, you can always count on me. I see my role in the department as pater familias as much as possible. And practical. Obviously most of you are old enough to handle your own affairs, but sometimes a sympathetic ear, a surrogate for the authority we all long for in our reminiscences of youth . . . I'm sure you know what I mean?"

"I know what you mean."

"Well, then. Solomon, where is she?"

"Rumor has it she's under the forsythia bush in the back yard."

"Under . . . You mean dead?"

"Obviously."

"But—how?"

"The lieutenant's favorite hypothesis is that she was murdered by her husband."

"Now, wait. Wait a moment. This is not rational. This is absurd. My professors are not the kind of men who kill their wives. I shall have to call him back, he can't possibly believe . . . I will not have him slandering a member of my department. You mustn't worry, Solomon. I shall stand beside you. I shall take care of this presumptuous—it would help if you knew where she is."

"But I don't."

"You have no idea?"

"No."

"Incredible. I don't like to say this, Solomon, but the whole affair smacks of bad management; at the very least a lack of foresight on your part. We are trained to use knowledge in the formulation of generalizations and predictions. You seem to have neglected your own skills in your family."

"Are they applicable?"

The chairman frowned. "An odd word, coming from you. The application of scientific method to all aspects of human intercourse and endeavor is the foundation of our lives. To question that is to doubt the validity of all you have done, all you have written and taught for—how long?"

Sorge moved his hands and wondered at his boredom. His world was suddenly peopled with fools. Either he had wakened to a new perception or he was determined to deepen his own sense of isolation. He shrugged his shoulders. In the end, it made no difference: he was still alone.

"But it does matter," said the chairman. "As in a marriage, we mark our anniversaries: they measure staying power and expertise. About thirty years?"

"About."

"Well. In conjunction with your books and teaching record—an impressive achievement; one to look at with pride, something to lean on in times of—ah—difficulties. You must not underestimate yourself, Solomon. Nor must you doubt your work because, at the moment, you doubt yourself. Nothing is more stable, more comforting than science: it will outlast both of us and our petty problems. Not, I assure you, that I think your problem small. It is serious, quite serious. But let us analyze it. Our first concern, of course, must be the department. I think you might take a brief sabbatical from teaching; we don't want curiosity seekers or scandal mongers using the department for their own satisfaction. Fortunately, summer is almost here. You might cancel your summer school course and forget about the University for a few months. Perhaps we could extend it through the fall quarter. By next winter people will have forgotten; it will be quite safe to come back. As I say, this is not final. I think we should discuss it. Now, as to your physical well being. You'll get a maid, of course; my wife will help you. And there are, fortunately, laundry and dry cleaning establishments to take care of your clothing. As for meals, I have spoken to your sons and daughter—what?"

"I said, what right did you have—"

"The right of pater familias, my dear Solomon. It is my duty to keep my department functioning smoothly, to maintain its image in the University and before the layman. The department, in my planning, is all-important. Surely you know of my plans? It cannot be possible that you are unaware of my goals for the department. Have I been so subtle? I thought it obvious that all my efforts are now bent toward the creation of an entity, a whole, a unit that will make its name in the social sciences for all time to come. This is something new: scientists will refer not to the work of one man, but to the work of the department; they will recognize the contributions of the department; their programs will follow the programs of the department.''

''Under your name.''

''Obviously under my name. I am the chairman; the department is my creation. Eventually all projects will be printed with the signature of the department, rather than an individual professor. Books will be published and the author will be the department. Courses will be devised under the aegis of the entire department. This is my life, my work: the molding of this department into a creative entity, all projects coordinated, all personal quirks submerged, disharmony eliminated.''

''Rule by committee.''

''Not at all. I am surprised at you, Solomon. Rule by community, if you like. One of the aims of science, as you well know, or ought to—I would be most shocked if you did not—is the elimination of personal preferences, the normative approach, the anthropomorphic element in terms and hypotheses. We cannot afford them. In my department they will be at a minimum as we all work together, checking on each other, canceling out the personal touches. Forgive me for lecturing, Solomon; I get carried away by the—I have to call it this—the beauty of the future. We have an enormous responsibility; we are the only ones who can rescue mankind from chaos, the only ones to end war and hatred and fear. No one else can do it, not the politicians, not the military, not the industrial establishment. Only we have the tools, and we are beginning to gain the knowledge. When the day comes that the social sciences have caught up with the physical sciences, we will live in a new world. Meanwhile, of course, we move slowly. Often we are frustrated. It saddens me, for example, to see that we know how to start a race riot, but we do not yet have the necessary knowledge to stop one. You find that amusing?''

Sorge's smile faded and he looked away. Something was happening to him: a shifting of sand beneath his feet, a loosening of bonds. As if she were beside him, he could hear Trudi's mockery—all the comments she had made over the past years which he had either ignored or attacked.

Now, with Trudi absent, he felt himself taking her part, her words insinuating themselves into his reactions, his defenses crumbling. His hands itched with a new recklessness; he was cold, tight, and uncaring. ''Did you ever hear the story of the scientist and the trained bug?''

''I don't think so, but—''

''When the scientist said 'hup' the bug jumped over a pencil. The scientist pulled off one of the bug's legs and said 'hup' and the bug jumped over the pencil. He pulled off another leg and said 'hup' and the bug jumped over the pencil. He continued pulling off legs and the bug continued to jump over the pencil, until there were only two legs left. The scientist pulled off one of them and said 'hup.' The bug staggered forward and lurched over the pencil. The scientist pulled off the last leg and said 'hup.' The bug did not move. Again he said 'hup.' Still the bug did not move. Finally he shouted his command but the bug remained unmoving. So the scientist published a paper in a learned journal. His hypothesis: When you pull the legs off a bug it becomes deaf.''

In the heavy silence, Sorge rose and mixed two drinks. ''It amuses the students,'' he said, despising the apologetic whine in his voice. With anyone else, at any other time, the joke would have received a small laugh. But here and now, both he and the chairman were looking for excuses.

"Does it indeed?" murmured the chairman, accepting the glass from Sorge's hand. "Does it indeed. You know, Solomon, I have detected a streak of rebellion in you at various times in the past. I have been tempted to offer my services, but each time I felt you were able to overcome yourself and continue to make a contribution to our community. Your wife must have made things difficult for you; I often wondered why you were not more firm with her. But I made it a rule long ago not to interfere in the marriages of my professors as long as they did not interfere with the well-being of the department. Jests—even well-meaning ones—are seeds that sprout into discord, for they give a certain dignity to the hangers-on, the wastrels, the paupers of behavioral science. This I cannot allow. And so I must interfere, if only in the aftermath of a marriage and not the marriage itself."

"There's another story about a scientist, a married one—"

"I do not wish to hear it. I will not hear it. You are playing the fool and I have no intention of aiding you. Whatever guilt you feel toward your wife is your own burden; I will help you carry it only if you can assure me of your continued loyalty."

"My signature on the dotted line. There's anthropomorphism for you."

"If you cannot so assure me, we shall have to get rid of you. Reluctantly, because you have done fine work. But I cannot tolerate an ignorant woman's attitude in my department. If you adopt this attitude—a childish way of atoning for whatever you think you have done—I will no longer be responsible for you, I will no longer be interested in you. You will be a danger to me. Do you understand that?"

"My past work will count for—"

"I am not interested in the past, only the future. I would not be a true scientist if I let the past determine my actions. I am concerned only with the future, and with the present insofar as it predicts the future. I have no curiosity for obsolescence; I leave that to the historian. I see my department afresh each day, weighing each man's worth as of that day, and the days to come, as far as I can see them. This is part of my responsibility; the constant reassessment of value, a mature refusal to be bound by the emotional trappings of a past, even as recent as yesterday, that might weigh us down as we forge ahead. We are bringing glory to behavioral science! Do you honestly believe I would let anyone hamper us in our work?''

''Cheaper than ideology, but no less stringent.''

The chairman put down his glass, pushing it away in solemn rejection. ''You force me to say you will have to leave, Solomon.''

''Now wait a minute. Just a minute. The attributes of a scientist are doubt, curiosity, openness, awe, and—''

''No, no, no, no, no. We leave awe to the priests and rabbis. If you had said amazement, I might—just might have agreed with you. But not awe. There is no wonder about measurement; just a steady persevering, a satisfaction with statistical order. Nothing is beyond our province; pick up any newspaper, point to any story, and you have the stuff of behavioral science—material that lends itself to analysis, to measurement in formulated units, to filing for cross reference. The time for curiosity is when you open the newspaper. After that you have work to do, and you have no right, as a scientist and as a member of our community, to doubt the value of your work or the validity of your method. *No right*. First, because they did not originate with you, nor will they end with you. And second because you become a canker in our midst, eating at the core of soundness and harmony I have created. Now, I know you are under a strain at the moment, and I assume there have been difficulties here for some time;

one's wife does not disappear without established reason. But I cannot excuse you on those grounds since, as I have said, on occasion I have been concerned about you before this. I have sometimes wondered how well you fit in with the rest of us. Today's restlessness, *recklessness*, would seem to bear me out. Much of science is a dull plodding from one operation to the next; up to now you have been as good a plodder as anyone, but today I have the feeling you are about to *leap* somewhere."

"Unforgivable."

"My dear Solomon, I am immune to sarcasm. As far as I am concerned, and I say this with sadness, you have already left the department."

Sorge felt his body relax, floating, oozing in his chair. He looked down on the enormous hulk of himself sprawled before the sparkling eyes of the chairman and restrained a groan. There was no reality here, nothing to try him, no serious challenge to force him into evaluation. Poor Leonard made a more permanent contribution to my dissolution than this machine-age scholar-messiah who would rob me of my last niche. L. My last nichel. Rob me of my last nickel. This is no time for puns. This is a time for solemn reflection, a recapitulation of meaning. But he was a child again: I find the whole fucking world rather amusing. No pity, no compassion; screw them all. It was not even a question of integrity: I no longer care because I cannot see a future. Once his father had tried to point the way; now his father was gone, his wife was gone, his brothers dead, his children foreign. There was no continuity, no sense, no pressure of necessity. And so we will have some fun with this creature, this chairman who envisions himself as a cross between Father Zeus and Father Zossima. He laughed: I'm beginning to sound like Leonard with his dictionaries.

"You are amused," said the chairman, alert and defensive.

Sorge shrugged. "You can't get rid of me so easily. All my years of faithful service . . . tenure . . ."

The chairman smiled. He was on comfortable ground now: the uses of power. There were several ways, he gently instructed Sorge; several means open to those who knew how to gain and hold power in a structure formulated, in part, to deal with aberrations. Sorge could get an offer from another college or university; a good one. The chairman could always find someone willing to pay for him; he did have a good background and every school recognized the problem of personal differences. For this purpose, the chairman, benevolent and wishing only the best for his alumni, would even—well, not lie, but certainly stretch a point when it came to describing Sorge's devotion to science and his potential for further fruitful endeavor. Of course, Sorge might reject the offer. Then the day would come when the professor would appear for the first class of the quarter to find he had no students. A pity, but registrars are amenable to suggestions from department chairmen, and they have a certain skill in influencing students to avoid particular courses. And if there are no students—or perhaps only the one or two who persisted in signing up for the course—why, then, there can be no course. The University cannot afford such luxuries as seminars with no students. There was such a case once at an Eastern school: the poor fellow, the professor nobody wanted, sat for a semester with nothing to do. Humiliating. Naturally he left at the end of the term.

Now a bitter man, a sick man, might think he could use such a period of leisure to write a book attacking those who had sheltered him for these many years. But that would be ill-advised. Publishers depend upon professors to use their books. Who would adopt an author, publish his book, and alienate the scholarly community? The professor would be alone: isolated, unpublished, scorned.

And if, after all this, Solomon Sorge was still a thorn in the flesh of the chairman's community, the chairman had time on his side. How long would it be before the generous Susan Hazlitt paid another visit to the lonely professor? How long before there was a string of Susan Hazlitts, a veritable parade through the front door and bedroom of a man who could not be content with one woman when she was his wife and, supposedly, available at all times? Immorality was not condoned at any school, no matter how long or well established the tenure of any professor.

Sorge searched for the response that would have been Trudi's. Who steals my tenure steals trash. No; Leonard might have written that in his little notebook, but Trudi would have been sharper, turning the chairman's suppressed glee into a weapon against him. Think of your own retorts: you don't need Trudi. But as the silence lengthened, he knew he did. I have no wit, no resources; this little man will think he has beaten me: he is only the last in a long line that begins with myself. When is a haven no longer a haven? When it takes more than an E to make it heaven. When it takes the whole alphabet, all man's words and knowledge, all man's effort. I'm too old, too tired to try. I don't care anymore. Not even enough to separate the chairman from his—my—life work: not even enough to defend science—myself—against his outrages.

He tried to feel anger and failed. What he felt was destructiveness, a vicious urge to damage something, anything, even himself, as if, looking into a mirror and seeing no reflection, he wanted to kick out to shatter the glass. "Finish your drink," he said.

"I've had enough," said the chairman, making his words weighty, portentous.

"How much have you drunk?"

"About half. What difference does it make? Solomon, I don't dislike you, you must understand . . ."

"Well, half is enough."

"Enough for what?"

Sorge arranged a leer on his face and leaned forward. "I put poison in it."

"My dear Solomon, you seem to have taken my words too personally. I assure you . . ."

"It works slowly, like your mind, but half the drink is sufficient to do its job, again like your mind."

The chairman put his hands to his mouth, frowning over clenched fingers. "You don't mean any of this. You're angry. Like a child."

"I give you about ten minutes before the pains begin."

"There was nothing in that drink! I would have tasted it."

"A subtle poison. What would you like it to be? Nicotine is a good one; tasteless, I believe. Or chloral hydrate. That, of course, would only knock you out, but then I could put *you* under the forsythia bush."

"You're mad."

Sorge nodded; his head bobbed up and down. To stop it, he put one hand on his chin, the other on his hair. "Look at it scientifically. What is the probability that I might kill you?"

"But you would gain nothing."

"Revenge," Sorge said amiably. "Or perhaps for the experience. Empirical evidence. Perhaps that was why I killed Trudi."

"But you didn't kill her."

"Did I ever say so?"

"I don't know . . ."

"You said so. 'None of my professors would kill.' Perhaps I'm striking a blow for sanity in science."

"You didn't kill her."

"No, I don't think I did. But she didn't rob me of my last nickel."

"What are you talking about?"

"My last niche. Never mind. Don't you have any profound last words you want me to record for posterity?"

"There was nothing in that drink!"

"Posterity won't be interested in those words. Hope or hypothesis, by the way?"

The chairman stood, holding his hands to his stomach. "I intend to report this to the police."

"Scandal in the department."

"I'll call a psychiatrist. God knows you need one."

"You'll need a doctor sooner than I'll need a psychiatrist."

"There was nothing in that drink."

Sorge pondered. "That had the tentative ring a good hypothesis should have. Why not say, nothing tended to be in that drink?"

"You are never to set foot in my department again. You understand? Never again. I'll send your papers and books to you."

"You won't have time."

The chairman turned, scuttling from the house. Sorge watched him run down the walk, pause briefly to look around for observers, straighten and take a deep breath. He began to walk, then trot down the street, toward the campus, one hand still on his stomach as if he could feel the first of the pains that would never come. Sorge picked up the chairman's glass and drained it. He began to laugh, a rasping heh-heh-heh that turned quickly to choking and then to sobs.

16

THE RABBI CAME. Sorge greeted him with frantic relief: he had been alone for almost twenty-four hours. "Leo, come in. Sit down. Can you stay long? I've been meaning to call you."

Not true. He never thought of calling Leo Fox, particularly not the past few days; he had been calling Felix Gold every half hour around the clock. He could not remember when he had last been in his bed; he dozed on the couch, in armchairs, sometimes on Harriet's old bed, or David's or Nathan's. He ate sporadically, bowls of cereal or soup, tuna fish, fruit, spaghetti, baked beans out of the can. The cupboards were almost empty but he was putting off a trip to the grocery store: the final truth of Trudi's abdication would be his adoption of this most wifely task. He still straightened the house in bursts of mindless activity, but there was little mess; everything was in its place, dull, dusty, suddenly grown old.

And my place? It was still here, in this house, a stable center waiting for Trudi to return and give it meaning. He and Trudi owned it; the income from his books, a modest portfolio of stocks, and his savings would pay the taxes and buy what little food and clothing he needed. He did not have to work, though there was no reason to assume he would not write again when he settled down. No reason except a loss of faith which might or might not be permanent. And if he in his place, like his possessions in theirs, was dull, dusty, suddenly grown old—that may be the future I could not see yesterday; a silent moldering without even the consolation of a satisfying past.

"Go upstairs and shave," the rabbi said. "I'll wait for you."

Sorge went. The occasion for obedience pleased him; he had never paid much attention to Rabbi Leo Fox but now he felt gratitude and some hope. He was pleased, too, by the act of shaving: he rejected his electric shaver to indulge in the luxury of warm water, soft foam and the sensual strokes of the blade across his face. The silent bathroom, scene of so many morning ablutions, recalled other days, other hours when Trudi slept across the hall or created the comforting clatter of breakfast for a family. Hypnotized by the cleansing ritual, Sorge could almost believe it was his wife who awaited him downstairs, prepared to send him off for the day, instead of a rabbi who came bearing God for his consolation.

He rubbed his clean cheeks with pleasure, pulling the skin with his fingers, mouthing silent words at his reflection. He looked a new man, fresh, youthful, prepared. He stripped off his clothes and stepped into the shower, turning on the hot water until it steamed. His huge, gray body turned pink, glowing under the heavy spray. He lathered again and again, washing a week's dirt and apprehension down the drain; he stood, head back, and let the boiling water beat on his face, his chest, his long, dangling arms. He washed his hair, scratching the scalp with his fingernails until it was sore. And then he turned the water to cold, feeling his body chill, the pores close, his wrinkled fingertips contract and turn numb. When he stepped out he was exhausted, hollow: it no longer mattered who waited downstairs.

He dressed in clean underclothes and a starched shirt, fastening the cuffs with silver links. He put on a silk tie Yetta had bought for his last birthday, and a lightweight dacron and wool suit. With a brush he took a few swipes at his shoes; he combed his hair with finicky detail; he put a clean handkerchief in his pocket. In the mirror, he approved of his image; I'll put on a good front for God and His rabbi.

"An improvement," the rabbi said, looking up from his book. "Trudi would recognize you now."

But I didn't dress for Trudi. I thought of her only in connection with what was and what might have been. I have given up on Trudi. "I didn't dress for Trudi."

"No," the rabbi remarked. "You dressed as you would upon awakening. A good sign; a necessary sign. She left no note? No word of explanation?"

"None."

"And her actions prior to leaving? She gave no clues?"

"None."

"You are not on trial, Solomon. You may elaborate your answers."

Sorge shrugged. "Of course I'm on trial. My guilt is equal to hers and as hers increases so does mine."

The rabbi frowned. "Faced with a mystery can you still cling to your methods? Must everything be measured, fitted to a scale?"

"In this case, yes. Guilt may range from knowledge to complicity to instigation. If you begin with a low point for simple knowledge—"

"And your guilt?"

"Mine? I'm not sure yet. I hope nothing worse than complicity."

"You are not a victim?"

"I don't think so."

The rabbi nodded. "And what do you want of me?"

"I? I didn't ask you to come."

"But you were meaning to call me. No, never mind; I

know you were not. It is a convenient line I hear frequently, after the fact. *I was meaning to call you, rabbi.* Never earlier, when the troubles begin or the problems first arise. You know, this will interest you, Solomon. In your terminology, my role has become confused. I have an impressive temple, a comfortable home, a car; my children's college education is assured. What I do not have is the spirit of my congregation. Few of them come to me with problems or fears—they want me as a social guest, a symbolic redeemer with whom they are on a first-name basis. How can they unburden their weaknesses and ugliness before a man to whom they send an engraved dinner invitation? They do not want, as many of their forebears did, intimacy with religion; the only kind of intimacy most of them have is purchased at twenty-five dollars an hour from their analysts or therapists. They do not want mystery; they want assurance. They do not want grandeur; they want support for the petty."

They were silent. The rabbi said, "You probably are thinking I would deny the validity of psychoanalysis and therapy. I do not. Nor do I deny the validity of your polls and questionnaires, though I believe they are too often confused with guides for behavior and belief. They all have their place. But where is the place for mystery? Where is the wonder? What has become of belief in something simply because it is unknowable? You may be thinking I am jealous. That I want a piece of the worship you engender. And it is just possible. But I would like to think my concern is based on something a little more special than my own pique. I would like to offer my knowledge, my self, when my congregation is in need, rather than attend a dinner party to discuss Kinsey, to whom they have turned in place of me. But my motives often do bewilder me. I would like, not to alter the world so much as to affect it. My portion of it. We are somewhat alike in that, are we not?"

"Trudi once said—"

"Ah, but Trudi understood much of my dilemma. We spoke of it. She was one who came to me. Not with personal troubles, family troubles—I thought you and she had made peace with each other; of course now I know I was mistaken—no, she came to me with the impossible questions that a rabbi awaits with eagerness and some fear. She wanted to ally the past with the present, faith with knowledge, the unknowable with your all-too-measurable. I think I may have helped her with a sense of perspective, of admitted longing in an era of satiety. I thought I was helping her find a place. Perhaps—I hope not—I only helped her to leave one."

"I gave her a place."

"But that was still a question: whether I really helped her. I know you want to talk about yourself, Solomon; I know you are troubled. But this will interest you: the question of a man's function. Would you call it role playing? I'm not happy with that phrase; it makes me wonder whether I am in truth a rabbi or only acting like one. I prefer position: my position is a rabbi, a teacher, a guide. If Judaism is an assumption of responsibility, as of course it is, my position, my duty, is to guide Jews in this most difficult of all tasks: the sharing of responsibility with God. But it is a responsibility with limited authority, a narrow catwalk for those who would grasp at easy concepts like blame and guilt and victimization. I cannot, nor would I, bring God in my fingertips and place Him before a questioner. What I *can* do, if I perform well, is lead others to an acceptance of mystery—you would call it faith but it is hardly as easy as that—as well as the full realization of power to move. We cannot simply respond to the unknowable; we must instigate. Now, you are probably thinking that I justify your work, that by telling you to instigate I ask you to go ahead with your charting and measuring and reducing. Of course I am telling you no such thing. Oh, go ahead by yourselves, if you wish, talking to yourselves in your private tongue and amusing each other with your playthings. But as for the world, your audience, you must cease. There must be an end, a visible limit to your claims. Otherwise mine are absurd. I know this no time to be taxing you, Solomon, but you should find this interesting: the effects of your profession on mine. I function in an area of doubt and insecurity: I must provide antidotes in the form of crutches. Of course this surprises you: it is so fashionable these days to sneer at crutches. But that is your fault. You and your fellow magicians who tell a gullible public that anything can be solved by measuring it, placing it on a scale or graph, reducing it to a commonplace of any of the disciplines, and then composing a homily—you call it theory or hypothesis—to catalogue it for future reference. You claim to be morally neutral; you may limit ends but you refuse to set them. Utopia! Between sufficient and necessary causes there is no need to search for a first; we can indulge or ignore morality—on one of your scales I suppose it would be puritanism measured in units of anxiety—we can feel ourselves at once the master of that which we measure and the non-responsible gull of that in us which is measurable. And where does that leave me? Not with a congregation that doesn't believe in God: most of them think they do. But with a congregation that doesn't know what it is talking about—an ignorant mass that denies its heritage, its responsibility, its awareness and thus, though never admitting this, denies God. And Judaism. A mass that sees religion as a social state, denying it as a buoy, a pillar, a bridge. They come to Temple because they seek an inner group with its own language—you see? I must use your orientation even as I castigate it—and because of a vague feeling that what goes on there has something to do with them. They forget that the reverse must be true or there is no meaning in Judaism, the Temple, or in me. You do not come to Temple."

In the sudden silence, Sorge looked up. "What?"

Gently the rabbi repeated his observation. "I realize I've given you a great deal to think about and at an awkward time . . ."

Sorge shook his head. He had heard little since his brief remark that he had given Trudi a place. What few phrases had crept in had annoyed him: the conflict between science and religion was a dead horse, a debate adopted by those who understood neither, or who wanted to denigrate one or the other. There had been no such conflict in his own life; he was surprised to hear of Trudi's: he had not known she consulted Leo Fox. Had she really been disturbed, in need of advice? Or had she been looking for someone, like poor Leonard, to use against her husband? She had never enforced her parents' forms of worship after leaving their home; Sorge was not sure now just what she had wanted, how she would have organized the spiritual life of the family had his own laxity not prevailed. ("Solomon," asked Yetta when their father died. "Do you believe in God?" "I don't know; I've never tried.") The children attended religious school; the boys were confirmed; there were no chalk talks on Judaism. "The world will never let you forget you are Jews; you should know something about your religion. Beyond that, it is a convenience: you will believe what you must to satisfy your own needs." ("Do scientists believe in God?" asked Nathan. "Scientists believe in God and God believes in scientists. They have learned to coexist.") There should be more public flippancy about religion and less public practice, less visible consumption as opposed to private belief. The kind of flippancy displayed by my sons in the biblical quotations they chose to decorate their walls. Think: we might have avoided the crusades, the pogroms, the massacres, the inquisitions. But that was a little like his mother-in-law and her dreams of a salon that would alter the face of Europe; he was not flippant to change the course of history but because, in an ordering of values, religion was always near the bottom. He simply couldn't be bothered. He had chosen a field that reduced, simplified, measured and charted because he found there a middle way between flippancy and fanaticism. Until he spoke to the chairman of his department the day before, he had felt sure-footed and satisfied. Now, faced with fanaticism of a new kind, he was uncomfortable; he would have liked to brood over it with someone like Rabbi Leo Fox—after having discussed Trudi and possible variations on the theme of guilt and innocence—but Fox was not prepared to brood over anyone but himself. Much of Sorge's contempt was thus confirmed, but he felt helpless, nothing left save a confrontation with Felix Gold and then a withdrawal into some form of neoscholarship that would save, if nothing else, some dignity and, eventually perhaps, meaning.

"How would you measure Job's sufferings?" said the rabbi. "You have a Settembrinian scale of sorrow, I suppose, and like that poor man in his attic room you reduce tragedy to a compendium of reactions." He stood and paced the room. "Distorted nineteenth century liberalism adopted by those who would give us a perfect state willy-nilly and ignore the mystery, the beauty of the unknowable. Not understanding is a form of understanding. Settembrini would sneer; you would sneer. You would both be wrong, you in your training, and he in his ignorance. Poor man!"

Another time, Sorge might have enjoyed the rabbi's unintentional pun, his incoherence, his misreading of Settembrini; might even have found a friend in Leo Fox. But not today. Not now. Nor, perhaps, ever again. I have to start from the beginning. And I'm not really young enough for that.

"It is not even as simple as a desire to destroy God. You are too clever for that. Or too stupid to recognize your potential. No, you simply destroy the need for Him with your simple-minded solutions. You make belief in Him seem rather childish, naïve, fumbling; worse, in an age of Science, complicated where straightforward graphs would suffice. The only sin now is not understanding, the only morality a proper ordering of facts; belief, faith, love, devotion have all become variables, and mystery is something to put in the movies. In your efforts to swell to omnipotence, you have made us atoms in some sociologist's perfect state. You have robbed us of glory." He stopped pacing and stood before Sorge's chair. "And I am being displaced!"

Sorge laughed. "Sorry," he said. "I'm sorry. I only wanted to talk about Trudi, not the glory of the rabbinate."

"I was not speaking of the glory of the rabbinate," said Leo Fox sadly. "I was speaking of yours."

"Gone," Sorge murmured. "Or never there. I'm afraid I can't help you."

"You stand for something—"

"Damn it, I stand for nothing. Don't force me to be a symbol to fit your distortions."

"Nothing?" said the rabbi. "You disappoint me."

Sorge was suddenly, startlingly infuriated. That this rabbi should dare put him in the position of disappointing him! He had disappointed one rabbi in his lifetime, that was enough. He would not be made over by this rabbi, used, loved, admired, or created in a disappointing image. Fox was a damn fool if he thought Sorge was his son, or a surrogate, and thus, in failure, or assumed failure, a disappointment. His hands shook; as yesterday, with the chairman, he wanted to strike out, to do violence; once again, he wanted to destroy. "I think," he said tightly, "I can help you after all."

Fox smiled weakly. "I came here to help you."

"You have a problem," Sorge continued, wishing for his blackboard. "You have an impressive Temple, a comfortable home, a car; your children's education is assured. What you do not have is the spirit of your congregation. Is that a fair assessment?"

The rabbi became wary. "You could say—"

"I already have. Well, then, why not find out what your congregation wants? What your flock expects of you? How you should respond to best serve their needs and, so to speak, sell your product."

"I don't think I would word it quite—"

"We can reword it in the questionnaire."

"Questionnaire?"

"We'll do a study of your congregation. We'll find out precisely what their relationship is to you and the Temple."

"And to God?" asked Fox faintly.

"And to God," said Sorge firmly. "When we are through your role will be clearly delineated, the needs of your congregation will be established, the interaction between you will allow for variables, an ordering of values, responses, effect. We will remove your doubts and give you a steady base from which to preach and prophesy. Even to counsel."

"No," said the rabbi.

Sorge's eyebrows went up. "You don't think I could do it?"

"I am sure you could."

"Then I'll need your help. A list of the congregation so a random sample may be selected—"

"I don't think—"

"A set of questions *you* would ask, a brief outline of your ideas as a rabbi, a short statement of your concept of the congregation and your vision of the ideal congregation. I could also use a capsule history of the Temple. I already have a socio-economic picture of the area. I think that will be enough. Get that to me as soon as possible, will you? I'll get right to work on the questionnaire and show it to you before I administer it."

The rabbi resumed his pacing. "You really think something could come of this?"

"I'm sure of it. You would know exactly where you stand."

"And where I need to go."

"And where you need to go. Your path would be clear, your role would be—"

"Clearly delineated. I understand. How would you choose the respondents? Out of three thousand people—"

"Random sample. Every fourth name, perhaps. Or all those with phone numbers beginning with a certain digit. Any number of ways. Leave that to me."

"I don't know," the rabbi mused. "It's true I often wonder what they really think—"

"What they really want."

"What they expect. They don't tell me."

"They just invite you to dinner."

"They don't talk about their needs."

"Just about Kinsey."

"It might work."

"Of course it would work."

"It *is* your field."

"I'm highly trained for this sort of thing."

"And it couldn't do any harm."

"Quite the contrary."

"What would it cost?"

"Nothing."

"Nothing? But . . ."

"As a member of the congregation I would contribute my services. We might even make some money out of it. If I publish an article on my findings, I'll contribute the proceeds to the Temple building fund."

The rabbi paced in silence. ''You could do it? In a dignified way?''

''Absolutely.''

Another short silence. Then: ''All right. All right, we'll try it.''

Sorge, exhausted, slumped in his chair. Trudi, you should be here now.

17

FELIX GOLD was historian to the masses, mixing metaphor, morals and manners with dates, bloody battles, and backstairs intrigue. He could dazzle an admirer at a cocktail party with the details of Aaron Aaronsohn's agricultural and political exploits, and confound a somber professor with the allegation that the finest job of historical reconstruction was Tey's *The Daughter of Time.* He was Everyman's author and guest: charming, civilized, possessive of his interpretations, open as to his methods, available for impromptu after-dinner remarks, a bachelor. He was forty-nine years old and lived in the converted elegance of a coach house on the near-north side, alone save for a housekeeper whose like had been immortalized in numberless novels and plays. He had been married twice, once briefly in college, then for eighteen years to an expatriate Estonian who gave piano recitals to raise money to free her country, called herself the female Chopin, and finally left him for a Lithuanian engineer who had started an underground movement, with her money, to infiltrate the Baltic states. Their target date for UN armies to support their revolution was 1968 and they had written their plans in a manifesto—one copy to the Secretary General, one to the President of the United States, one in a safety deposit box in the First National Bank of Chicago. Gold wished them well;

they had provided him with years of amusement and entertainment. They had also provided him with a notarized statement that he was to be the official historian of the revolution. He kept it in his desk. There was no sense in ignoring the kernel of reality nestled in each man's fantasy.

Sorge arrived on his doorstep, unannounced, to find him unpacking from a research trip to Israel: he had mined the field of recent Jewish history and now was reaching further back. He received Sorge incuriously; they had been casual friends for fifteen years since meeting on a radio panel discussion of whatever crises were considered paramount in 1949.

"Help yourself to a drink. You don't mind if I finish?" He was extraordinarily neat: his clothes folded symmetrically, socks and ties rolled, shoes wrapped in tissue paper. His rooms were subdued, more so since the day was cloudy: neat and uncluttered with startling flashes—a Tunisian wall hanging, a Mexican onyx horse, an early-American copper washtub holding magazines. There was no trace of Estonia. "Trudi not with you?"

Sorge looked at the closed guest room door. "No." He watched Gold through the door of the other bedroom, moving with smooth precision from open suitcase to dressers to closets. He moved his head to test the tension in the air: there was none. He was more relaxed than he had been all week. It was difficult in the man's presence to judge degrees of anger or apprehension or justified resentment: though he had never been sure it was reciprocated, he liked Felix Gold.

"Anything wrong?"

"Why?"

"You look like a man about to propose. Calculating, in a last leap of fancy, past and future tense."

Sorge did not answer. He was finding it difficult to frame words: an accusation seemed impossible (what disservice would he do himself by confessing to a rifling of Trudi's papers, and what to her by betraying her private babblings to a lover who might—a sudden shift of thought here—have grown cold before she disappeared?). Nor could he plead for information; he might be fond of Felix Gold but not so fond that he could cede all advantage to him. Where is my wife? Good God, how ask a lover that? "Where is my wife?"

Gold's hands stilled on the edge of the suitcase; his back to Sorge, head cocked as if listening, he stood until at last turning, head still bent to one side. "Gone?"

Sorge's eyes went to the guest room door and Gold, with a wry smile, opened it and gestured inside. "Not for almost a month."

Sorge nodded in confirmed pain and the quick sympathy he felt for Gold: she has left both of us. "Did she love you?"

"I think so. Yes."

They became active. Sorge, who had tried to stimulate anger by refusing to drink his host's liquor, went to the cabinet and poured Scotch; he waited while Gold brought ice from the kitchen. "For how long?"

"Nearly two years."

They toasted each other in silence and drained their glasses, rising together to refill them: a smoothly working team. Sorge, towering over Gold, looked down upon the straight sandy hair his wife had lyricized and briefly contemplated murder. But it would be such a waste: he is a good historian. The irrelevancy of his own emotions startled him: I could not chart myself.

"You haven't heard from her?"

"I've been in Israel."

"But she might have tried to call you."

"Possibly. She didn't tell me her plans."

"You knew nothing?"

"Nothing."

"Not even that she *wanted* to leave?"

Gold, newly restless, walked to the door and back, fingering objects along the way. "How did you find out?"

"She wrote about you. I went through her things after she left."

"She never wrote me letters."

"A profile. Trying to see you and herself, to fit things together."

Gold's mouth went slack: Sorge could not be sure whether it was in tenderness or amusement. "She was trying to make up her mind."

"To go away with you?"

"Much simpler. To go to bed with me."

A wave of terrible disappointment swept Sorge. "She never did?"

"She never did. We came close but—no. It was a measure of her charm that I stuck it as long as I did. Or the charm of her obduracy. She revived an ancient rite: the pursuit of woman. I rather enjoyed it."

"Bitch," Sorge muttered. He was furious. "Bitch."

"On my account?" asked Gold, plainly amused. "I knew what I was doing; it was Trudi who was confused. You know, Sol, you took a perfectly lovely girl and raised her to a miserable woman. There wasn't much I could do for her except love her; in time she might have let me. Something must have happened while I was gone. Or maybe I simply set her up for someone else. Was there someone else in those papers you were in such a hurry to read?"

"Miserable?"

"Was there someone else?"

"No. Not in her papers. No. She was miserable?"

"I didn't think there could be. She had enough trouble coping with me. Poor girl, she couldn't fit me into a scheme of things. She was afraid—she told me this—she was afraid she would want to marry me. 'I'm no Lucy Tantamount,' she said. 'I wouldn't be able to discard you, or what I had done.' Poor child; I should have sent her away long ago."

"Go on."

"With what? You want a detailed description? Yes, by God, that's just what you do want. Felix Gold: intellectual pimp. Is there any reason why I should do this for you?"

"Not for me; to me."

"In that case, I'll be delighted. I didn't quite love your wife, Sol; I was charmed by her and I enjoyed disturbing her. She gave the impression of malleability: a major attraction after her beauty. I'm not so sure, now that she's left us for some presumably more attractive third choice. I would say she wanted to be affected by men but couldn't adapt herself to what they demanded even though she tried, or wanted to try. I don't mean she was complex or mysterious; she wasn't. In most respects she was an ordinary Jewish housewife—eternal and rocklike: impossible to budge. Probably very much like your mother."

"That's not true."

"No? You prefer her as a complicated syndrome fit for analysis? My poor Sol, you never looked at her. She was a beautiful woman who didn't want to use her beauty; an intelligent woman who wanted only to channel her intelligence into a home; a motherly person who couldn't like her own children; a sexual creature ashamed of her own desires because they seemed at variance with the failures of the rest of her life. She didn't like you anymore."

Sorge rose abruptly. "Bastard." He searched for more scatological terms but his chest was tight and his mind crowded with images of Trudi spreadeagled beneath Gold. For Gold had lied. Why he did not know, but he had lied; no man could pretend to know a woman so well unless he had bedded her and listened to her in the drowsy confessional that followed orgasm. So Felix Gold had made love to his wife, then fed him Scotch and acted out amused objectivity. Felix Gold, a failure with two wives, took the role of reverse counselor to a man he had cuckolded without even the pretense of love. Felix Gold: "Bastard," he said again and reached out, almost casually, to take the taut neck between his hands.

"Then why did she leave?" asked Gold, unmoving, watching Sorge's enormous hands with dispassion. "The role of wife is a creation of women: they determine its limits, its obligations, its pleasures. They rule themselves: priests without bishops, planters without overseers, mechanics without supervisors. They have refined self-employment to a pitch of perfection. Why would any of them leave?"

Sorge's concept of Trudi's role had been one of drudgery, unrelieved, degrading. That it might be a condition of freedom he felt an obscure insult to himself: nothing to do with Gold, or even Trudi, but as a measure of his own evaluations. His hands fell, thumbs twitching, and he turned back to his chair. It had been a weakness in Trudi that she enjoyed housework, that she measured her days with the same pleasure he took in measuring his, that her satisfactions soothed her, as his did himself. Was it a weakness, then, if she added to dusting and vacuuming a toss in the hay every afternoon at two or three while her husband taught the principles of political science? That she had a freedom he never saw and used it as—face it, Solly—he did his?

Gold shook his head. "I told you; she never did. You want it all? She came here for fairy tales. The lovely princess and her savior in a world of potions, incantations, and spells. I was the savior. No, don't smile: she was quite serious. Why not? She was afraid of your statistics, your methodology, your neat hypotheses that all tended to say something. She was terrified of impersonality, of being lost: Snow White in a forest of the inanimate. She wanted sense, meaning, a place.

She went to your rabbi and ended up as counselor, a feminine shoulder. So she came to me. Because she thought I could re-create her in the past and find her in the present. Because I am an historian and the word was magic to her."

"Magic."

"My dear Sol, it is hardly your place to scoff. You lost her in your own mumbo-jumbo, in your refusal to build on anything solid, in your unwillingness to look back, or let her look back, to find meaning. She wanted to find some tie, some reason for a continuous line from Esther, Bathsheba, Ruth to Lady Montefiore and Lady de Hirsch, to Henrietta Szold, Lilian Wald, Sarah Aaronson, Emma Lazarus, to a million nameless refugees, to Trudi Loeffler. She wanted to know where she belonged, how she fitted in. When I told her about Lady Montague—you've heard of Lady Montague, of course?"

Sorge shook his head. "I didn't come here for a lesson in—"

"Lady Montague was a Jew turned Christian. The original family name had been Montague Samuel; conveniently reversible. But one of the later Lady Montagues publicly re-embraced Judaism during the Hitler era to show her solidarity with the Jews of Germany. Trudi liked that: it demonstrated, to her, a trust, a depth of knowledge, an enviable awareness of possibilities and power and self. She would have liked to be tested so that she could know herself. She would have liked to be Sarah Aaronsohn, to find out whether she would have committed suicide rather than betray her fellow Jews. She would have liked to live in Germany in the thirties."

"Then she was a fool."

Gold smiled gently. "The only kind of fool. One who is not satisfied. She was a child looking for kinship with lesser gods; she wanted a family."

"And found a lover."

Gold's amiability vanished. "You stupid ass. You aren't worth her anguish, her indecision. She no longer loved you but couldn't let go enough to come into my bed, to turn on you with your own arsenal."

"Wait." Sorge struggled upright in his chair. Harriet had said the same thing. "She knew I had—"

"Names and dates. You have good taste, Sol: Trudi said most of them were good-looking. Not clever, perhaps, or wise; they didn't disguise much in looking at you or condescending to make veiled conversation with your wife. But then none of them had respect for your wife. Why should they? You didn't, and attitudes are pervasive in bed."

"She never indicated . . ."

"This is evidently difficult for you to believe: your wife was not stupid. Quite ordinary in many ways, but with her own brand of wisdom. While she loved you she was afraid of forcing you to lie. When she stopped caring for you, she felt she had no right to demand faithfulness."

"But she told you."

"Why not? I had no special brief. I would neither defend or damn. For once I could practice some of your damned objectivity and for once she could welcome it."

Sorge sat very still, attempting to revive dead conversations, to pick out loaded words in the innocuous sentences he had exchanged with his wife at key periods during the past ten years; they were all gone. He had lost not only Trudi—the sound of her voice, the expressions on her face—he had lost the millions of words that had passed between them, that had bound them in the commonality of a shared life. Flashing, silent images—Trudi lifting a heavy pan from the stove; Trudi bent to cut a flower; Trudi opening the car door to step out—these were all that remained of his marriage. These and a residual anger at the man who had had the opportunity to replace him whether in fact he had or not.

"She didn't make love to you?"

"She didn't come to my bed."

"So, in that, too, she got her own back. First Leonard, then the rabbi, then you. To prove how much better—"

"No. Not to set herself up against you. To see what kind of a person she was before becoming the most elemental. She wanted the complex first, and was barely capable of understanding it. She came to me, I told you, to find her place. We could have glossed over it by lying together; we did once, as a matter of fact—"

"You did—"

"As a preliminary never concluded. We didn't ignore sex; it was always there. I enjoyed kissing her, holding her, moving my hands along her and feeling her response—you don't want to hear this."

"I want to hear it."

Gold shrugged. "You don't need the details. I might have married Trudi, given time. I intend to marry again; I've gotten used to it. But it would have taken time, perhaps too much time for me. I didn't know she was planning to walk out; if I had I might not have gone to Israel; I might have gone to your party instead."

"She invited you?"

"You didn't know? I told her I might come; she expected me, I suppose. But I felt we were approaching some time of decision—that much she did indicate—and I thought it better if I went away for awhile, to give her a chance as well as myself. I didn't want her to be forced into anything. Whatever she wanted, I think I would have done for her; she had created a dependency and I'm not young enough to have ignored it. Besides, I was fond of her. But I went away without telling her how long I would be gone; without telling her I was going, in fact. I suppose she waited for me at your party. If she had let me know what she was planning . . . But for some reason she didn't. Perhaps she knew I would marry her if she wanted it; perhaps she wasn't ready for me yet. Perhaps she wanted some time alone; I wouldn't blame her. She was growing up."

Growing up. Sorge put back his head and closed his eyes. He had met her, married her when she was sixteen. She had borne his children, kept his house, cooked his food. And grown up when she was forty-five years old. A sadness swept him, a foretaste of self-pity and loneliness and longing for the things he might have done that he still could not understand. A sadness for the non-understanding. A sadness for the weeks ahead when he would do nothing to find her.

He opened his eyes. Gold had returned to his unpacking; the room had changed. Lazily, he waited to comprehend the difference. It struck him: the sun had come out. Bars of golden, dust-flecked light lay across the room, gleaming on walnut surfaces, burnishing the teak with dull brilliance. A corner of light touched his face; he could feel the warmth. Sunlight; a new day: he felt like an ancient worshipper. Sunlight; an ending. Trudi, he thought; forgive me. He sat unmoving, feeling the touch of warmth move across his skin, and in a few moments he was asleep.

About the Author

JUDITH BARNARD was born in Colorado. She attended Antioch College and was graduated from Ohio State University. After receiving her M.A. degree in English Literature from Northwestern, she became a literary critic and journalist. *The Past and Present of Solomon Sorge,* her first work of fiction, received The Award of Excellence of the Friends of American Writers. She has since collaborated on several novels with her husband, Michael Fain. They currently live in Chicago.